A QUESTION OF UPBRINGING

And so we turned about towards the fields, passing the house again, and entering an area of dusty cow-parsley and parched meadows. While still on the road the figure of Widmerpool appeared in front of us. He was tramping along in the sunlight, swinging arms and legs like an automaton of which the mechanism might be slightly out of order. We walked behind him for a time, Stringham doing an imitation of the way Widmerpool put his feet to the ground. From an unreasoning fear of the embarrassment that would be caused me if Widmerpool should look back and himself observe Stringham's agitated pantomime, I persuaded him to stop this improvisation. I had remained in some odd manner interested in Widmerpool since that night in the fog; and, although Stringham's imitation was ludicrously exact, to think that Widmerpool might see it was for some reason painful to me; though I was almost sorry when the time came to turn off the road and leave Widmerpool to disappear in a distant cloud of dust.

'I don't know what I should do without Widmerpool,' Stringham said. 'He keeps me young.'

'I sometimes wonder whether he is a human being at all,' Templer said. 'He certainly doesn't move like one.'

A Dance to the Music of Time

A Question of Upbringing
A Buyer's Market
The Acceptance World
At Lady Molly's
Casanova's Chinese Restaurant
The Kindly Ones
The Valley of Bones
The Soldier's Art
The Military Philosophers
Books Do Furnish a Room
Temporary Kings
Hearing Secret Harmonies

All the books in the series
are available from Mandarin Paperbacks

ANTHONY POWELL

A Question of Upbringing

Mandarin

This edition published in the United Kingdom in 1991 by
Mandarin Paperbacks

7 9 10 8

First published in the United Kingdom in 1951 by William Heinemann

Mandarin Paperbacks
Random House UK Limited
20 Vauxhall Bridge Road, London SW1V 2SA

Random House Australia (Pty) Limited
20 Alfred Street, Milsons Point, Sydney, New South Wales 2061, Australia

Random House New Zealand Limited
18 Poland Road, Glenfield, Auckland 10, New Zealand

Random House South Africa (Pty) Limited
Endulini, 5a Jubilee Road, Parktown 2193, South Africa

Random House UK Limited Reg. No. 954009

A CIP catalogue record for this book is available from the British Library

Papers used by Random House UK Limited
are natural, recyclable products made from wood grown in
sustainable forests. The manufacturing processes conform to
the environmental regulations of the country of origin

Printed and bound in the United Kingdom by
Cox & Wyman Ltd, Reading, Berkshire

ISBN 0 7493 0658 0

For T. R. D. P.

A DANCE TO THE MUSIC OF TIME

★

A QUESTION OF UPBRINGING

1

THE men at work at the corner of the street had made a kind of camp for themselves, where, marked out by tripods hung with red hurricane-lamps, an abyss in the road led down to a network of subterranean drain-pipes. Gathered round the bucket of coke that burned in front of the shelter, several figures were swinging arms against bodies and rubbing hands together with large, pantomimic gestures: like comedians giving formal expression to the concept of extreme cold. One of them, a spare fellow in blue overalls, taller than the rest, with a jocular demeanour and long, pointed nose like that of a Shakespearian clown, suddenly stepped forward, and, as if performing a rite, cast some substance—apparently the remains of two kippers, loosely wrapped in newspaper—on the bright coals of the fire, causing flames to leap fiercely upward, smoke curling about in eddies of the north-east wind. As the dark fumes floated above the houses, snow began to fall gently from a dull sky, each flake giving a small hiss as it reached the bucket. The flames died down again; and the men, as if required observances were for the moment at an end, all turned away from the fire, lowering themselves laboriously into the pit, or withdrawing to the shadows of their tarpaulin shelter. The grey, undecided flakes continued to come down, though not heavily, while a harsh odour, bitter and gaseous, penetrated the air. The day was drawing in.

For some reason, the sight of snow descending on fire always makes me think of the ancient world—legionaries in sheepskin warming themselves at a brazier: mountain altars where offerings glow between wintry pillars; centaurs with torches cantering beside a frozen sea—scattered, unco-ordinated shapes from a fabulous past, infinitely removed from life; and yet bringing with them memories of things real and imagined. These classical projections, and something in the physical attitudes of the men themselves as they turned from the fire, suddenly suggested Poussin's scene in which the Seasons, hand in hand and facing outward, tread in rhythm to the notes of the lyre that the winged and naked greybeard plays. The image of Time brought thoughts of mortality: of human beings, facing outward like the Seasons, moving hand in hand in intricate measure: stepping slowly, methodically, sometimes a trifle awkwardly, in evolutions that take recognisable shape: or breaking into seemingly meaningless gyrations, while partners disappear only to reappear again, once more giving pattern to the spectacle: unable to control the melody, unable, perhaps, to control the steps of the dance. Classical associations made me think, too, of days at school, where so many forces, hitherto unfamiliar, had become in due course uncompromisingly clear.

As winter advanced in that river valley, mist used to rise in late afternoon and spread over the flooded grass; until the house and all the outskirts of the town were enveloped in opaque, chilly vapour, tinted like cigar-smoke. The house looked on to other tenement-like structures, experiments in architectural insignificance, that intruded upon a central concentration of buildings, commanding and antiquated, laid out in a quadrilateral, though irregular, style. Silted-up residues of the years smouldered uninterruptedly—and not without melancholy—in the maroon brickwork of these medieval closes: beyond the cobbles and archways of which (in a more northerly direction) memory also brooded, no less enigmatic and inconsolable, among water-meadows and avenues of trees: the sombre demands of the past becoming at times almost suffocating in their insistence.

Running westward in front of the door, a metalled road continued into open country of a coarser sort than these gothic parklands—fields: railway arches: a gas-works: and then more fields—a kind of steppe where the climate seemed at all times extreme: sleet: wind: or sultry heat; a wide territory, loosely enclosed by inflexions of the river, over which the smells of the gasometer, recalled perhaps by the fumes of the coke fire, would come and go with intermittent strength. Earlier in the month droves of boys could be seen drifting in bands, and singly, along this trail, migrating tribes of the region, for ever on the move: trudging into exile until the hour when damp clouds began once more to overwhelm the red houses, and to contort or veil crenellations and pinnacles beyond. Then, with the return of the mist, these nomads would reappear again, straggling disconsolately back to their deserted habitations.

By this stage of the year—exercise no longer contestable five days a week—the road was empty; except for Widmerpool, in a sweater once white and cap at least a size too small, hobbling unevenly, though with determination, on the flat heels of spiked running-shoes. Slowly but surely he loomed through the dusk towards me as I walked back—well wrapped-up, I remember—from an expedition to the High Street. Widmerpool was known to go voluntarily for 'a run' by himself every afternoon. This was his return from trotting across the plough in drizzle that had been falling since early school. I had, of course, often seen him before, because we were in the same house; even spoken with him, though he was a bit older than myself. Anecdotes relating to his acknowledged oddness were also familiar;

but before that moment such stories had not made him live. It was on the bleak December tarmac of that Saturday afternoon in, I suppose, the year 1921 that Widmerpool, fairly heavily built, thick lips and metal-rimmed spectacles giving his face as usual an aggrieved expression, first took coherent form in my mind. As the damp, insistent cold struck up from the road, two thin jets of steam drifted out of his nostrils, by nature much distended, and all at once he seemed to possess a painful solidarity that talk about him had never conveyed. Something comfortless and inelegant in his appearance suddenly impressed itself on the observer, as stiffly, almost majestically, Widmerpool moved on his heels out of the mist.

His status was not high. He had no colours, and, although far from being a dunce, there was nothing notable about his work. At this or any other time of year he could be seen training for any games that were in season: in winter solitary running, with or without a football: in summer, rowing 'courses' on the river, breathing heavily, the sweat clouding his thick lenses, while he dragged his rigger through the water. So far as I know he never reached even the semi-finals of the events for which he used to enter. Most of the time he was alone, and even when he walked with other boys he seemed in some way separate from them. About the house he was more noticeable than in the open air, because his voice was pitched high and he articulated poorly: as if tongue were too big for mouth. This delivery made his words always appear to protest, a manner of speaking almost predictable from his face. In addition to that distinctly noisy manner of utterance, thick rubber reinforcements on soles and heels caused his boots—he wore boots more often than what Stringham used to call 'Widmerpool's good sensible shoes'—to squeal incessantly: their shrill rhythmic bursts of sound, limited in compass like the notes of a barbaric orchestra, giving warning of his approach along the linoleum of distant passages; their sullen whining dirge seeming designed to express in musical terms the mysteries of an existence of toil and abnegation lived apart from the daily life of the tribe. Perhaps he sounds a grotesque and conspicuous figure. In excess, Widmerpool was neither. He had his being, like many others, in obscurity. The gap in age caused most of my knowledge of him to have come second-hand; and, in spite of this abrupt realisation of him as a person that took place on that winter evening, he would have remained a dim outline to me if he had not at an earlier date, and before my own arrival, made himself already memorable, as a new boy, by wearing the wrong kind of overcoat.

At this distance of time I cannot remember precisely what sort of an overcoat Widmerpool was said to have worn in the first instance. Stories about it had grown into legend: so much so that even five or six years later you might still occasionally hear an obtrusive or inappropriate garment referred to as 'a Widmerpool'; and Templer, for example, would sometimes say: 'I am afraid I'm wearing rather Widmerpool socks today', or, 'I've bought a wonderfully Widmerpool tie to go home in'. My impression is that the overcoat's initial deviation from normal was slight, depending on the existence or absence of a belt at the back, the fact that the cut was single- or double-breasted, or, again, irregularity may have had something to do with the collar; perhaps the cloth, even, was of the wrong colour or texture.

As a matter of fact the overcoat was only remarkable in itself as a vehicle for the comment it aroused, insomuch that an element in Widmerpool himself had proved indigestible to the community. An overcoat (which never achieved the smallest notoriety) belonging to a boy called Offord whose parents lived in Madeira, where they had possibly purchased the garment, was indeed once pointed out to me as 'very like Widmerpool's'. There was on no occasion the slightest question of Widmerpool being bullied, or even seriously ragged about the matter. On the contrary, his deviation seems scarcely to have been mentioned to him, except by cruder spirits: the coat becoming recognised almost immediately as a traditionally ludicrous aspect of everyday life. Years later, if you questioned his contemporaries on the subject, they were vague in their answers, and would only laugh and say that he wore the coat for a couple of terms; and then, by the time winter came round again, he was found to possess an overcoat of a more conventional sort.

This overcoat gave Widmerpool a lasting notoriety which his otherwise unscintillating career at school could never wholly dispel. How fully he was aware of this reputation it was hard to say. His behaviour certainly indicated that he hoped for more substantial credit with other people than to be known solely on account of a few months given over to out-of-the-way dress. If such was his aim, he was unsuccessful; and the only occasion when I heard these exertions of his receive some small amount of public recognition had been about a month before this, so to speak transcendental, manifestation of himself to me in the mist. Everyone had been summoned to the house library to listen to complaints that Parkinson, captain of games, wanted to make on the subject of general slackness. Parkinson, rather a feeble figure who blushed easily, had ended his little speech with the words: 'It is a pity that some of you are not as keen as Widmerpool.' There had been loud laughter at this. Parkinson himself grinned sheepishly, and, as usual, went red, as if he had said something that might be considered, even in his own eyes, more than a little indecent:

lightly touching, as his habit was, a constellation of spots accumulated on one of his cheekbones.

Widmerpool himself had not smiled, though he could hardly have failed to notice the laughter. He had stared seriously at his boots with their thick rubber reinforcements, apparently trying to avoid any imputation of priggishness. While he did this, his fingers twitched. His hands were small and gnarled, with nails worn short and cracked, as if he spent his spare time digging with them deep down into the soil. Stringham had said that the nails of the saint who had hollowed his own grave without tools might fairly have competed against Widmerpool's in a manicure contest. If Widmerpool had not developed boils soon after this crumb of praise had been let fall, he would, by the end of the season, have scraped into the house football team. This achievement, however, was not to be; though from the moment that his ailment began to abate he was training again as hard as ever. Some more popular figure was made twelfth man.

Still pondering on this vision of Widmerpool, I entered the house, encountering in the hall its familiar exhalation of carbolic soap, airing blankets, and cold Irish stew—almost welcoming after the fog outside—and mounted the staircase towards tea. A thick black stripe of paint divided the upper, and yellow, half of the wall from the magenta dado beneath. Above this black line was another, mottled and undulating, where passers-by, up and down the stairs, rested arm or shoulder, discolouring the distemper in a slanting band of grey. Two or three boys were as usual standing in front of the notice-board on the first floor, their eyes fixed on the half-sheets of paper attached by drawing-pins to the green baize, gazing at the scrawled lists and regulations as if intent on a tape-machine liable at any moment to announce the winner. There was nothing more recent than one of the recurrent injunctions emanating from Le Bas, our house-master, requiring that all boots should be scraped on the scraper, and then once more scoured on the door-mat on entering the hall, to avoid dispersion of mud throughout the house. On the corner of this grubby fiat Stringham, some days before, had drawn a face in red pencil. Several pairs of eyes were now resting glassily on that outward protest against the voice of authority.

Since the beginning of the term I had messed with Stringham and Templer; and I was already learning a lot from them. Both were a shade older than myself, Stringham by about a year. The arrangement was in part a matter of convenience, dictated by the domestic economy of the house: in this case the distribution of teas. I liked and admired Stringham: Templer I was not yet sure about. The latter's boast that he had never read a book for pleasure in his life did not predispose me in his favour: though he knew far more than I of the things about which books are written. He was also an adept at breaking rules, or diverting them to ends not intended by those who had framed them. Having obtained permission, ostensibly at his parents' request, to consult an oculist, Templer was spending that day in London. It was unlikely that he would cut this visit short enough to enable him to be back in time for tea, a meal taken in Stringham's room.

When I came in, Stringham was kneeling in front of the fire, employing a paper-knife shaped like a scimitar as a toasting-fork. Without looking up, he said: 'There is a jam crisis.'

He was tall and dark, and looked a little like one of those stiff, sad young men in ruffs, whose long legs take up so much room in sixteenth-century portraits: or perhaps a younger—and far slighter—version of Veronese's Alexander receiving the children of Darius after the Battle of Issus:

with the same high forehead and suggestion of hair thinning a bit at the temples. His features certainly seemed to belong to that epoch of painting: the faces in Elizabethan miniatures, lively, obstinate, generous, not very happy, and quite relentless. He was an excellent mimic, and, although he suffered from prolonged fits of melancholy, he talked a lot when one of these splenetic fits was not upon him: and ragged with extraordinary violence when excited. He played cricket well enough to rub along: football he took every opportunity of avoiding. I accepted the piece of toast he held out towards me.

'I bought some sausages.'

'Borrow the frying-pan again. We can do them over the fire.'

The room contained two late eighteenth-century coloured prints of racehorses (Trimalchio and The Pharisee, with blue-chinned jockeys) which hung above a picture, cut out of one of the illustrated weeklies and framed in passe-partout, of Stringham's sister at her wedding: the bridegroom in khaki uniform with one sleeve pinned to his tunic. Over the fireplace was a large, and distinctly florid, photograph of Stringham's mother, with whom he lived, a beauty, and an heiress, who had remarried the previous year after parting from Stringham's father She was a South African. Stuck in the corner of the frame was a snapshot of the elder Stringham, an agreeable-looking man in an open shirt, smoking a pipe with the sun in his eyes. He, too, had remarried, and taken his second, and younger, wife, a Frenchwoman, to Kenya. Stringham did not often talk about his home, and in those days that was all I knew about his family; though Templer had once remarked that 'in that direction there was a good deal of money available', adding that Stringham's parents moved in circles that lived 'at a fairly rapid pace'.

I had been so struck by the conception of Widmerpool, disclosed almost as a new incarnation, shortly before on the road in front of the house, that I described, while the sausages cooked, the manner in which he had materialised in a series of jerks out of the shadows, bearing with him such tokens of despondency. Stringham listened, perforating each of the sausages with the scimitar. He said slowly: 'Widmerpool suffers—or suffered—from contortions of the bottom. Dickinson told me that, in the days when the fags used to parade in the library at tea-time, they were all standing by the wall one evening when suddenly there were inarticulate cries. Owing to this infirmity of his, Widmerpool's legs had unexpectedly given way beneath him.'

'Did he fall?'

'He clung to the moulding of the wall, his feet completely off the ground.'

'What next?'

'He was carted off.'

'I see. Have we any mustard?'

'Now I'll tell you what I saw happen last summer,' Stringham went on, smiling to himself, and continuing to pierce the sausages. 'Peter Templer and I had—for an unaccountable reason—been watching the tail-end of some cricket, and had stopped for a drink on the way back. We found Widmerpool standing by himself with a glass of lemonade in front of him. Some of the Eleven were talking and ragging at the far end of the counter and a skinned banana was thrown. This missed its target and hit Widmerpool. It was a bull's-eye. The banana was over-ripe and it burst all over his face, knocking his spectacles sideways. His cap came off and he spilt most of the lemonade down the front of his clothes.'

'Characteristic of the Eleven's throwing-in.'

'Budd himself was responsible. Widmerpool took out his handkerchief and began to clean up the mess. Budd came down the shop, still laughing, and said: "Sorry, Widmerpool. That banana wasn't intended for you." Widmerpool was obviously astonished to hear himself addressed by name, and so politely, by no less a person than the Captain of the Eleven—who could only have known what Widmerpool was called on account of the famous overcoat. Budd stood there smiling, showing a lot of those film-star teeth of his, and looking more than ever like the hero of an adventure story for boys.'

'That noble brow.'

'It doesn't seem to help him to pile up runs,' said Stringham, 'any more than do those fine cutting shots of his which photograph so well.'

He paused and shook his head, apparently in sadness at the thought of Budd's deficiencies as a cricketer; and then continued: 'Anyway, Budd—exuding charm at every pore—said: "I'm afraid I've made you in a bit of a mess, Widmerpool," and he stood there inspecting the havoc he had just caused. Do you know an absolutely *slavish* look came into Widmerpool's face. "I don't mind," he said, "I don't mind at all, Budd. It doesn't matter in the least." '

Stringham's dexterity at imitating the manner in which Widmerpool talked was remarkable. He stopped the narrative to put some bread into the fat in which the sausages were frying, and, when this was done, said: 'It was as if Widmerpool had experienced some secret and awful pleasure. He had taken off his spectacles and was wiping them, screwing up his eyes, round which there were still traces of banana. He began to blow on the glasses and to rub them with a great show of good cheer. The effect was not at all what might have been hoped. In fact all this heartiness threw the most appalling gloom over the shop.

Budd went back to his friends and finished whatever he was eating, or drinking, in deathly silence. The other members of the Eleven—or whoever they were—stopped laughing and began to mutter self-consciously to themselves about future fixtures. All the kick had gone out of them. I have never seen anything like it. Then Budd picked up his bat and pads and gloves and other belongings, and said: "I must be getting along now. I've got the Musical Society tonight," and there was the usual business of "Good-night, Bill, good-night——" '

' "Good-night, Guy . . . good-night, Stephen . . . good-night, John . . . good-night, Ronnie . . . good-night, George . . ." '

'Exactly,' said Stringham. ' "Good-night, Eddie . . . good-night, Simon . . . good-night, Robin . . ." and so on and so forth until they had all said good-night to each other collectively and individually, and shuffled off together, arm-in-arm. Templer wanted to move because he had to go down-town before lock-up; so we left Widmerpool to himself. He had put on his spectacles again, and straightened his cap, and as we went through the door he was rubbing his gritty little knuckles together, still smiling at his great encounter with Budd.'

The account of this incident, illustrating another of Widmerpool's aspects, did not at that moment make any deep impression on me. It was like a number of other anecdotes on the subject that circulated from time to time, differing only in the proficiency with which Stringham told his stories. My own renewed awareness of Widmerpool's personality seemed to me closer and more real. Stringham, however, had not finished with the matter. He said: 'As we walked past the fives courts, Templer remarked: "I'm glad that ass Widmerpool fielded a banana with his face." I asked why he did not like him—for after all there is little harm in the poor old boy—and it turned out that it was Widmerpool who got Akworth sacked.'

Stringham paused to allow this statement to sink in, while he arranged the sausages in a new pattern. I could not recall at all clearly what Akworth's story had been: though I remembered that he had left the school under a cloud soon after my arrival there, and that various rumours regarding his misdoings had been current at the time.

'Akworth tried to set fire to his room, didn't he? Or did he steal everything that was not nailed down?'

'He well may have done both,' said Stringham; 'but he was principally shot out for sending a note to Peter Templer. Widmerpool intercepted the note and showed it to Le Bas. I must admit that it was news to me when Peter told me.'

'And that was why Peter had taken against Widmerpool?'

'Not only that but Widmerpool got hold of Peter and gave him a tremendous jaw on morals.'

'That must have been very good for him.'

'The jaw went on for so long, and Widmerpool came so close, that Templer said that he thought Widmerpool was going to start something himself.'

'Peter always thinks that about everybody.'

'I agree his conceit is invincible,' said Stringham, turning the sausages thoughtfully, as if contemplating Templer's vanity.

'Did Widmerpool start anything?' I asked.

'It is a grim thought, isn't it?'

'What is the answer?'

Stringham laughed. He said: 'Peter made an absolutely typical Templer remark when I asked him the same question. He said: "No, thank God, but he moved about the room breathing heavily like my sister's white pekinese. Did you see how pleased he was just now to be noticed by Budd? He looked as if he had just been kissed under the mistletoe. Bloody fool. He's so wet you could shoot snipe off him." Can you imagine a more exquisitely Templer phrase? Anyhow, that is how poor old Widmerpool looks to our little room-mate.'

'But what is he like really?'

'If you are not sure what Widmerpool is like,' said Stringham, 'you can't do better than have another look at him. You will have an opportunity at prayers tonight. These sausages are done.'

He stopped speaking, and, picking up the paper-knife again, held it upright, raising his eyebrows, because at that moment there had been a kind of scuffling outside, followed by a knock on the door: in itself a surprising sound. A second later a wavering, infinitely sad voice from beyond said: 'May I come in?'

Obviously this was no boy: the approach sounded unlike a master's. The hinge creaked, and, as the door began to open, a face, deprecatory and enquiring, peered through the narrow space released between the door and the wall. There was an impression of a slight moustache, grey or very fair, and a well-worn, rather sporting tweed suit. I realised all at once, not without apprehension, that my Uncle Giles was attempting to enter the room.

I had not seen my uncle since the end of the war, when he had been wearing some sort of uniform, though not one of an easily recognisable service. This sudden appearance in Stringham's room was an unprecedented incursion: the first time that he had found his way here. He delayed entry for a brief period, pressing the edge of the door against his head, the other side of which touched the wall: rigid, as if imprisoned in a cruel trap specially designed to catch him and his like: some ingenious snare, savage in mechanism, though at the same time calculated to preserve from injury the skin of such rare creatures. Uncle Giles's skin was, in point of fact, not easily injured, though experience of years had made him cautious of assuming as a matter of course that his company would be welcome anywhere—anywhere, at least, where other members of his family might be gathered together. At first, therefore, he did not venture to advance farther into the room, meekly conscious that his unexpected arrival might, not unreasonably, be regarded by the occupants as creating a pivot for potential embarrassment.

'I was just passing through on the way to Reading,' he said. 'Thought I might look you up.'

He stood by the door and appeared a little dazed, perhaps overcome by the rich smell of sausages that permeated the atmosphere of the room: possibly reminding him of what might easily have been a scanty luncheon eaten earlier in the day. Why he should be going to Reading was unguessable. If he had come from London, this could hardly be termed 'on the way'; but it might well be that Uncle Giles had not come from London. His locations were not, as a rule, made public. Stringham stood up and pushed the sausages on to a plate.

'This is my uncle—Captain Jenkins.'

Checking the sausages with the paper-knife, Stringham said: 'I'll get another cup. You'll have tea with us, won't you?'

'Thank you, I never take tea,' said Uncle Giles. 'People who eat tea waste half the afternoon. Never wanted to form the habit.' He added: 'Of course, I'm not speaking of *your* sort of tea.'

He looked round at us, as if for sympathy, a bit uncertain as to whether or not this declaration expressed a justifiable attitude towards tea; unsure—and with good reason—if an assertion that he made efforts, however small, to avoid waste of time would prove easily credible, even in the company in which he now found himself. We borrowed a hard chair from next door, and he sat down, blowing his nose into a bandana handkerchief in a series of little grunts.

'Don't let me keep you fellows from your sausages,' he said. 'They will be getting cold. They look damned good to me.'

Neat, and still slightly military in appearance—though he had not held a commission for at least twenty years and 'captain' was probably a more or less honorary rank, gazetted to him by himself and the better disposed of his relations—my father's brother was now about fifty. His arrival that night made it clear that he had not emigrated: a suggestion put forward at one moment to explain his disappearance for a longer period than usual from public view. There had also been some rather uneasy family jokes regarding the possibility of his having overstepped the limits set by the law in the transaction of everyday business, some slip in financial dealings that might account for an involuntary absence from the scene; for Uncle Giles had been relegated by most of the people who knew him at all well to that limbo where nothing is expected of a person, and where more than usually outrageous actions are approached, at least conversationally, as if they constituted a series of practical jokes, more or less enjoyable, according to where responsibility for clearing up matters might fall. The curious thing about persons regarding whom society has taken this largely self-defensive measure is that the existence of the individual himself reaches a pitch when nothing he does can ever be accepted as serious. If he commits suicide, or murder, only the grotesque aspects of the event dominate the circumstances: on the whole, avoidance of such major issues being an integral part of such a condition. My uncle was a good example of the action of this law; though naturally I did not in those days see him with anything like this clearness of vision. If Reading were his destination, there could be no hint of immediate intention to leave the country: and, unless on ticket-of-leave, he was evidently under no sort of legal restraint. He finished blowing his nose, pushed the handkerchief back up his sleeve, and, using without facetious implication a then popular catchword. said: 'How's your father?'

'All right.'

'And your mother?'

'Very well.'

'Good,' said Uncle Giles, as if it were a relief to him personally that my parents were well, even when the rest of the world might feel differently on the same matter.

There was a pause. I asked how his own health had been, at which he laughed scornfully.

'Oh, me,' he said, 'I've been about the same. Not growing any younger. Trouble with the old duodenal. I rather wanted to get hold of your father about signing some papers. Is he still in Paris? I suppose so.'

'That bit of the Conference is finished.'

'Where is he?'

'London.'

'On leave?'

'Yes.'

'The War Office haven't decided where they are going to send him?'

'No.'

My uncle looked put out at this piece of news. It was most unlikely, hardly conceivable, that he really intended to impose his company on my father, who had for many years discouraged close association with his brother, except when possessed with an occasional and uncontrollable desire to tell Uncle Giles to his face what he thought of him, a mood that rarely lasted more than thirty-six hours; by the end of which period of time the foredoomed inefficacy of any such contact made itself clear.

'In London, is he?' said Uncle Giles, wrinkling the dry, reddish skin at the sides of his nostrils, under which a web of small grey veins etched on his nose seemed to imply preliminary outlines for a game of noughts-and-crosses. He brought out a leather cigarette-case and—before I could prevent him—lighted a cigarette.

'Visitors are not really supposed to smoke here.'

'Oh, aren't they?' said Uncle Giles. He looked very surprised. 'Why not?'

'Well, if the place smells of smoke, you can't tell if someone else smokes too.'

'Of course you can't,' said Uncle Giles readily, blowing outward a long jet of smoke. He seemed puzzled.

'Le Bas might think a boy had been smoking.'

'Who is Le Bas?'

'Our housemaster.'

How he had managed to find the house if he were ignorant of Le Bas's identity was mysterious: even inexplicable. It was, however, in keeping with the way my uncle conducted his life that he should reach his destination without knowing the name of the goal. He continued to take small puffs at his cigarette.

'I see,' he said.

'Boys aren't allowed to smoke.'

'Quite right. Stunts the growth. It is a great mistake to smoke before you are twenty-one.'

Uncle Giles straightened his back and squared his shoulders. One had the impression that he was well aware that young people of the day could scarcely attempt to compete with the rigorous standards that had governed his own youth. He shook his head and flicked some ash on to one of the dirty plates.

'It is a hundred to one Le Bas won't come in,' said Stringham. 'I should take a chance on it.'

'Take a chance on what?' Uncle Giles asked.

'On smoking.'

'You mean I really ought to put this out?'

'Don't bother.'

'Most certainly I shall bother,' said Uncle Giles. 'I should not dream of breaking a rule of that sort. Rules are made to be obeyed, however foolish they may sometimes seem. The question is where had I best put this, now that the regulation has been broken?'

By the time my uncle had decided to extinguish the cigarette on the sole of his shoe, and throw the butt into the fire, there was not much left of it. Stringham collected the ash, which had by now found its way into several receptacles, brushing all of this also into the cinders. For the rest of tea, Uncle Giles, who, for the time being at least, had evidently dismissed from his mind the question of discussing arrangements for meeting my father, discoursed, not very lucidly, on the possibility of a moratorium in connexion with German reparations and the fall of the mark. Uncle Giles's sympathies were with the Germans. 'They work hard,' he said. 'Therefore they have my respect.' Why he had suddenly turned up in the manner was not yet clear. When tea came to an end he muttered about wanting to discuss family matters, and, after saying good-bye—for my uncle, almost effusively—to Stringham, he followed me along the passage.

'Who was that?' he asked, when we were alone together.

As a rule Uncle Giles took not the slightest interest in

anyone or anything except himself and his own affairs—indeed was by this time all but incapable of absorbing even the smallest particle of information about others, unless such information had some immediate bearing on his own case. I was therefore surprised when he listened with a show of comparative attention to what I could tell him about Stringham's family. When I had finished, he remarked:

'I used to meet his grandfather in Cape Town.'

'What was he doing there?'

'His mother's father, that was. He made a huge fortune. Not a bad fellow. Knew all the right people, of course.'

'Diamonds?'

I was familiar with detective stories in which South African millionaires had made their money in diamonds.

'Gold,' said Uncle Giles, narrowing his eyes.

My uncle's period in South Africa was one of the several stretches of his career not too closely examined by other members of his family—or, if examined, not discussed—and I hoped that he might be about to give some account of experiences I had always been warned not to enquire into. However, he said no more than: 'I saw your friend's mother once when she was married to Lord Warrington and a very good-looking woman she was.'

'Who was Lord Warrington?'

'Much older than she was. He died. Never a good life, Warrington's. And so you always have tea with young Stringham?'

'And another boy called Templer.'

'Where was Templer?' asked Uncle Giles, rather suspiciously, as if he supposed that someone might have been spying on him unawares, or that he had been swindled out of something.

'In London, having his eyes seen to.'

'What is wrong with his eyes?'

'They ache when he works.'

My uncle thought over this statement, which conveyed in Templer's own words his personal diagnosis of this ocular complaint. Uncle Giles was evidently struck by some similarity of experience, because he was silent for several seconds. I spoke more about Stringham, but Uncle Giles had come to the end of his faculty for absorbing statements regarding other people. He began to tap with his knuckles on the window-pane, continuing this tattoo until I had given up attempting, so far as I knew it, to describe Stringham's background.

'It is about the Trust,' said Uncle Giles, coming abruptly to the end of his drumming, and adopting a manner at once accusing and seasoned with humility.

The Trust, therefore, was at the bottom of this visitation. The Trust explained this arrival by night in winter. If I had thought harder, such an explanation might have occurred to me earlier; but at that age I cannot pretend that I felt greatly interested in the Trust, a subject so often ventilated in my hearing. Perhaps the enormous amount of time and ingenuity that had been devoted by other members of my family to examining the Trust from its innumerable aspects had even decreased for me its intrinsic attraction. In fact the topic bored me. Looking back, I can understand the fascination that the Trust possessed for my relations: especially for those, like Uncle Giles, who benefited from it to a greater or lesser degree. In those days the keenness of their interest seemed something akin to madness.

The money came from a great-aunt, who had tied it up in such a way as to raise what were, I believe, some quite interesting questions of legal definition. In addition to this, one of my father's other brothers, Uncle Martin, also a beneficiary, a bachelor, killed at the second battle of the Marne, had greatly complicated matters, although there was not a great deal of money to divide, by leaving a will of his own devising, which still further secured the capital without making it absolutely clear who should enjoy the interest. My father and Uncle Giles had accordingly come to a 'gentleman's agreement' on the subject of their respective shares (which brought in about one hundred and eighty-five pounds annually, or possibly nearly two hundred in a good year); but Uncle Giles had never been satisfied that he was receiving the full amount to which he was by right entitled: so that when times were hard—which happened about every eighteen months—he used to apply pressure with a view to squeezing out a few pounds more than his agreed portion. The repetition of these tactics, forgotten for a time and then breaking out again like one of Uncle Giles's duodenal ulcers, had the effect of making my father exceedingly angry; and, taken in conjunction with the rest of my uncle's manner of life, they had resulted in an almost complete severance of relations between the two brothers.

'As you probably know,' said Uncle Giles, 'I owe your father a small sum of money. Nothing much. Decent of him to have given me the use of it, all the same. Some brothers wouldn't have done as much. I just wanted to tell him that I proposed to let him have the sum in question back.'

This proposal certainly suggested an act to which, on the face of it, there appeared no valid objection; but my uncle, perhaps from force of habit, continued to approach the matter circumspectly. 'It is just a question of the trustees,' he said once or twice; and he proceeded to embark on explanations that seemed to indicate that he had some idea of presenting through myself the latest case for the adjustment of his revenue: tacking on repayment of an ancient debt as a piece of live bait. Any reason that might have been advanced earlier for my becoming the medium in these negotiations, on the grounds that my father was still out of England, had been utterly demolished by the information that he was to be found in London. However, tenacity in certain directions—notably that of the Trust—was one of Uncle Giles's characteristics. He was also habitually unwilling to believe that altered circumstances might affect any matter upon which he had already made up his mind. He therefore entered now upon a comprehensive account of the terms of the Trust, his own pecuniary embarrassment, the forbearance he had shown in the past—both to his relations and the world at large—and the reforms he suggested for the future.

'I'm not a great business expert,' he said, 'I don't claim to be a master brain of finance or anything of that sort. The only training I ever had was to be a soldier. We know how much use that is. All the same, I've had a bit of experience in my day. I've knocked about the world and roughed it. Perhaps I'm not quite so green as I look.'

Uncle Giles became almost truculent for a man with normally so quiet a manner when he said this; as if he expected that I was prepared to argue that he was indeed 'green', or, through some other similar failing, unsuited to run his own affairs. I felt, on the contrary, that in some ways it had to be admitted that he was unusually well equipped for looking after himself: in any case a subject I should not have taken upon myself to dispute with him. There was, therefore, nothing to do but agree to pass on anything he had to say. His mastery of the hard-luck story was of a kind never achieved by persons not wholly concentrated on themselves.

'Quand même,' he said at the end of a tremendous parade

of facts and figures, 'I suppose there is such a thing as family feeling?'

I mumbled.

'After all there was the Jenkins they fought the War of Jenkins's Ear about.'

'Yes.'

'We are all descended from him.'

'Not directly.'

'Collaterally then.'

'It has never been proved, has it?'

'What I mean is that he was a relation and that should keep us together.'

'Well, our ancestor, Hannibal Jenkins, of Cwm Shenkin, paid the Hearth Tax in 1674——'

Perhaps justifiably, Uncle Giles made a gesture as if to dismiss pedantry—and especially genealogical pedantry—in all its protean shapes: at the same time picking up his hat. He said: 'All I mean is that just because I am a bit of a radical, it doesn't mean that I believe tradition counts for nothing.'

'Of course not.'

'Don't think that for a moment.'

'Not a bit.'

'Then you will put it to your father?'

'All right.'

'Can you get leave to walk with me as far as the station?'

'No.'

We set off together down the stairs, Uncle Giles continually stopping on the way to elaborate points omitted in his earlier argument. This was embarrassing, as other boys were hanging about the passages, and I tried, without success, to hurry him along. The front door was locked, and Cattle, the porter, had to be found to obtain the key. For a time we wandered about in a kind of no-man's-land of laundry baskets and coke, until Cattle, more or less asleep, was at last discovered in the boot-room. A lumbering, disagreeable character, he unlocked the door under protest, letting into the house a cloud of fog. Uncle Giles reached the threshold and plunged his hand deep into his trouser pocket as if in search of a coin: stood for what seemed an age sunk in reverie: thought better of an earlier impulse: and stepped briskly out into the mist with a curt 'Good-night to you'. He was instantly swallowed up in the gloom, and I was left standing on the steps with Cattle, whose grousing, silenced for the passage of time during which there had seemed hope of money changing hands, now began to rumble again like the buzz of distant traffic. As I returned slowly up the stairs, this sound of complaint sank to a low growling, punctuated with sharp clangs as the door was once more laboriously locked, bolted, and chained.

On the whole it could not be said that one felt better for Uncle Giles's visit. He brought with him some fleeting suggestion, always welcome at school, of an outside world: though against this had to be weighed the disturbing impact of home-life in school surroundings: even home-life in its diminished and undomestic embodiment represented by my uncle. He was a relation: a being who had in him perhaps some of the same essence that went towards forming oneself as a separate entity. Would one's adult days be spent in worrying about the Trust? What was he going to do at Reading? Did he manage to have quite a lot of fun, or did he live in perpetual hell? These were things to be considered. Some apology for his sudden appearance seemed owed to Stringham: after that, I might try to do some work to be dealt with over the week-end.

When I reached the door I heard a complaining voice raised inside the room. Listening for a moment, I recognised the tone as Le Bas's. He was not best pleased. I went in. Le Bas had come to find Templer, and was now making a fuss about the cigarette smoke.

'Here is Jenkins, sir,' said Stringham. 'He has just been seeing his uncle out of the house.'

He glanced across at me, putting on an expression to indicate that the ball was now at my foot. The room certainly smelt abominably of smoke when entered from the passage. Le Bas was evidently pretty angry.

He was a tall, untidy man, clean-shaven and bald with large rimless spectacles that gave him a curiously Teutonic appearance: like a German priest. Whenever he removed these spectacles he used to rub his eyes vigorously with the back of his hand, and, perhaps as a result of this habit, his eyelids looked chronically red and sore. On some occasions, especially when vexed, he had the habit of getting into unusual positions, stretching his legs far apart and putting his hands on his hips; or standing at attention with heels together and feet turned outwards so far that is seemed impossible that he should not overbalance and fall flat on his face. Alternatively, especially when in a good humour, he would balance on the fender, with each foot pointing in the same direction. These postures gave him the air of belonging to some highly conventionalised form of graphic art: an oriental god, or knave of playing cards. He found difficulty with the letter 'R', and spoke—like Widmerpool—rather as if he were holding an object about the size of a nut in his mouth. To overcome this slight impediment he was careful to make his utterance always slow and very distinct. He was unmarried.

'Stringham appears to think that you can explain, Jenkins, why this room is full of smoke.'

'I am afraid my uncle came to see me, sir. He lit a cigarette without thinking.'

'Where is your uncle?'

'I have just been getting Cattle to let him out of the house.'

'How did he get in?'

'I think he came in at the front door, sir. I am not sure.'

I watched Stringham, from where he stood behind Le Bas, make a movement as of one climbing a rope, following these gestures with motions of his elbows to represent the beating of wings, both dumb-shows no doubt intended to demonstrate alternative methods of ingress possibly employed by Uncle Giles.

'But the door is locked.'

'I suppose he must have come in before Cattle shut the door, sir.'

'You both of you—' he turned towards Stringham to include him in the indictment '—know perfectly well that visitors are *not allowed to smoke in the house.*'

He certainly made it sound a most horrible offence. Quite apart from all the bother that this was going to cause, I felt a twinge of regret that I had not managed to control Uncle Giles more effectively: insomuch that I had been brought up to regard any form of allowing him his head as a display of weakness on the part of his own family.

'Of course as soon as he was told, sir . . .'

'But why is there this *smell?*'

Le Bas spoke as if smoking were bad enough in all conscience: but that, if people must smoke, they might at least be expected to do so without the propagation of perceptible fumes. Stringham said: 'I think the stub—the fag-end, sir—may have smouldered. It might have been a *Turkish* cigarette. I believe they have a rather stronger scent than Virginian.'

He looked round the room, and lifted a cushion from one of the chairs, shaking his head and sniffing. This was not the sort of conduct to improve a bad situation. Le Bas, although he disliked Templer, had never showed any special animus against Stringham or myself. Indeed Stringham was rather a favourite of his, because he was quick at knowing the sources of the quotations that Le Bas, when in a good temper, liked to make. However, like most schoolmasters, he was inclined to feel suspicious of all boys in his house as they grew older; not because he was in any sense an unfriendly man, though abrupt and reserved, but simply on account of the increased difficulty in handling the daily affairs of creatures who tended less and less to fit into a convenient and formalised framework: or, at least, a framework that was convenient to Le Bas because he himself had formalised it. That was how Le Bas's attitude of mind appeared to me in later years. At the time of his complaint about Uncle Giles's cigarette, he merely seemed to Stringham and myself a dangerous lunatic, to be humoured and outwitted.

'How am I to know that neither of you smoked too?' he said, sweeping aside the persistent denials that both of us immediately offered. 'How can I possibly tell?'

He sounded at the same time angry and despairing. He said: 'You must write a letter to your uncle, Jenkins, and ask him to *give his word* that neither of you smoked.'

'But I don't know his address, sir. All I know was that he was on his way to Reading.'

'By car?'

'By train, I think, sir.'

'Nonsense, nonsense,' said Le Bas. 'Not know your own uncle's address? Get it from your parents if necessary. I shall make myself very objectionable to you both until I see that letter.'

He raised his hands from his sides a little way, and clenched his fists, as if he were about to leap high into the air like an athlete, or ballet dancer; and in this taut attitude he seemed to be considering how best to carry out his threat, while he breathed heavily inward as if to imbibe the full savour of sausages and tobacco smoke that still hung about the room. At that moment there was a sound of talking, and some laughter, in the passage. The door was suddenly flung open, and Templer burst into the room. He was brought up short by the sight of Le Bas: in whom Templer immediately called up a new train of thought.

'Ah, Templer, there you are. You went to London, didn't you? What time did your train get in this evening?'

'It was late, sir,' said Templer, who seemed more than usually pleased with himself, though aware that there might be trouble ahead: he dropped his voice a little: 'I couldn't afford a cab, sir, so I walked.'

He had a thin face and light blue eyes that gave out a perpetual and quite mechanical sparkle: at first engaging: then irritating: and finally a normal and inevitable aspect of his features that one no longer noticed. His hair came down in a sharp angle on the forehead and his large pointed ears were like those attributed to satyrs, 'a race amongst whom Templer would have found some interests in common', as Stringham had said, when Templer's ears had been dignified by someone with this classical comparison. His eyes flashed and twinkled now like the lamps of a lighthouse as he fixed them on Le Bas, while both settled down to a duel about the railway time-table. Although Templer fenced with skill, it seemed pretty clear that he would be forced, in due course, to admit that he had taken a train later than that prescribed by regulations. But Le Bas, who not uncommonly forgot entirely about the matter in hand, suddenly seemed to lose interest in Templer's train and its time of arrival (just as he had for the moment abandoned the subject of Uncle Giles's cigarette); and he hurried away, muttering something about Greek unseens. For the moment we were free of him. Templer sat down in the armchair.

'Did he come in when you were having a gasper?' he said. 'The room reeks as if camels had been stabled in it.'

'You don't suppose we should be such fools as to smoke in the house,' said Stringham. 'It was Jenkins's uncle. But my dear Peter, why do you always go about dressed as if you were going to dance up and down a row of naked ladies singing "Dapper Dan was a very handy man", or something equally lyrical? You get more like an advertisement for gents' tailoring every day.'

'I think it is rather a good get-up for London,' said Templer, examining a handful of his suit. 'Every item chosen with thought, I can assure you.'

Stringham said: 'If you're not careful you will suffer the awful fate of the man who always knows the right clothes to wear and the right shop to buy them at.'

Templer laughed. He had a kind of natural jauntiness that seemed to require to be helped out by more than ordinary attention to what he wore: a quality that might in the last resort save him from Stringham's warning picture of the dangers of dressing too well. As a matter of fact, although he used to make fun of him to his face, Stringham was stimulated, perhaps a little impressed, by Templer; however often he might repeat that: 'Peter Templer's affectation that he has to find time to smoke at least one pipe a day bores me to death: nor did it cut any ice with me when he pointed out the empty half-bottle of whisky he had deposited behind the conservatory in Le Bas's garden.' The previous summer, Stringham and Templer had managed to attend a race-meeting together one half-holiday afternoon without being caught. Such adventures I felt to be a bit above my head, though I enjoyed hearing about them. I was, as I have said, not yet sure that I really liked Templer. His chief subjects of conversation were clothes, girls, and the persecutions of Le Bas, who, always sensitive to the possibility of being ragged, tended to make himself unnecessarily disagreeable in any quarter that might reasonably be thought to arouse special apprehension. Besides this, Templer could not possibly be looked upon as a credit to the house. He was not much of a hand at the sort of games that are played at school (though his build made him good at tennis and golf), so that he was in a weak position, being fairly lazy at work, to withstand prolonged aggression from a housemaster. Consequently Templer was involved in a continuous series of minor rows. The question of the train was evidently to become the current point for Le Bas's attack.

'Well, that all seems to have blown over for the moment,' Stringham said. 'You ought to keep your uncles in better order, Jenkins.'

I explained that Uncle Giles was known for being impossible to keep in order, and that he always left trouble in his wake. Templer said: 'I suppose Le Bas will go on pestering about that train. You know, I used to be a great pet of his. Now his only object seems to be to get me sacked.'

'He ought to be able to bring that off sooner or later with your help,' said Stringham. 'After all he is not an absolute fool: though pretty near it.'

'I believe he was quite an oar in his youth,' said Templer. 'At least he won the Diamond Sculls. Still, past successes at Henley don't make him any more tolerable to deal with as a housemaster.'

'He started life as a poet,' Stringham said. 'Did you know that? Years ago, after coming back from a holiday in Greece, he wrote some things that he thought were frightfully good. He showed them to someone or other who pointed out that, as a matter of fact, they were frightfully bad. Le Bas never got over it.'

'I can't imagine anything more appalling than a poem by Le Bas,' said Templer, 'though I'm surprised he doesn't make his pupils learn them.'

'Who did he show them to?' I asked.

'Oh, I don't know,' said Stringham. 'Henry James, or Robert Louis Stevenson, or someone like that.'

'Who on earth told you?'

'An elderly character who came to lunch. I believe he is an ambassador somewhere; or was. He used to run round with the same gang as Le Bas. He said Le Bas used to be tremendously promising as a young man. He was good at everything.'

'I can't imagine he was ever much good with the girls,' said Templer.

'Maybe not,' said Stringham. 'Not everyone has your singleness of aim. As a matter of fact do you think Le Bas has any sex life?'

'I don't know about Le Bas,' said Templer, who had evidently been waiting since his arrival back from London for the right moment to make some important announcement about himself, 'but I have. The reason I took the later train was because I was with a girl.'

'You devil.'

'I was a devil, I can assure you.'

'I suppose we shall have to hear about it,' said Stringham. 'Don't spare my feelings. Did you hold hands at the cinema? Where did you meet?'

'In the street.'

'Do you mean you picked her up?'

'Yes.'

'Fair or dark?'

'Fair.'

'And how was the introduction effected?'

'She smiled at me.'

'A tart, in other words.'

'I suppose she was, in a kind of way,' said Templer, 'but quite young.'

'You know, Peter, you are just exactly the sort of boy my parents warned me against.'

'I went back to her flat.'

'How did you acquit yourself?'

'It was rather a success; except that the scent she used was absolutely asphyxiating. I was a bit afraid Le Bas might notice it on my clothes.'

'Not after the cigarette smoked by Jenkins's uncle. Was it a well appointed apartment?'

'I admit the accommodation was a bit on the squalid side,' said Templer. 'You can't have everything for a quid.'

'That wasn't very munificent, was it?'

'All I had. That was why I had to walk from the station.'

'You seem to have been what Le Bas would call "a very unwise young man".'

'I see no reason why Le Bas should be worried by the matter, if he didn't notice the scent.'

'What an indescribably sordid incident,' said Stringham. 'However, let's hear full details.'

'Not if you don't want to be told them.'

'We do.'

Templer was supplying further particulars when Le Bas appeared in the room again. He seemed increasingly agitated, and said: 'Templer, I want you to come and show me in the time-table which train you took. I have telephoned to the station and have been told that the one you should have travelled on was *not* late—and Jenkins, don't forget that I shall expect to see that letter from your uncle by the end of the week. You had better keep him up to it, Stringham, as it is just as much in your interests as his that the matter should be cleared up.'

He tore off up the passage with Templer following behind at a slower pace. Stringham said: 'Peter is crazy. He really will get shot out sooner or later.'

Although incomplete, the story of Templer's London adventure—to be recapitulated on countless future occasions—had sufficiently amplified the incident for its significance to be inescapably clear to Stringham and myself. This was a glimpse through that mysterious door, once shut, that now seemed to stand ajar. It was as if sounds of far-off conflict, or the muffled din of music and shouting, dimly heard in the past, had now come closer than ever before. Stringham smiled to himself and whistled. I think he felt a little uneasy in the awareness that Templer was one up on him now. He did not discuss the matter further: I too had no comment to make before thinking things over. After a time Templer returned to the room. He said: 'What an infernal nuisance that man Le Bas is. I think he is going to write to my father. I particularly do not want trouble at this moment.'

'He seems to have developed a mania for letters flying in all directions,' said Stringham. 'However, I feel competent to deal with his puny onslaughts. Meanwhile, I should like to hear more of this unfortunate incident which you were in the course of describing with such a wealth of colour. Begin at the beginning, please.'

The episode that Stringham continued to call 'Templer's unfortunate incident', not startlingly interesting in itself, somehow crystallised my impression of Templer's character: rather in the same way that seeing Widmerpool coming home from his 'run' had established a picture of him in my mind, not different from the earlier perception held there, but one set in a clearer focus. Templer's adventure indicated the lengths to which he was prepared to go, and behaviour that had previously seemed to me needless—and even rather tiresome—bravado on his part harmonised with a changing and widening experience. I found that I suddenly liked him better. His personality seemed to have fallen into place. There could be no doubt that he himself felt a milestone to have been passed; and, probably for this reason, became in some ways a quieter, more agreeable, friend. In due course, though not before the end of the term had been reached, Le Bas agreed to some sort of a compromise about the train: Templer admitting that he had been wrong in not returning earlier, at the same time producing evidence to show that alterations in the time-table might reasonably be supposed to have misled him. This saved Le Bas's face, and the matter was allowed to drop at the expense of some minor penalty. The question of Uncle Giles's cigarette was, however, pursued with extraordinary relentlessness into the New Year. My uncle's lapse seemed in some manner to have brought home to Le Bas the suspicion that Stringham and I might have developed a tendency, no less pernicious than Templer's, to break rules; and he managed in a number of small ways to make himself, as he had promised, decidedly obnoxious to both of us. I wrote twice to Uncle Giles, though without much hope of hearing from him. Months later, the second letter arrived back from his last address marked 'Gone Away': just as if—as Stringham had remarked—my uncle had been a fox. This envelope finally satisfied Le Bas; but in future he was never quite the same either to Stringham or myself, the deterioration of his relations with Stringham leading ultimately to the incident of 'Braddock alias Thorne', an occasion which illustrated, curiously enough, another aspect of Widmerpool, though in it he played an entirely subordinate part.

This rather absurd affair, which did no one great credit, took place the following summer. Stringham, Templer and I were still messing together; and by then both of them had become so much part of my existence at school that it seemed strange to me that I had ever had doubts about either as a companion: though Stringham remained the one with whom I had most in common. Even now it seems to me that I spent a large proportion of my life in their close company, although the time that we were all three together was less than eighteen months. Their behaviour exemplified two different sides of life, in spite of some outward similarity in their tastes. For Templer, there was no truth except in tangible things: though he was not ambitious. Stringham, as I now see him, was romantic, and would perhaps have liked to play a somewhat different rôle from that which varying moods, and love of eccentricity, entailed upon him. Personally, I was aware of no particular drift to my life at that time. The days passed, and only later could their inexorable comment be recorded; and, pointless in some respects as was the Braddock alias Thorne episode, it retains a place, though not a specially admirable one, in my recollections of Stringham especially.

The three of us had gone for a walk one Sunday afternoon and were wandering about, rather aimlessly, in the heat; Stringham and Templer having wished to proceed in opposite directions. Passing the police-station, which we had finally reached without yet deciding on a line of march, Stringham had paused to read the posters pasted up outside: where, among a collection of notices referring to lost dogs, stolen jewellery, and foot-and-mouth disease, was reproduced the likeness of a man wanted for fraud. He was called 'Braddock alias Thorne', and his portrait showed one of those blurred, nondescript countenances, familiar in advertisements depicting persons who testify that patent medicine has banished their uric acid, or that application of some more efficacious remedy has enabled them to dispense with the use of a truss. The writing under the picture said that Braddock alias Thorne (who seemed to have committed an unusually large number of petty offences) was a man of respectable appearance, probably dressed in a black suit. The description was hardly borne out by what could be resolved from the photograph, which showed a bald, middle-aged criminal in spectacles, who looked capable of any enormity. Stringham remarked that the picture resembled President Woodrow Wilson. Templer said: 'It is much more like Le Bas.'

'More of a poet,' said Stringham, who loved to emphasise this side of Le Bas's personality; and had indeed built up a picture of his housemaster as a man whose every spare moment was spent in scribbling verses with the help of a rhyming dictionary. He said: 'There is a touch of distinction about Braddock alias Thorne, and absolutely none about Le Bas.'

'Must we spend the whole afternoon reading this stuff?' said Templer. 'It is about as interesting as the house notice-board. Let's go somewhere where I can have my pipe. There is no point in trudging about the town on Sunday.'

And so we turned about towards the fields, passing the house again, and entering an area of dusty cow-parsley and parched meadows. While still on the road the figure of Widmerpool appeared in front of us. He was tramping along in the sunlight, swinging arms and legs like an automaton of which the mechanism might be slightly out of order. We walked behind him for a time, Stringham doing an imitation of the way Widmerpool put his feet to the ground. From an unreasoning fear of the embarrassment that would be caused me if Widmerpool should look back and himself observe Stringham's agitated pantomime, I persuaded him to stop this improvisation. I had remained in some odd manner interested in Widmerpool since that night in the fog; and, although Stringham's imitation was ludicrously exact, to think that Widmerpool might see it was for some reason painful to me; though I was almost sorry when the time came to turn off the road and leave Widmerpool to disappear in a distant cloud of dust.

'I don't know what I should do without Widmerpool,' Stringham said. 'He keeps me young.'

'I sometimes wonder whether he is a human being at all,' Templer said. 'He certainly doesn't move like one.'

We passed beyond the railway line to pasture, where Templer lit up his horrible, stubby pipe, and argued as we walked along about the age of the Dolly Sisters, one of whom Stringham held to be the mother of the other. The sun was too hot to make our way straight across the grass, so that we moved along by hedges, where there was some little shade. Templer was still vigorously contesting Stringham's theory of relationship, when we came through some trees and faced a low bank, covered with undergrowth, which stood between us and the next field. The road was by this time fairly far away. Stringham and Templer now ceased to discuss the Dolly Sisters, and both took a run at this obstacle. Stringham got over first, disappearing down the far side: from which a sort of cry, or exclamation, sounded. As Templer came to the top of the mound of grass, I noticed him snatch his pipe from his mouth and jump. I came up the slope at my leisure, behind the other two, and, reaching the crest, saw them at the foot of the bank. There was an unexpectedly deep drop to the ground. In the field below, Stringham and Templer were talking to Le Bas, who was reclining on the ground, leaning on one elbow.

Stringham was bending forward a little, talking hard. Templer had managed to get his pipe back into his pocket, or was concealing it in his hand, because, when I reached the level of the field, it had disappeared: although the rank, musty odour of the shag which he was affecting at that period swept from time to time through the warm air, indicating that the tobacco was still alight in the neighbourhood. Le Bas had in his hand a small blue book. It was open. I saw from the type face that it contained verse. His hat hung from the top of his walking stick, which he had thrust into the ground, and his bald head was sweating a bit on top. He crouched there in the manner of a large animal—some beast alien to the English countryside, a yak or sea-lion—taking its ease: marring, as Stringham said later, the beauty of the summer afternoon. However, Le Bas appeared to be in a moderately good humour. He was saying to Stringham: 'I don't know why I should tolerate this invasion of my favourite spot. Cannot you all understand that I come here to get away from people like you and Jenkins and Templer? I want peace and quiet for once: not to be surrounded by my pupils.'

'It is a nice place, sir,' said Stringham, smiling, though not in the least committing himself by too much friendliness all at once.

Le Bas turned without warning to his book, and, picking it up from the ground, began to read aloud in his guttural, controlled voice:

> '"Ah! leave the smoke, the wealth, the roar
> Of London, and the bustling street,
> For still, by the Sicilian shore,
> The murmur of the Muse is sweet,

Still, still, the suns of summer greet
The mountain-grave of Helikê,
And shepherds still their songs repeat,
Where breaks the blue Sicilian sea.

' "Theocritus! thou canst restore
The pleasant years, and over-fleet;
With thee we live as men of yore,
We rest where running waters meet:
And then we turn unwilling feet
And seek the world—so must it be—
We may not linger in the heat
Where breaks the blue Sicilian sea!" '

He shut the book with a snap, and said: 'Now can any one of you tell me who wrote that?'

We made various suggestions—Templer characteristically opting for Shakespeare—and then Stringham said: 'Matthew Arnold.'

'Not a bad shot,' said Le Bas. 'It is Andrew Lang as a matter of fact. Fine lines, you know.'

Another fetid whiff of Templer's shag puffed its way through the ether. It seemed impossible that Le Bas should remain much longer unaware that a pipe was smoking somewhere near him. However, he seemed to be getting into his stride on the subject of poetry. He said: 'There are descriptive verses by Arnold somewhat similar in metre that may have run in your head, Stringham. Things like:

' "The clouds are on the Oberland,
The Jungfrau's snows look faint and far;
But bright are those green fields at hand,
And through those fields comes down the Aar."

'Rather a different geographical situation, it is true, but the same mood of invoking melancholy by graphic description of natural features of the landscape.'

Stringham said: 'The Andrew Lang made me think of:

> ' "O singer of Persephone!
> In the dim meadows desolate
> Dost thou remember Sicily?"

'Do you know that, sir? I don't know how it goes on, but the lines keep on repeating.'

Le Bas looked a little uneasy at this. It was evident that Stringham had displeased him in some way. He said rather gruffly: 'It is a villanelle. I believe Oscar Wilde wrote it, didn't he? Not a very distinguished versifier.'

Quickly abandoning what had apparently been taken as a hostile standpoint, Stringham went on: 'And then Heraclitus——'

The words had an instantaneous effect. Le Bas's face cleared at once, and he broke in with more reverberance even than before:

> ' "Still are thy pleasant voices, thy nightingales awake,
> For Death he taketh all away, but them he cannot take."

'I think you are right, Stringham. Good. Very good. In fact, alpha plus. It all has the same note of nineteenth-century nostalgia for a classical past largely of their own imagining.'

Le Bas sighed, and, removing his spectacles, began in his accustomed manner to massage his eyelids, which appeared to be a trifle less inflamed than normally.

'I looked up Heraclitus in the classical dictionary, sir,' said Stringham, 'and was rather surprised to find that he fed mostly on grass and made his house on a dung-hill. I can quite understand his wanting to be a guest if that is how he lived at home, but I shouldn't have thought that he would have been a very welcome one. Though it is true that one would probably remember him afterwards.'

Le Bas was absolutely delighted at this remark. He laughed aloud, a rare thing with him. 'Splendid, Stringham, splendid,' he said. 'You have confused the friend of Callimachus with a philosopher who lived probably a couple of centuries earlier. But I quite agree that if the other Heraclitus's habits had been those you describe, he would not have been any encouragement to hospitality.'

He laughed a lot, and this would have been the moment to leave him, and go on our way. We should probably have escaped without further trouble if Templer—feeling no doubt that Stringham had been occupying too much of the stage—had not begun to shoot out radiations towards Le Bas, long and short, like an ocular Morse code, saying at the same time in his naturally rather harsh voice: 'I am afraid we very nearly jumped on you, sir.'

Le Bas at once looked less friendly. In any case it was an unwise remark to make and Templer managed to imply a kind of threat in the tone, probably the consequence in some degree of his perpetual war with Le Bas. As a result of this observation, Le Bas at once launched into a long, and wholly irrelevant, speech on the topic of his new scheme for the prevention of the theft of books from the slab in the hall: a favourite subject of his for wearing down resistance in members of his house. It was accordingly some time before we were at last able to escape from the field, and from Le Bas: who returned to his book of verse. Fortunately the pipe seemed to have extinguished itself during the latter period of Le Bas's harangue; or perhaps its smell was absorbed by that of the gas-works, which, absent in the earlier afternoon, had now become apparent.

Behind the next hedge Templer took the pipe from his pocket and tapped it out against his heel.

'That was a near one,' he said. 'I burnt my hand on that bloody pipe. Why on earth did you want to go on like that about poetry?'

'How Le Bas failed to notice the appalling stink from your pipe will always be a mystery,' Stringham said. 'His olfactory sense must be deficient—probably adenoids. Why, therefore, did he make so much fuss about Jenkins's uncle's cigarette? It is an interesting question.'

'But Heraclitus, or whoever it was,' said Templer. 'It was all so utterly unnecessary.'

'Heraclitus put him in a good temper,' said Stringham. 'It was your threatening to jump on him that made the trouble.'

'It was your talking about Oscar Wilde.'

'Nonsense.'

'Anyway,' said Templer, 'Le Bas has thoroughly spoiled my afternoon. Let's go back.'

Stringham agreed, and we pursued a grassy path bordered with turnip fields. A short distance farther on, this track narrowed, and traversed a locality made up of allotments, dotted here and there with huts, or potting-sheds. Climbing a gate, we came out on to the road. There was a garage opposite with a shack beside it, in front of which stood some battered iron tables and chairs. A notice offered 'Tea and Minerals'. It was a desolate spot. Stringham said: 'We might just drop in here for a cooling drink.'

Templer and I at once protested against entering this uninviting booth, which had nothing whatever to recommend it outwardly. All shops were out-of-bounds on

Sunday, and there was no apparent reason for running the risk of being caught in such a place; especially since Le Bas might easily decide to return to the house along this road. However, Stringham was so pressing that in the end we were persuaded to accompany him into the shack. The front room was empty. A girl in a grubby apron with untidy bobbed hair came in from the back, where a gramophone was playing:

Everything is buzz-buzz now,
Everything is buzz, somehow:
You ring up on your buzzer,
And buzz with one anozzer,
Or, in other words, pow-wow.

The girl moved towards us with reluctance. Stringham ordered ginger-beer. Templer said: 'This place is too awful. Anyway, I loathe sweet drinks.'

We sat down at one of the iron tables, covered with a cloth marked with jagged brown stains. The record stopped: the needle continuing to scratch round and round its centre, revolving slower and slower, until at last the mechanism unwound itself and ceased to operate. Stringham asked the girl if there was a telephone. She made some enquiries from an unseen person, still farther off than the gramophone, and an older woman's voice joined in discussion of the matter. Then the girl came back and told Stringham he could use the telephone in the office of the garage, if he liked to come with her to the back of the building. Stringham disappeared with the girl. Templer said: 'What on earth is happening? He can't be trying to get off with that female.'

We drank our ginger-beer.

'What the hell is he up to?' said Templer again, after

some minutes had passed. 'I hope we don't run into Le Bas coming out of here.'

We finished our drinks, and Templer tried, without success, to engage the girl in conversation, when she came to clear plates and glasses from another table. At last Stringham reappeared, rather hurriedly, his usually pale face slightly flushed. He drank off his ginger-beer at a gulp and said: 'We might be getting along now. I will pay for this.'

Out on the road again, Templer said: 'First we are rushed into this horrible place: then we are rushed out again. What is supposed to be on?"

Stringham said: 'I've just had a word with the police.'

'What about?'

'On the subject of Braddock alias Thorne.'

'Who's that?'

'The chap they wanted for fraud.'

'What about him?'

'Just to inform them of his whereabouts.'

'Is this a joke?'

'Yes.'

'Where did you tell them to look?'

'In a field beyond the railway line.'

'Why?'

'Set your mind to it.'

'Le Bas?'

'Neat, wasn't it?'

'What did they say?'

'I rang up in the character of Le Bas himself,' Stringham said. 'I told them that a man "described as looking rather like me" had been piling up bills at various shops in the town where I had accounts: that I had positive information that the man in question had been only a few minutes earlier at the place I described.'

'Did the police swallow that?'

'They asked me to come to the station. I pretended to get angry at the delay, and—in a really magnificent Le Bas outburst—I said that I had an urgent appointment to address the confirmation candidates (although, as far as I can remember, it is the wrong time of year to be confirmed): that I was late already and must set off at once: and that, if the man were not arrested, I should hold the local police responsible.'

'I foresee the hell of a row,' said Templer. 'Still, one must admit that it was a good idea. Meanwhile, the sooner we get back to the house and supply a few alibis, the better.'

We walked at a fairly smart pace down the road Widmerpool had traversed when I had seen him returning from his run at the end of the previous year: the tar now soft under foot from the heat of the summer sun. Inside, the house was quiet and comparatively cool. Templer, who had recently relaxed his rule of never reading for pleasure, took up *Sanders of the River,* while Stringham and I discussed the probable course that events would take if the police decided to act as a result of the telephone message. We sat about until the bell began to ring for evening chapel.

'Come on,' said Stringham. 'Let's see if there is any news.'

At the foot of the stairs, we met Widmerpool in the hall. He had just come in from outside, and he seemed unusually excited about something. As we passed—contrary in my experience to all precedent so far as his normal behaviour was concerned—he addressed himself to Stringham, in point of age the nearest to him, saying in his shrillest voice: 'I say, do you know Le Bas has been *arrested?'*

He stood there in the shadowy space by the slab in a setting of brown-paper parcels, dog-eared school books, and crumbs—a precinct of which the moral and physical cleansing provoked endless activity in the mind of Le Bas—and stood with his feet apart and eyes expanded, his panting, as Templer had justly described it, like that of an elderly lap-dog: his appearance suggesting rather some unusual creature actually bred in those depths by the slab, amphibious perhaps, though largely belonging to this land-world of blankets and carbolic: scents which attained their maximum density at this point, where they met and mingled with the Irish stew, which, coming from the territories of laundry baskets and coke, reached its most potent force on the first step of the stairs.

Stringham turned to Widmerpool. 'I am not surprised,' he said coldly. 'How did it happen?'

'I was coming back from my walk,' said Widmerpool, in spite of his excitement lowering his voice a little, as though touching on a very sacred subject in thus referring to his personal habits, 'I was coming back from my walk,' he repeated, dwelling on the words, 'and, as I strolled across one of the fields by the railway line, I saw Le Bas lying on the ground reading a book.'

'I hope you weren't smoking, Widmerpool,' said Templer.

Widmerpool ignored this interpolation, and went on: 'Then I noticed that there was a policeman making across the field towards Le Bas. When the policeman—a big, fat fellow—reached Le Bas he seemed to begin reading something from a notebook. Anyway, Le Bas looked very surprised at first. Then he began to get up. I suppose he must have caught his foot in something, because he stumbled. Evidently the policeman thought he was going to try and escape.'

'What happened when he stumbled?' asked Stringham.

'The policeman took his arm.'

'Did he handcuff him?'

'No; but he grabbed him rather roughly.'

'What did Le Bas say?'

'I couldn't hear. It looked as if he were making an awful

fuss. You know the way he stutters when he is angry.'

'And so the policeman led him off?'

'What *could* he have done?' said Widmerpool, who seemed utterly overwhelmed at the idea that his housemaster should have been arrested.

Stringham asked: 'Did anyone else see this?'

'A soldier and a girl appeared from a ditch and watched them go off together.'

'Did Le Bas notice you?'

'I kept behind the hedge. I didn't want to get mixed up with anything awkward.'

'That was wise of you, Widmerpool,' said Stringham. 'Have you told anyone what you saw?'

'Only F. F. Fletcher and Calthorpe Major. I met them on the way back. What can Le Bas have done?'

'Do you mean to tell me you don't know?' said Stringham.

Widmerpool looked taken aback. His breathing had become less heavy while he unburdened himself of his story. Now once more it began to sound like an engine warming up.

'What do you mean?' he asked.

"I don't *mean* anything,' said Stringham, 'except that I am not particularly surprised.'

'But tell me what you think it is.'

Widmerpool spoke almost beseechingly.

'Now look here, Widmerpool,' said Stringham, 'I am awfully sorry. If you have never noticed for yourself anything about our housemaster, it is hardly my place to tell you. You are higher up in the house than I am. You have to shoulder a certain amount of additional responsibility on that account. It is not for me to spread scandals in advance. I fear that we shall all be reading about Le Bas quite soon enough in the papers.'

We left Widmerpool on the steps of the house: to all intents and purposes, a fish recently hauled from the water, making powerful though failing efforts at respiration.

'That boy will be the death of me,' said Stringham, as we walked quickly together up the road.

Most of the crowd who paced up and down by the chapel, passing backwards and forwards over the cobbles, while masters tried to herd them into the building, already knew something of Le Bas's arrest: though only Calthorpe Major, armed with advanced information from Widmerpool, seemed yet to have had time to write home on the subject. 'I sat straight down and sent off a letter to my people about Le Bas having been removed to prison at last,' Calthorpe Major was saying. 'They never liked him. He got his Leander the same time as my father. I've promised to let them know further details as soon as I can get them.' He moved on, repeating the story to friends who had not yet heard the news. Stringham, too, pushed his way through the mob of boys, collecting versions of the scene that had taken place. These were many in number. The bell quickened its ring and stopped with a kind of explosion of sound as the clock began to strike the hour. We were swept up the steps. Stringham said: 'I am afraid it was all in rather doubtful taste. In some ways I regret having been concerned in it. One is such a creature of impulse.'

Although the air under the high vault struck almost chill after the warmth outside in the yard, the evening sun streamed through the windows of the chapel. Rows of boys, fidgeting but silent, provoked, as always, an atmosphere of expectancy before the service began. The voluntary droned quietly for a time, gradually swelling into a bellow: then stopped with a jerk, and began again more gently: remaining for a time at this muted level of sound. Emotional intensity seemed to meet and mingle with an air of indifference, even of cruelty within these ancient walls. Youth and Time here had made, as it were, some compromise. Le Bas came in late, just before the choir, and strode unsteadily towards his stall under the high neo-gothic canopy of carved wood. He looked discomposed. The surface of his skull was red and shining, and, more than once, he seemed to mutter to himself.

Cobberton, another housemaster, and a parson, through gold-rimmed spectacles looked across from the far side of the aisle, lips tightly caught together and eyebrows raised. He and Le Bas had chronically strained relations with one another, and, as it turned out, by one of those happy, or unhappy, chances, Cobberton had finally been the man to establish Le Bas's identity with the police. This fact was subsequently revealed by Cobberton, who also disclosed generally that the policeman who had taken down Stringham's telephone message on the subject of Braddock alias Thorne had remarked to Le Bas, after the matter had been cleared up: 'He'd fair got your manner of speech to a T, sir, whoever he was.'

The congregation rose to sing a hymn. I looked round the packed seats, and lines of faces arranged in tiers. Stringham was opposite, standing with his arms folded, not singing. His cheeks had lost the flush they had taken on during the excitement of all that had followed his telephoning the police-station and had now returned to their usual pallor. He looked grave, lost in thought, almost seraphic: a carved figure symbolising some virtue Resignation or Self-sacrifice. Templer I could not see, because he sat on the same side of the aisle as myself and was too far distant to be visible from my place. On the other side, away to the left, Widmerpool was holding a book in front of him, singing hard: his mouth opening and shutting sharply, more than ever like some uncommon specimen of marine life. He turned his eyes from time to time towards the rafters and high spaces of the roof. I could see his lips forming the syllables. The words of the verse seemed especially applicable to his case, since he was leaving at the end of the term; and I wondered whether the same thought was passing through his own mind:

> As o'er each continent and island
> The dawn leads on another day,
> The voice of prayer is never silent
> Nor dies the strain of praise away.

Somehow I felt rather moved as the hymn rolled on. A group of boys sitting behind me began to chant a descant of their own; making a good deal of noise, not entirely disagreeable. Cobberton noticed the sound, and frowned. Widmerpool also stopped singing for a second and he too glanced across reprovingly. That was my last memory of him at school, because he left, for good, a few weeks later; although owing to some misunderstanding—perhaps Le Bas's mind was more confused than usual on account of the trick played on him—Widmerpool's name continued to appear in the house-list of the following September: a final assertion of the will to remain and strive further for unattainable laurels.

2

It is not easy—perhaps not even desirable—to judge other people by a consistent standard. Conduct obnoxious, even unbearable, in one person may be readily tolerated in another; apparently indispensable principles of behaviour are in practice relaxed—not always with impunity—in the interests of those whose nature seems to demand an exceptional measure. That is one of the difficulties of committing human action to paper, a perplexity that really justifies the alternations of comedy with tragedy in Shakespearian drama: because some characters and some deeds (Uncle Giles's, as I have mentioned) may be thought of only in terms appropriate to themselves, irrespective of their consequence. On the stage, however, masks are assumed with some regard to procedure: in everyday life, the participants act their parts without consideration either for suitability of scene or for the words spoken by the rest of the cast: the result is a general tendency for things to be brought to the level of farce even when the theme is serious enough. This disregard for the unities is something that cannot be circumvented in human life; though there are times when close observation reveals, one way or another, that matters may not have been so irreconcilable at the close of the performance as they may have appeared in the First Act.

For example, in the course of having tea for nine months of the year with Stringham and Templer, the divergent nature of their respective points of view became increasingly clear to me, though compared with some remote figure like

Widmerpool (who, at that time, seemed scarcely to belong to the same species as the other two) they must have appeared, say to Parkinson, as identical in mould: simply on account of their common indifference to a side of life—notably football—in which Parkinson himself showed every sign of finding absorbing interest. As I came gradually to know them better, I saw that, in reality, Stringham and Templer provided, in their respective methods of approaching life, patterns of two very distinguishable forms of existence, each of which deserved consideration in the light of its own special peculiarities: both, at the same time, demanding adjustment of a scale of values that was slowly taking coherent shape so far as my own canons of behaviour were concerned. This contrast was in the main a matter of temperament. In due course I had opportunities to recognise how much their unlikeness to each other might also be attributed to dissimilar background.

The autumn of the year of Le Bas's arrest turned to winter. Stringham was leaving at Christmas. Before going up to the university, he was to stay for some months with his father in Kenya, a trip for which he showed little enthusiasm, his periods of gloom becoming, if anything, of longer duration and more intense. As the time drew near, he used to give prolonged imitations of his father's probable demeanour in handling the natives of his new African home, in the course of which the elder Stringham—reputed to drink too much, though noted for elaborately good manners—employed circumlocutions a little in the manner of Lord Chesterfield to faithful coloured retainers envisaged in terms of Man Friday or Uncle Tom. 'I imagine everyone in Kenya will be terribly hearty and wear shorts and drink sun-downers and all that sort of thing,' Stringham used to say. 'However, it will be nice to leave school and be on one's own at last, even though it is to be one's own in darkest Africa in those great open spaces where men are men.' It was arranged that I should lunch at his mother's house on my way through London on the first day of the holidays. The weather, from being wet and mild, had changed to frost and bright sun; and we travelled up together through white and sparkling fields.

'You will probably meet Buster at lunch,' Stringham said.

'Who is Buster?'

'My mother's current husband.'

I knew nothing of this figure except that he was called Lieutenant-Commander Foxe, and that Stringham had once described him as 'a polo-playing sailor'. When asked what Buster was like, Stringham had replied that he preferred naval officers who were 'not so frightfully grand'. He had not elaborated this description, which did not at that time convey much to me, most of the naval officers I had come across being accustomed to speak of themselves as far from grand and chronically hard-up; though he added in amplification—as if the presence of a husband in his mother's house was in itself odd enough in all conscience—that Buster was 'always about the place'.

'Doesn't he ever go to sea?'

'At present he is at the Admiralty; and, I believe, starting some leave at any moment. However, I suppose it is better to have him living in the house than arriving there at all hours of the day and night disturbing the servants.'

This sketch of Buster evoked an impression of behaviour decidedly unsatisfactory; and for the rest of the journey I was curious to meet someone of mature years and such apparently irregular habits. When we arrived in London, Stringham explained that he wanted to buy some tropical clothes; and, as this proved an amusing occupation, we did not reach the house again until late in the morning; having delivered the luggage there on our arrival. It was a rather gloomy double-fronted façade in a small street near Berkeley Square: the pillars of the entrance flanked on either side with hollow cones for the linkmen to extinguish their torches.

'Come up to the library,' Stringham said. 'We shall probably find Buster there.'

I followed up the stairs into a room on the first floor, generally crimson in effect, containing a couple of large Regency bookcases. A female portrait, by appearance a Romney, hung over the fireplace, and there was a malachite urn of immense size on a marble-topped table by the window: presented, I learnt later, by the Tsar to one of the Warringtons who had headed some diplomatic mission to Russia at the beginning of the nineteenth century. Buster was standing beside this urn, cleaning a cigarette-holder with the end of a match-stick. He was tall, and at once struck me as surprisingly young; with the slightly drawn expression that one recognises in later life as the face of a man who does himself pretty well, while not ceasing to take plenty of exercise. His turn-out was emphatically excellent, and he diffused waves of personality, strong, chilling gusts of icy air, a protective element that threatened to freeze into rigidity all who came through the door, before they could approach him nearer.

'Hullo, you fellows,' he said, without looking up from his cigarette-holder, at which he appeared to be sneering, as if this object were not nearly valuable enough to presume to belong to him.

'Hullo.'

Stringham took a step forward, and, without moving farther into the room, stood for a moment looking more than ever like Veronese's Alexander. Then he introduced me. Buster slipped his cigarette-holder into his pocket, and nodded. He had a way of making one feel remarkably ill at ease. He said: 'It's a blow, but I have to leave you.'

'Aren't you lunching here?' said Stringham.

'I am trying to buy a Bentley from a man awfully cheap. I've got to keep him sweet.'

'Did you sell the Isotta?'

'I had to.'

Buster smiled a little sadly, as if in half public acknowledgment that he himself had long since seen through any illusions once possessed regarding the extent of his wife's fortune; but indicating by the same smile that he had learnt how to bear disappointment. Stringham said: 'Where are you taking him?'

'Claridge's.'

'Will you ply him with drink?'

'Hock, I think. That is what I am feeling like myself. Are you coming to the Russian Ballet tonight?'

'I didn't know I was asked,' Stringham said. 'I'd like to.'

'Do.'

'Anyone for lunch?'

'Only Tuffy. She will be glad to see you.'

'Then we will wish you good luck with your deal.'

I was conscious that some sort of a duel had been taking place, and that Stringham had somehow gained an advantage by, as it were, ordering Buster from the room. Buster himself began to smile, perhaps recognising momentary defeat, to be disregarded from assurance of ultimate victory. Like a man effortlessly winning a walking-race, he crossed the carpet with long, easy strides: at the same time separating from himself some of the eddies of cold air that surrounded him, and bequeathing them to the atmosphere of the room after he had left it. I was relieved at his departure. Stringham moved across to the window.

He said: 'He gets himself up rather like Peter Templer, doesn't he?'

'Have they ever met?'

To my surprise, Stringham laughed aloud.

'Good Lord, no,' he said.

'Wouldn't they like each other?'

'It is an interesting question.'

'Why not try it?'

'I am devoted to Peter,' Stringham said, 'but really I'm not sure one could have him in the house, could one?'

'Oh?'

'Well, I don't really mean that,' said Stringham. 'Not literally, of course. But you must admit that Peter doesn't exactly fit in with home life.'

'I suppose not.'

'You agree?'

'I see what you mean.'

I certainly saw what Stringham meant; even though the sort of home life that included Buster provided a picture rather different from that which the phrase ordinarily suggested to me from my own experience. At the moment, however, I was chiefly conscious of a new balance of relationship between Stringham and Templer. Although their association together possessed a curiously unrelenting quality, like the union of partners in a business rather than the intimacy of friends, I had always thought of Templer as a far closer and more established crony of Stringham's than was I myself; and it had never crossed my mind that Stringham might share at all the want of confidence that, at least in the earlier stages of our acquaintance, I had sometimes felt towards Templer. Templer certainly did not appear to be designed for domestic life: though for that matter the same might be said of Stringham. Before I could ponder the question further, someone descending the stairs passed in through the door left ajar by Buster. Catching sight of this person, Stringham called out: 'Tuffy, how are you?'

The woman who came into the room was about thirty or thirty-five, I suppose, though at the time she impressed me as older. Dressed in black, she was dark and not bad-looking, with a beaky nose. 'Charles,' she said; and, as she smiled at him, she seemed so positively delighted that her face took on a sudden look of intensity, almost of anxiety, the look that women's faces sometimes show at a moment of supreme pleasure.

That quick, avid glance disappeared immediately, though she continued to smile towards him.

'This is Miss Weedon,' said Stringham, laughing in a friendly way, as he took her left hand in his right. 'How have you been, Tuffy?'

Though less glacial than Buster, Miss Weedon was not overwhelmingly affable when she gave me a palm that felt cool and brittle. She said in an aside: 'You know they nearly forgot to take a ticket for you for the Russian Ballet tonight.'

'Good gracious,' said Stringham. 'What next?'

However, he did not show any sign of being specially put out by this lapse on the part of his family.

'I saw to it that they got an extra one.'

'Thank you, Tuffy.'

She had perhaps hoped for something more exuberant in the way of gratitude, because her face hardened a little, while she continued to fix him with her smile.

'We have just been talking to Buster,' Stringham said, plainly dismissing the subject of the tickets.

She put her head a little on one side and remarked: 'I am sure that he was as charming as ever.'

'If possible, even more so.'

'Buster has been behaving *very* well,' she said.

'I am glad to hear it.'

'Now I must rush off and do some things for your mother before luncheon.'

She was gone in a flash. Stringham yawned. I asked about Miss Weedon. Stringham said: 'Tuffy? Oh, she used to be my sister's governess. She stays here a lot of the time. She does all my mother's odd jobs—especially the Hospital.'

He laughed, as if at the thought of the preposterous amount of work that Miss Weedon had to undertake. I was not very clear as to what 'the Hospital' might be; but accepted it as an activity natural enough for Mrs. Foxe.

'Tuffy is a great supporter of mine,' Stringham added: as if in explanation of something that needed explaining.

He did not extend this statement. A moment or two later his mother appeared. I thought her tremendously beautiful: though smaller than the photograph in Stringham's room had suggested. Still wearing a hat, she had just come into the house. She kissed him, and said: 'Everything is in a terrible muddle. I really can't decide whether or not I want to go to Glimber for Christmas. I feel one ought to; but it is so frightfully cold.'

'Come to Kenya with me, instead,' said Stringham. 'Glimber is much too draughty in the winter. Anyway, it would probably kill Buster, who is used to snug cabins.'

'It would be rather fun to spend Christmas on the boat.'

'Too jolly for words,' said Stringham.

'Buster had to lunch out. Did you see him?'

'I hear he is buying a new car.'

'He really did need one,' she said.

This could hardly have been meant for an apology, but her voice sounded a little apprehensive. Changing the subject, she turned to me and said: 'I think poor Mr. Le

Bas must be so glad that Charles has left at last. He used to write the most pathetic letters about him. Still, you weren't expelled, darling. That was clever of you.'

'It took some doing,' Stringham said.

In view of their relationship, this manner of talking was quite unlike anything I had been used to; though, in a general way, fitting the rough outline pieced together from scraps of information regarding his home, or stories about his mother, that Stringham had from time to time let fall. He had, for example, once remarked that she liked interfering in political matters, and I wondered whether some startling intrigue with a member, or members, of the Cabinet would be revealed during luncheon, which was announced a minute or two later. Miss Weedon came down the stairs after us, and, before following into the dining-room, had some sort of a consultation with the footman, to whom she handed a sheaf of papers. As we sat down, Stringham said: 'I hear we are going to the Russian Ballet tonight.'

'It was Buster's idea. He thought you would like it.'

'That was kind of him.'

'I expect you boys—can I still call you boys?—are going to a matinée this afternoon.'

I told her that I had, unfortunately, to catch a train to the country.

'Oh, but that is too sad,' she said, seeming quite cast down. 'Where are you making for?'

I explained that the journey was to the west of England, where my father was on the staff of a Corps Headquarters. Thinking that the exigencies of army life might in all likelihood be unfamiliar to her, I added something about often finding myself in a place different from that in which I had spent previous holidays.

'I know all about the army,' she said. 'My first husband

was a soldier. That was ages ago, of course. Even apart from that we had a house on the Curragh, because he used to train his horses there—so that nothing about soldiering is a mystery to me.'

There was something curiously overpowering about her. Now she seemed to have attached the army to herself, like a piece of property rediscovered after lying for long years forgotten. Lord Warrington had, it appeared, commanded a cavalry brigade before he retired. She told stories of the Duke of Cambridge, and talked of Kitchener and his collection of china.

'Are you going to be a soldier too?' she asked.

'No.'

'I think Charles ought. Anyway for a time. But he doesn't seem awfully keen.'

'No,' said Stringham, 'he doesn't.'

'But your father liked his time in the Grenadiers,' she insisted. 'He always said it did him a lot of good.'

She looked so beseeching when she said this that Stringham burst out laughing; and I laughed too. Even Miss Weedon smiled at the notion that anything so transitory as service with the Grenadiers could ever have done Stringham's father good. Stringham himself had seemed to be on the edge of one of his fits of depression; but now he cheered up for a time: though his mother seemed to exhaust his energies and subdue him. This was not surprising, considering the force of her personality, which perhaps explained some of Buster's need for an elaborate mechanism of self-defence. Except this force, which had something unrestrained, almost alien, about it, she showed no sign whatever of her South African origin. It is true that I did not know what to expect as outward marks of such antecedents; though I had perhaps supposed that in some manner she would be less assimilated into the world in which she now lived. She said: 'This is the last time you will see Charles until he comes back from Kenya.'

'We meet in the autumn.'

'I wish I wasn't going,' Stringham said. 'It really is the most desperate bore. Can't I get out of it?'

'But, darling, you are sailing in two days' time. I thought you wanted to go. And your father would be so disappointed.'

'Would he?'

His mother sighed. Stringham's despondency, briefly postponed, was now once more in the ascendant. Miss Weedon said with emphasis: 'But you will be back soon.'

Stringham did not answer; but he shot her a look almost of hatred. She was evidently used to rough treatment from him, because she appeared not at all put out by this, and rattled on about the letters she had been writing that morning. The look of disappointment she had shown earlier was to be attributed, perhaps, to her being still unaccustomed to having him at home again, with the kindnesses and cruelties his presence entailed for her. The meal proceeded. Miss Weedon and Mrs. Foxe became involved in a discussion as to whether or not the head-gardener at Glimber was selling the fruit for his own profit. Stringham and I talked of school affairs. The luncheon party—the whole house—was in an obscure way depressing. I had looked forward to coming there, but was quite glad when it was time to go.

'Write and tell me anything that may happen,' said Stringham, at the door. 'Especially anything funny that Peter may do.'

I promised to report any of Templer's outstanding adventures, and we arranged to meet in nine or ten months' time.

'I shall long to come back to England,' Stringham said. 'Not that I specially favour the idea of universities. Undergraduates all look so wizened, and suède shoes appear to be compulsory.'

Berkeley Square, as I drove through it, was cold and bright and remote: like Buster's manner. I wondered how it would be to return to school with only the company of Templer for the following year; because there was no one else with any claim to take Stringham's place, so that Templer and I would be left alone together. Stringham's removal was going to alter the orientation of everyday life. I found a place in a crowded compartment, next to the engine, beside an elderly man wearing a check suit, who, for the whole journey, quarrelled quietly with a clergyman on the subject of opening the window, kept on taking down a dispatch-case from the rack and rummaging through it for papers that never seemed to be there, and in a general manner reminded me of the goings-on of Uncle Giles.

Uncle Giles's affairs had, in fact, moved recently towards something like a climax. After nearly two years of silence—since the moment when he had disappeared into the fog, supposedly on his way to Reading—nothing had been heard of him; until one day a letter had arrived, headed with the address of an hotel in the Isle of Man, the contents of which implied, though did not state, that he intended to get married. In anticipation of this contingency, my uncle advocated a thorough overhaul of the conditions of the Trust; and expressed, not for the first time, the difficulties that lay in the path of a man without influence.

This news caused my parents some anxiety; for, although Uncle Giles's doings during the passage of time that had taken place were unknown in detail, his connection with

Reading had been established, with fair certainty, to be the result of an association with a lady who lived there: some said a manicurist: others the widow of a garage-proprietor. There was, indeed, no reason why she should not have sustained both rôles. The topic was approached in the family circle with even more gloom, and horrified curiosity, than Uncle Giles's activities usually aroused: misgiving being not entirely groundless, since Uncle Giles was known to be almost as indiscriminate in dealings with the opposite sex as he was unreliable in business negotiation. His first serious misadventure, when stationed in Egypt as a young man, had, indeed, centred upon a love affair.

It was one of Uncle Giles's chief complaints that he had been 'put' into the army—for which he possessed neither Mrs. Foxe's romantic admiration nor her hard-headed grasp of military realities—instead of entering some unspecified profession in which his gifts would have been properly valued. He had begun his soldiering in a line regiment: later, with a view to being slightly better paid, exchanging into the Army Service Corps. I used to imagine him wearing a pill-box cap on the side of his head, making assignations under a sub-tropical sun with a beautiful lady dressed in a bustle and sitting in an open carriage driven by a coloured coachman; though such attire, as a matter of fact, belonged to a somewhat earlier period; and, even if circumstances resembled this picture in other respects, the chances were, on the whole, that assignations would be made, and kept, 'in mufti'.

There had been, in fact, two separate rows, which somehow became entangled together: somebody's wife, and somebody else's money: to say nothing of debts. At one stage, so some of his relations alleged, there had even been question of court-martial: not so much to incriminate my unfortunate uncle as to clear his name of some of the rumours in circulation. The court-martial, perhaps fortunately, was never convened, but the necessity for Uncle Giles to send in his papers was unquestioned. He travelled home by South Africa, arriving in Cape Town a short time before the outbreak of hostilities with the Boers. In that town he made undesirable friends—no doubt also encountering at this period Mrs. Foxe's father—and engaged in unwise transactions regarding the marketing of diamonds: happily not involving on his part any handling of the stones themselves. This venture ended almost disastrously; and, owing to the attitude taken up by the local authorities, he was unable to settle in Port Elizabeth, where he had once thought of earning a living. However, like most untrustworthy persons, Uncle Giles had the gift of inspiring confidence in a great many people with whom he came in contact. Even those who, to their cost, had known him for years, sometimes found difficulty in estimating the lengths to which he could carry his lack of reliability—and indeed sheer incapacity—in matters of business. When he returned to England he was therefore seldom out of a job, though usually, in his own words, 'starting at the bottom' on an ascent from which great things were to be expected.

In 1914 he had tried to get back into the army, but his services were declined for medical reasons by the War Office. Not long after the sinking of the Lusitania he obtained a post in the Ministry of Munitions; later transferring himself to the Ministry of Food, from which he eventually resigned without scandal. When the United States entered the war he contrived to find some sort of a job in the provinces at a depot formed for supplying 'comforts' to American troops. He had let it be known that he had made business connexions on the other side of the Atlantic, as a result of this employment. That was why there had been a suggestion—in which wish may have been father to thought in the minds of his relations—that he might take up a commercial post in Philadelphia. The letter from the Isle of Man, with its hint of impending marriage, seemed to indicate that any idea of emigration, if ever in existence, had been abandoned; whilst references throughout its several pages to 'lack of influence' brought matters back to an earlier, and more fundamental, stage in my uncle's presentation of his affairs.

This business of 'influence' was one that played a great part in Uncle Giles's philosophy of life. It was an article of faith with him that all material advancement in the world was the result of influence, a mysterious attribute with which he invested, to a greater or lesser degree, every human being on earth except himself. That the rich and nobly born automatically enjoyed an easy time of it through influence was, of course, axiomatic; and—as society moved from an older order—anybody who might have claims to be considered, at least outwardly, of the poor and lowly was also included by him among those dowered with this almost magic appanage. In cases such as that of the window-cleaner, or the man who came to read the gas-meter, the advantage enjoyed was accounted to less obvious—but, in fact, superior—opportunity for bettering position in an increasingly egalitarian world. '*That* door was banged-to for me at birth,' Uncle Giles used to say (in a phrase that I found, much later, he had lifted from a novel by John Galsworthy) when some plum was mentioned, conceived by him available only to those above, or below, him in the social scale.

It might be imagined that people of the middle sort—people, in other words, like Uncle Giles himself—though he would have been unwilling to admit his attachment to any recognisable social group, could be regarded by him as substantially in the same boat. Nothing could be farther from the truth. Such persons belonged to the class, above all others, surveyed with misgiving by him, because members of it possessed, almost without exception, either powerful relations who helped them on in an underhand way, or business associations, often formed through less affluent relations, which enabled them—or so he suspected—to buy things cheap. Any mention of the City, or, worse still, the Stock Exchange, drove him to hard words. Moreover, the circumstances of people of this kind were often declared by him to be such that they did not have to 'keep up the same standards' in the community as those that tradition imposed upon Uncle Giles himself; and, having thus secured an unfair advantage, they were one and all abhorrent to him.

As a result of this creed he was unconquerably opposed to all established institutions on the grounds that they were entirely—and therefore incapably—administered by persons whose sole claim to consideration was that they could command influence. His own phrase for describing briefly this approach to all social, political and economic questions was 'being a bit of a radical': a standpoint he was at pains to make abundantly clear to all with whom he came in contact. As it happened, he always seemed to find people who would put up with him; and, usually, people who would employ him. In fact, at his own level, he must have had more 'influence' than most persons. He did not, however, answer the enquiries, and counter-proposals, put forward in a reply to his letter sent to the address in the Isle of Man; and, for the time being, no more was heard of his marriage, or any other of his activities.

Settling down with Templer at school was easier than I had expected. Without Stringham, he was more expansive, and I began to hear something of his life at home. His father and uncle (the latter of whom—for public services somewhat vaguely specified—had accepted a baronetcy at the hands of Lloyd George, one of the few subjects upon which Templer showed himself at all sensitive) had made their money in cement. Mr. Templer had retired from business fairly recently, after what his son called 'an appalling bloomer over steel.' There were two sisters: Babs, the eldest of the family, who towards the end of the war had left a husband in one of the dragoon regiments in favour of a racing motorist; and Jean, slightly younger than her brother. Their mother had died some years before I came across Templer, who displayed no photographs of his family, so that I knew nothing of their appearance. Although not colossally rich, they were certainly not poor; and whatever lack of appreciation Peter's father may at one moment have shown regarding predictable fluctuations of his own holdings in the steel industry, he still took a friendly interest in the market; and, by Peter's account, seemed quite often to guess right. I also knew that they lived in a house by the sea.

'Personally I wouldn't mind having a look at Kenya,' said Templer, when I described the luncheon with Stringham and his mother.

'Stringham didn't seem to care for the idea.'

'My elder sister had a beau who lived in the Happy Valley. He shot himself after having a lot of drinks at the club.'

'Perhaps it won't be so bad then.'

'Did you lunch with them in London or the country?'

'London.'

'Stringham says Glimber is pretty, but too big.'

'Will he come into it?'

'Good Lord, no,' said Templer. 'It is only his mother's

for life. He will come into precious little if she goes on spending money at her present rate.'

I was not sure how much of this was to be believed; but, thinking the subject of interest, enquired further. Templer sketched in a somewhat lurid picture of Mrs. Foxe and her set. I was rather surprised to find that he himself had no ambition to become a member of that world, the pleasures of which sounded of a kind particularly to appeal to him.

'Too much of a good thing,' he said. 'I have simpler tastes.'

I was reminded of Stringham's disparagement of Buster on the ground that he was 'too grand'; and also of the reservations he had expressed regarding Templer himself. Clearly some complicated process of sorting-out was in progress among those who surrounded me: though only years later did I become aware how early such voluntary segregations begin to develop; and of how they continue throughout life. I asked more questions about Templer's objection to house-parties at Glimber. He said: 'Well, I imagine it was all rather pompous even at lunch, wasn't it?'

'Buster seemed rather an ass. His mother was awfully nice.'

Even at the time I felt that the phrase was not a very adequate way of describing Mrs. Foxe's forceful, even dazzling, characteristics.

'Oh, she is all right, I have no doubt,' said Templer. 'And damned good-looking still. She gave Stringham's sister absolute hell, though, until she married the first chap that came along.'

'Who was he?'

'I can't remember his name. A well-known criminal with one arm.'

'Stringham certainly seemed in bad form when she was there.'

'She led his father a dance, too.'

'Still, he need not join in all that if he doesn't want to.'

'He will want to,' said Templer. 'Take my word for it, he will soon disappear from sight so far as we are concerned.'

Armed, as I have said, with the knowledge of Stringham's admission regarding his own views on Templer, I recognised that there must be some truth in this judgment of Stringham's character; though some of its implications—notably with regard to myself—I failed, rather naturally, to grasp at that period. That was the only occasion when I ever heard Templer speak seriously about Stringham, though he often used to refer to escapades in which they had shared, especially the incident of Le Bas's arrest.

So far as Templer and I were concerned, nothing further had taken place regarding this affair; though Templer's relations with Le Bas continued to be strained. Although so little involved personally in the episode, I found myself often thinking of it. Why, for example, should Stringham, singularly good-natured, have chosen to persecute Le Bas in this manner? Was it a matter for regret or congratulation: had it, indeed, any meaning at all? The circumstances revealed at once Stringham's potential assurance, and the inadequacy of Le Bas's defences. If Stringham had been brutal, Le Bas had been futile. In spite of his advocacy of the poem, Le Bas had not learnt its lesson:

> 'And then we turn unwilling feet
> And seek the world—so must it be—
> *We* may not linger in the heat
> Where breaks the blue Sicilian sea!'

He was known for a long time after as 'Braddock alias Thorne', especially among his colleagues, whose theory was that the hoaxer had recently left the school, and, while passing through the town, probably in a car, had decided to tease Le Bas. Certainly Stringham would never have been thought capable of such an enormity by any master who had ever come in contact with him. Not unnaturally, however, Le Bas's tendency to feel that the world was against him was accentuated by an experience in many ways humiliating enough; and he persecuted Templer—or, at least, his activities in this direction were represented by Templer as persecution—more energetically than ever.

Finally Templer's habitual carelessness gave Le Bas an opportunity to close the account. This conclusion was the result of Templer leaving his tobacco pouch—on which, characteristically, he had inscribed his initials—lying on the trunk of a tree somewhere among the fields where we had happened on Le Bas. Cobberton, scouting round that neighbourhood, had found the pouch, and passed it on to Le Bas. Nothing definite could be proved against Templer: not even the ownership of a half-filled tobacco pouch, though no one doubted it was his. However, Le Bas moved heaven and earth to be rid of Templer, eventually persuading the headmaster to the view that life would be easier for both of them if Templer left the school. In consequence, Peter's father was persuaded to remove him a term earlier than previously intended. This pleased Templer himself, and did not unduly ruffle his father; who was reported to take the view that schools and universities were, in any case, waste of time and money: on the principle that an office was the place in which to learn the realities of life. And so I was left, as it seemed to me, alone.

Templer was not a great hand at letter-writing after his departure; though an occasional picture post-card used to arrive, stating his score at the local golf tournament, or saying that he was going to Holland to learn business methods.

Before he left school, he had suggested several times that I should visit his home, always qualifying his account of the amusements there offered by a somewhat menacing picture of his father's habitually cantankerous behaviour. I did not take these warnings about his father too seriously because of Templer's tendency to impute bad temper to anyone placed in a position of authority in relation to himself. At the same time, I had the impression that Mr. Templer might be a difficult man to live with; I even thought it possible that Peter's dealings with Le Bas might derive from experience of similar skirmishes with his father. Peter's chief complaint, so far as his father was concerned, seemed directed not towards any violent disagreement between them in tastes, or way of life, so much as to the fact that his father, in control of so much more money than himself, showed in his son's eyes on the whole so little capacity for putting this favourable situation to a suitable advantage. 'Wait till you see the car we have to use for station work,' Peter used to say. 'Then you will understand what sort of a man my father is.'

The invitation arrived just when the mechanical accessories of leaving school were in full swing. Later in the summer it had been arranged that, before going up to the university, I should spend a period in France; partly with a view to learning the language: partly as a solution to that urgent problem—inviting one's own as much as other people's attention—of the disposal of the body of one of those uneasy, stranded beings, no longer a boy and hardly yet a man. The Templer visit could be fitted in before the French trip took place.

Stringham's letters from Kenya reported that he liked the place better than he had expected. They contained drawings of people met there, and of a horse he sometimes rode. He could not really draw at all, but used a convention of blobs and spidery lines, effective in expressing the appearance of persons and things. One of these was of Buster selling a car; another of Buster playing polo. I used to think sometimes of the glimpse I had seen of Stringham's life at home; and—although this did not occur to me at once—I came in time to regard his circumstances as having something in common with those of Hamlet. His father had, of course, been shipped off to Kenya rather than murdered; but Buster and his mother were well adapted to play the parts of Claudius and Gertrude. I did not manage to get far beyond this, except to wonder if Miss Weedon was a kind of female Polonius, working on Hamlet's side. I could well imagine Stringham stabbing her through the arras. At present there was no Ophelia. Stringham himself had a decided resemblance to the Prince of Denmark; or, as Templer would have said: 'It was the kind of part the old boy would fancy himself in.'

At first sight the Templers' house seemed to be an enormously swollen villa, red and gabled, facing the sea from a small park of Scotch firs: a residence torn by some occult power from more appropriate suburban setting, and, at the same time, much magnified. It must have been built about twenty or thirty years before, and, as we came along the road, I saw that it stood on a piece of sloping ground set about a quarter of a mile from the cliff's edge. The clouded horizon and olive-green waves lapping against the stones made it a place of mystery in spite of this outwardly banal appearance: a sea-palace for a version of one of those embarkation scenes of Claude Lorraine—the Queen of Sheba, St. Ursula, or perhaps The Enchanted Castle—where any adventure might be expected.

There were a pair of white gates at the entrance to the drive, and a steep, sandy ascent between laurels. At the summit, the green doors of a row of garages faced a cement platform. As we drove across this open space a girl of about sixteen or seventeen, evidently Peter's unmarried sister, Jean, was closing one of the sliding doors. Fair, not strikingly pretty, with long legs and short, untidy hair, she remained without moving, intently watching us, as Peter shut off the engine, and we got out of the car. Like her legs, her face was thin and attenuated, the whole appearance given the effect of a much simplified—and somewhat self-conscious—arrangement of lines and planes, such as might be found in an Old Master drawing, Flemish or German perhaps, depicting some young and virginal saint; the racquet, held awkwardly at an angle to her body, suggesting at the same time an obscure implement associated with martyrdom. The expression of her face, although sad and a trifle ironical, was not altogether in keeping with this air of belonging to another and better world. I felt suddenly uneasy, and also interested: a desire to be with her, and at the same time, an almost paralysing disquiet at her presence. However, any hopes or fears orientated in her direction were quickly dissolved, because she hardly spoke when Peter introduced us, except to say in a voice unexpectedly deep, and almost as harsh as her brother's: 'The hard court needs re-surfacing.'

Then she walked slowly towards the house, humming to herself, and swinging her racquet at the grass borders. Peter shouted after her: 'Has Sunny arrived yet?'

'He turned up just after you left.'

She made this answer without turning her head. It conveyed no implication of disapproval; no enthusiasm either. I watched her disappear from sight.

'Leave your stuff here,' said Peter. 'Someone is bound to collect it. Let's have some tea. What bloody bad manners my sisters have.'

Wearing a soft felt hat squashed down in the shape of a pork-pie, he already showed signs of having freed himself from whatever remaining restraints school had imposed. He had spent a month or two in Amsterdam, where his father had business interests. Mr. Templer's notion was that Peter should gain in this way some smattering of commercial life before going into the City; as all further idea of educating or improving his son had now been abandoned by him. Peter could give no very coherent account of Dutch life, except to say that the canals smelt bad, and that there were two night-clubs which were much better than the others in that city. Apart from such slightly increased emphasis on characteristics already in evidence, he was quite unchanged.

'Who is Sunny?'

'He is called Sunny Farebrother, a friend of my father's. He was staying in the neighbourhood for a funeral and has come over to talk business.'

'Your father's contemporary?'

'Oh, no,' said Peter. 'Much younger. Thirty or thirty-five. He is supposed to have done well in the war. At least I believe he got rather a good D.S.O.'

The name 'Sunny Farebrother' struck me as almost redundant in its suggestion of clear-cut, straightforward masculinity. It seemed hardly necessary for Peter to add that someone with a name like that had 'done well' in the war, so unambiguous was the portrait conjured up by the syllables. I imagined a kind of super-Buster, in whom qualities of intrepidity and simplicity of heart had been added to those of dash and glitter.

'Why is he called Sunny?' I asked, expecting some confirmation of this imaginary personality with which I had invested Mr. Farebrother.

'Because his Christian name is Sunderland,' said Peter. 'I

expect we shall have to listen to a lot of pretty boring conversation between the two of them.'

We entered the house at a side door. The walls of the greater part of the ground floor were faced with panelling, coloured and grained like a cigar-box. At the end of a large hall two men were sitting on a sofa by a tea-table at which Jean was pouring out cups of tea. The elder of this couple, a wiry, grim little fellow, almost entirely bald, and smoking a pipe, was obviously Peter's father. His identity was emphasised by the existence of a portrait of himself hanging on the wall above him—the only picture in the room—representing its subject in a blue suit and hard white collar. The canvas, from the hand of Isbister, the R.A., had been tackled in a style of decidedly painful realism, the aggressive nature of the pigment intensified by the fact that each feature had been made to appear a little larger than life.

'Hullo, Jenkins,' said Mr. Templer, raising his hand. 'Have some tea. Pour him out some tea, Jean. Well, go on, Farebrother—but try and stick to the point this time.'

He turned again to the tall, dark man sitting beside him. This person, Sunny Farebrother presumably, had shaken hands warmly, and given a genial smile when I approached the table. At Mr. Templer's interpellation, this smile faded from his face in a flash, being replaced by a look of almost devotional intensity; and, letting drop my hand with startling suddenness, he returned to what seemed to be a specification of the terms and bearings of a foreign loan—apparently Hungarian—which he and Mr. Templer had evidently been discussing before our arrival. Jean handed me the plate of buttered toast, and, addressing herself to Peter, spoke once more of the hard tennis court.

During tea I had an opportunity of examining Sunny Farebrother more closely. His regular features and ascetic, serious manner did remind me in some way of Buster, curiously enough: though scarcely for the reasons I had expected. In spite of neatness and general air of being well-dressed, Farebrother had none of Buster's consciously reckless manner of facing the world; while, so far from dispensing anything that might be interpreted as an attitude of indirect hostility, his demeanour—even allowing for the demands of a proper respect for a man older than himself and at the same time his host—appeared to be almost unnecessarily ingratiating. I was not exactly disappointed with the reality of someone whose outward appearance I had, rather absurdly, settled already in my mind on such slender grounds; but I was surprised, continuing to feel that I should like to know more of Sunny Farebrother.

The train of thought engendered by this association with Buster took me on, fairly logically, to Miss Weedon; and, for a second, it even occurred to me that some trait possessed in common by Buster and Miss Weedon linked both of them with Sunny Farebrother; the two latter being the most alike, ridiculous as it might sound, of the three. This was certainly not on account of any suggestion, open or inadequately concealed, that Farebrother's temperament was feminine in any abnormal manner, either physically or emotionally; on the contrary; though Miss Weedon for her part might perhaps lay claim to some remotely masculine air. It was rather that both had in common some smoothness, an acceptance that their mission in life was to iron out the difficulties of others: a recognition that, for them, power was won by self-abasement.

Sunny Farebrother's suit, though well cut, was worn and a trifle dilapidated in places. The elbows of the coat were shiny, and, indeed, his whole manner suggested that he might be in distinctly straitened circumstances. I imagined him a cavalryman—something about his long legs and narrow trousers suggested horses—unable to support the expenses of his regiment, unwillingly become a stockbroker, or agent for some firm in the City, in an attempt to make two ends meet; though I learnt later that he had never been a regular soldier. With folded hands and head bent, he was listening, attentively, humbly—almost as if his life depended on it—to the words that Mr. Templer was speaking.

Years later, when I came to know Sunny Farebrother pretty well, he always retained for me something of this first picture of him; a vision—like Jean's—that suggested an almost saintly figure, ill-used by a coarse-grained world: some vague and uncertain parallel with Colonel Newcome came to mind, in the colonel's latter days in the Greyfriars almshouses, and it was easy to imagine Mr. Farebrother answering his name in such a setting, the last rays of sunset falling across his, by then, whitened hair. Everything about him supported claims to such a rôle: from the frayed ends of the evening tie that he wore later at dinner, to the immensely battered leather hat-box that was carried through the hall with the rest of his luggage while we sat at tea. He seemed to feel some explanation for the existence of this last object was required, saying that it contained the top-hat he had recently worn at his great-uncle's funeral, adding that it was the headgear that normally hung on a hook in his office for use as part of the uniform of his calling in the City.

'It cost me a tidy sum in lost business to pay that last tribute,' he said. 'But there aren't many of that grand old fellow's sort left these days. I felt I ought to do it.'

Mr. Templer, his hands deep in his trousers pockets, took scarcely any notice of such asides. He discoursed instead, in a rasping undertone, of redemption dates and capital requirements. Jean finished what she had to say to Peter regarding the hard tennis court, then scarcely spoke at all. Later she went off on her own.

This introduction to the Templer household was fairly representative of its prevailing circumstances for the next few days. Mr. Templer was gruff, and talked business most of the time to Sunny Farebrother: Jean kept to herself: Peter and I bathed, or lounged away the day. I discovered that Peter's account of his lack of accord with his father had been much exaggerated. In reality, they understood each other well, and had, indeed, a great deal in common. Mr. Templer possessed a few simple ideas upon which he had organised his life; and, on the whole, these ideas had served him well, largely because they fitted in with each other, and were of sufficiently general application to be correct perhaps nine times out of ten. He was very keen on keeping fit, and liked to describe in detail exercises he was in the habit of performing when he first rose from his bed in the morning. He was always up and about the house long before anyone else was awake, and he certainly looked healthy, though not young for his age, which was somewhere in the sixties. Sunny Farebrother continued to impress me as unusually agreeable; and I could not help wondering why he was treated by the Templers with so little consideration. I do not mean that, in fact, I gave much thought to this matter; but I noticed from time to time that he seemed almost to enjoy being contradicted by Mr. Templer, or ignored by Jean, whom he used to survey rather hungrily, and attempt, without much success, to engage in conversation. In this, as other respects, Jean remained in her somewhat separate world. Peter used to tease her about this air of existing remote from everything that went on round her. I continued to experience a sense of being at once drawn to her, and yet cut off from her utterly.

The party was increased a few days after my arrival by

the addition of the Striplings—that is to say Peter's married sister, Babs, and her husband, the racing motorist—who brought with them a friend called Lady McReith. These new guests radically altered the tone of the house. Babs was good-looking, with reddish fair hair, and she talked a lot, and rather loudly. She was taller than Jean, without her sister's mysterious, even melancholy, presence. Sitting next to her at dinner there was none of the difficulty that I used to experience in getting some scraps of conversation from Jean. Babs seemed very attached to Peter and asked many questions about his life at school. Her husband, Jimmy Stripling, was tall and burly. He wore his hair rather long and parted in the middle. Like his father-in-law he was gruff in manner, and always looked beyond, rather than at, the person he was talking to. Uncle Giles was, at that period, the only grumbler I had ever met at all comparable in volume: though Stripling, well-equipped financially for his pursuit of motor-racing, had little else in common with my uncle.

It is not unusual for people who look exceptionally robust, and who indulge in hobbies of a comparatively dangerous kind, to suffer from poor health. Stripling belonged to this category. On that account he had been unable to take an active part in the war; unless—as Peter had remarked—persuading Babs to run away with him while her husband was at the front might be regarded as Jimmy having 'done his bit'. This was no doubt an unkind way of referring to what had happened; and, if Peter's own account of Babs's early married life was to be relied upon, there was at least something to be said on her side, as her first husband, whatever his merits as a soldier, had been a far from ideal husband. It was, however, unfortunate from Stripling's point of view that his forerunner's conduct had been undeniably gallant; and this fact had left him with a consuming hatred for all who had served in the armed forces. Indeed, anyone who mentioned, even casually, any matter that reminded him that a war had taken place was liable to be treated by him in a most peremptory manner; although, at the same time, all his topics of conversation seemed, sooner or later, to lead to this subject. His state of mind was perhaps the outcome of too many persons like Peter having made the joke about 'doing his bit'. In consequence of this attitude he gave an impression of marked hostility towards Sunny Farebrother.

In spite of the circumstances of their marriage, outward relations between the Striplings were cool, almost formal; and the link which seemed most firmly to bind them together was, in some curious manner, vested in the person of their friend Lady McReith, known as 'Gwen', a figure whose origins and demeanour suggested enigmas that I could not, in those days, even attempt to fathom. In the first place I could form no idea of her age. When she came into the room on their arrival, I thought she was a contemporary of Jean's: this was only for a few seconds, and immediately after I supposed her to be nine or ten years older; but one afternoon, strolling across the lawn from tennis, when the air had turned suddenly cold and a chilly breeze from the sea had swept across the grass, she had shivered and changed colour, her face becoming grey and mottled, almost as if it were an old woman's. She was tall, though slightly built, with dark hair over a fair skin, beneath which the veins showed: her lips always bright red. Something about her perhaps hinted vaguely of the stage, or at least what I imagined theatrical people to be like. This fair skin with the blue veins running across had a look of extraordinary softness.

'She was married to a partner of my father's,' Peter said, when questioned. 'He had a stroke and died ten days after he was knighted—a remarkable instance of delayed shock.'

Although appearing to accept her as in some manner necessary for the well-being of their household, Jimmy Stripling seemed less devoted than his wife to Lady McReith. There was a certain amount of ragging between them, and Stripling liked scoring off her in conversation: though, for that matter, he liked scoring off anyone. Babs, on the other hand, seemed never tired of walking about the lawn, or through the rose garden, arm in arm with Lady McReith; and demonstrative kissing took place between them at the slightest provocation.

Lady McReith was also on excellent terms with the Templer family, especially Peter. Even Mr. Templer himself sometimes took her arm, and led her into dinner, or towards the drink tray in the evening. Sunny Farebrother, however, evidently regarded her without approval, though he was always scrupulously polite: so much so that Lady McReith was often unable to do more than go off into peals of uncontrollable laughter when addressed by him: the habit of giggling being one of her most pronounced characteristics. Personally, I found her rather alarming, chiefly because she talked, when she spoke at all, of people and things I had never heard of. The Striplings were always laughing noisily at apparently pointless remarks made by her on the subject of acquaintances possessed by them in common. Apart from this banter, she had little or nothing to say for herself; and, unlike Jean, her silences suggested to me no hidden depths. Mr. Templer used to say: 'Come on, Gwen, try and behave for once as if you were grown-up,' a request always followed by such immoderate fits of laughter from Lady McReith that she was left almost helpless. At dinner there would be exchanges between herself and Peter:

'Why aren't you wearing a clean shirt tonight, Peter?'

'I thought this one would be clean enough for you.'

'You ought to keep your little brother up to the mark, Babs.'

'He is always very grubby, isn't he?'

'What about those decomposing lip-sticks Gwen is always leaving about the house? They make the place look like the ladies' cloak-room in a third-rate night-club.'

'Do you spend much of your time in the ladies' cloak-rooms of third-rate night-clubs, Peter? What a funny boy you must be.'

Sunny Farebrother gave the impression of being not at all at his ease in the midst of this rough-and-tumble, in which he was to some degree forced to participate. Mr. Templer fell from time to time into fits of moroseness which made his small-talk at best monosyllabic: at worst, drying up all conversation. He treated his son-in-law with as little ceremony as he did Farebrother; evidently regarding the discussion of serious matters with Stripling as waste of time. He was, however, prepared to listen to Farebrother's views—apparently sensible enough—on how best to handle the difficulties of French reoccupation of the Ruhr (which had taken place earlier in the year), especially in relation to the general question of the shortage of pig-iron on the world market. When on one occasion Farebrother ventured to change the subject and give his opinion regarding professional boxing, Mr. Templer went so far as to say: 'Farebrother, you are talking through your hat. When you have watched boxing for forty years, as I have, it will be quite soon enough to start criticising the stewards of the National Sporting.'

Sunny Farebrother showed no sign of resenting this capricious treatment. He would simply nod his head, and chuckle to himself, as if in complete agreement; after a while giving up any attempt to soothe his host, and trying to join in whatever was happening at the other end of the table. It was at such moments that he sometimes became involved in cross-fire between Peter, Lady McReith, and the Striplings. I was not sure how often the Striplings had met Sunny Farebrother in the past. Each seemed to know a good deal about the other, though they remained on distant terms, Stripling making hardly an effort to conceal his dislike. They would sometimes talk about City matters, in which Stripling took an interest that was probably of a rather amateurish sort; for it was clear that Farebrother rarely agreed with his judgment, even when he outwardly concurred. After these mild contradictions, Stripling would raise his eyebrows and make faces at Farebrother behind his back. Farebrother showed no more sign of being troubled by this kind of behaviour than by Mr. Templer's gruffness; but he sometimes adopted a manner of exaggerated good-fellowship towards Stripling, beginning sentences addressed to him with the words: 'Now then, Jimmy——': and sometimes making a sweeping dive with his fist towards Stripling's diaphragm, as if in a playful effort to disembowel him. It was not Stripling so much as Lady McReith, and, to a lesser degree, Babs, who seemed to make Farebrother uncomfortable. I decided—as it turned out, correctly—that this was a kind of moral disapproval, and that some puritan strain in Farebrother rebelled against Lady McReith especially.

One evening, when Mr. Templer had come suddenly out of one of his gloomy reveries, and nodded curtly to Babs to withdraw the women from the dining-room, Sunny Farebrother jumped up to open the door, and, in the regrouping of seats that took place when we sat down again, placed himself next to me. The Templers, father and son, had begun to discuss with Stripling the jamming of his car's accelerator. Farebrother shifted the port in my direction, without pouring himself out a second glass. He said: 'Did I understand that your father was at the Peace Conference?'

'For a time.'

'I wonder if he and I were ever in the same show.'

I described to the best of my ability how my father had been wounded in Mesopotamia; and, after a spell of duty in Cairo, had been sent to Paris at the end of the war: adding that I was not very certain of the nature of his work. Farebrother seemed disappointed that no details were available on this subject; but he continued to chat quietly of the Conference, and of the people he had run across when he had worked there himself.

'Wonderfully *interesting* people, he said. 'After a time one thought nothing of lunching with, for example, a former Finance Minister of Rumania, as a matter of fact we reached the stage of my calling him "Hilarion" and he calling me "Sunny". I met Monsieur Venizelos with him on several occasions.'

I expressed the respect that I certainly felt for an appointment that brought opportunity to enjoy such encounters.

'It was a different world,' said Sunny Farebrother.

He spoke with more vehemence than usual; and I supposed that he intended to imply that hobnobbing with foreign statesmen was greatly preferable to touting for business from Peter's father. I asked if the work was difficult.

'When they were kind enough to present me with an O.B.E. at the end of it,' said Farebrother, 'I told them I should have to wear it on my backside because it was the only medal I had ever won by sitting in a chair.'

I did not know whether it was quite my place either to approve or to deprecate this unconventional hypothesis, daring in its disregard for authority (if 'they' were superiors immediately responsible for the conferment of the award) and, at the same time, modest in its assessment of its expositor's personal merits. Sunny Farebrother had the happy gift of suggesting by his manner that one had known him for a long time; and I began to wonder whether I had not, after all, been right in supposing that his nickname had been acquired from something more than having been named 'Sunderland'. There was a suggestion of boyishness —the word 'sunny' would certainly be applicable—about his frank manner; but, in spite of this manifest desire to get along with everyone on their own terms, there was also something lonely and inaccessible about him. It seemed to me, equally, that I had not been so greatly mistaken in the high-flown estimate of his qualities that I had formed on first hearing his name, and of his distinguished record. However, before any pronouncement became necessary on the subject of the most appropriate region on which to distribute what I imagined to be his many decorations, his voice took on a more serious note, and he went on: 'The Conference was, of course, a great change from the previous three and a half years, fighting backwards and forwards over the Somme and God knows where else—and fighting damned hard, too.'

Jimmy Stripling caught the word 'Somme', because his mouth twitched slightly, and he began chopping at a piece of pine-apple rind on his plate: though continuing to listen to his father-in-law's diagnosis of the internal troubles of the Mercedes.

'Going up to the university?' Farebrother asked.

'In October.'

'Take my advice,' he said. 'Look about for a good business opening. Don't be afraid of hard work. That was what I said to myself when the war was over—and here we are.'

He laughed; and I laughed too, though without knowing quite why anything should have been said to cause amusement. Farebrother had the knack, so it seemed to me, of making others feel that they were in some conspiracy with him; though clearly that was not how he was regarded by the Striplings. When Peter had asked the day before: 'What do you think of old Sunny?' I had admitted that Farebrother had made a good impression as a man-of-the-world who was at the same time mild and well disposed: though I had not phrased my opinion quite in that way to Peter, in any case never greatly interested in the details of what people thought about each other. Peter had laughed even at the guarded amount of enthusiasm I had revealed.

'He is a downy old bird,' Peter said.

'Is he very hard up?'

'I suppose he is doing just about as nicely in the City as anyone could reasonably expect.'

'I thought he looked a bit down at heel?'

'That is all part of Sunny's line. You need not worry about him. I may be going into the same firm. He is a sort of distant relation, you know, through my mother's family.'

'He and Jimmy Stripling don't care for each other much, do they?'

'To tell the truth, we all pull Sunny's leg when he comes down here,' said Peter. 'He'll stand anything because he likes picking my father's brains, such as they are.'

This picture of Sunny Farebrother did not at all agree with that which I had formed in my own mind; and I should probably have been more shocked at the idea of teasing him if I had entirely believed all Peter had been saying. The fact that I was not prepared fully to accept his commentary was partly because I knew by experience that he was in the habit of exaggerating about such matters: and, even more, because at that age (although one may be prepared to swallow all kinds of nonsense of this sort or that) personal assessment of individuals made by oneself is hard to shake: even when offered by those in a favourable position to know what they are talking about. Besides, I could hardly credit the statement that Peter himself—even abetted by Jimmy Stripling—would have the temerity to rag someone who looked like Sunny Farebrother, and had his war record. However, later on in the same evening on which we had talked together about the Peace Conference, I was given further insight into the methods by which the Stripling-Farebrother conflict was carried on.

Mr. Templer always retired early. That night he went upstairs soon after we had left the dining-room. Jean had complained of a headache, and she also slipped off to bed. Jimmy Stripling was lying in an armchair with his legs stretched out in front of him. He was an inch or two over six foot, already getting a bit fleshy, always giving the impression of taking up more than his fair share of room, wherever he might be standing or sitting. Farebrother was reading *The Times,* giving the sports page that special rapt attention that he applied to everything he did. Babs and Lady McReith were sitting on the sofa, looking at the same illustrated paper. Farebrother came to the end of the column, and before putting aside the paper shook down the sheets with his accustomed tidiness of habit to make a level edge. He strolled across the room to where Peter was looking through some gramophone records, and I heard him say: 'When you come to work in London, Peter, I should strongly recommend you to get hold of a little gadget I make use of. It turns your collars, and reduces laundry bills by fifty per cent.'

I did not catch Peter's reply; but, although Farebrother had spoken quietly, Stripling had noticed this recommendation. Rolling round in his chair, he said: 'What is that about cutting down your laundry bill, Sunny?'

'Nothing to interest a gentleman of leisure like yourself, Jimmy,' said Farebrother, 'but we poor City blokes find it comes pretty hard on white collars. They have now invented a little patent device for turning them. As a matter of fact a small company has been formed to put it on the market.'

'And I suppose you are one of the directors,' said Stripling.

'As a matter of fact I am,' said Farebrother. 'There are one or two other little odds and ends as well; but the collar-turner is going to be the winner in my opinion.'

'You thought you could plant one on Peter?'

'If Peter has got any sense he'll get one.'

'Why not tackle someone of your own size?'

'I'll plant one on you, Jimmy, once you see it work.'

'I bet you don't.'

'You get some collars then.'

The end of it was that both of them went off to their respective rooms, Stripling returning with a round leather collar-box; Farebrother with a machine that looked like a pair of horse-clippers made from wood. All this was accompanied with a great deal of jocularity on Stripling's part. He came downstairs again first, and assured us that 'Old Sunny's leg was going to be well and truly pulled'. Babs and Lady McReith now began to show some interest in what was going on. They threw aside *The Tatler* and each put up her feet on the sofa. Farebrother stood in the centre of the room holding the wooden clippers. He said: 'Now you give me one of your collars, Jimmy.'

The round leather box was opened, and a collar was inserted into the jaws of the machine. Farebrother closed the contraption forward along the edge of the collar. After proceeding about two inches, there was a ripping sound, and the collar tore. It was extracted with difficulty. Everyone roared with laughter.

'What did I say?' said Stripling.

'Sorry, Jimmy,' said Farebrother. 'That collar must have been washed too often.'

'But it was practically new,' said Stripling. 'You did it the wrong way.'

Stripling chose a collar, and himself ran the clippers along it. They slipped from his grip half-way down, so that the collar was caused to fold more or less diagonally.

'Your collars are a different shape from mine,' Farebrother said. 'They don't seem to have the same "give" in them.'

Farebrother had another try, with results rather similar to his first attempt; and, after that, everyone insisted on making the experiment. The difficulty consisted in holding the instrument tight and, at the same time, running it straight. Babs and Lady McReith both crumpled their collars: Peter and I tore ours on the last inch or so of the run. Then Farebrother tried again, bringing off a perfect turn.

'There you are,' he said. 'What could be better than that?'

However, as three collars were ruined and had to be thrown into the waste-paper basket, and three more had to be sent to the laundry, Stripling was not very pleased. Although the utility of Farebrother's collar-turner had certainly been called into question, he evidently felt that to some extent the joke had been turned against him.

'It is something about your collars, old boy,' Farebrother repeated. 'It is not at all easy to make the thing work on them. It might pay you in the long run to get a more expensive kind.'

'They are damned expensive as it is,' said Stripling. 'Anyway, quite expensive enough to have been made hay of like this.'

However, everyone, including his wife, had laughed a

great deal throughout the various efforts to make the machine work, so that, angry as he was, Stripling had to let the matter rest there. Farebrother, I think, felt that he had not provided a demonstration very satisfactory from the commercial point of view, so that his victory over Stripling was less complete on this account than it might otherwise have seemed. Soon after this he went upstairs, carrying the collar-turner with him, and saying that he had 'work to do', a remark that was received with a certain amount of facetious comment, which he answered by saying: 'Ah, Jimmy, I'm not a rich man like you. I have to toil for my daily bread.'

Stripling was, no doubt, glad to see him go. He probably wanted time to recover from what he evidently looked upon as a serious defeat over the collars. Peter turned on the gramophone, and Stripling retired to the corner of the room with him, where while Stripling's temper cooled they played some game with matches. It was soon after this that I made a decidedly interesting discovery about Lady McReith, who had begun to discuss dance steps with Babs, while I looked through some of the records that Peter had been arranging in piles. In order to illustrate some point she wanted to make about fox-trotting, Lady McReith suddenly jumped from the sofa, took my arm and, sliding it round her waist, danced a few steps. 'Like this?' she said, turning her face towards Babs; and then, as she continued to cling to me, tracing the steps back again in the other direction: 'Or like that?' The transaction took place so swiftly, and, so far as Lady McReith was concerned, so unselfconsciously, that Peter and Stripling did not look up from their game; but—although employed merely as a mechanical dummy—I had become aware, with colossal impact, that Lady McReith's footing in life was established in a world of physical action of which at present I knew little or nothing. Up to that moment I had found her almost embarrassingly difficult to deal with as a fellow guest: now the extraordinary smoothness with which she glided across the polished boards, the sensation that we were holding each other close, and yet, in spite of such proximity, she remained at the same time aloof and separate, the pervading scent with which she drenched herself, and, above all, the feeling that all this offered something further, some additional and violent assertion of the will, was—almost literally—intoxicating. The revelation was something far more universal in implication than a mere sense of physical attraction towards Lady McReith. It was realisation, in a moment of time, not only of her own possibilities, far from inconsiderable ones, but also of other possibilities that life might hold; and my chief emotion was surprise.

This incident was, of course, of interest to myself alone, as its importance existed only in my own consciousness. It would never have occurred to me to discuss it with Peter, certainly not in the light in which it appeared to myself, because to him the inferences would—I now realised—have appeared already so self-evident that he would have been staggered by my own earlier obtuseness: an obtuseness which he would certainly have disparaged in his own forceful terms. Keen awareness of Peter's point of view on the subject followed logically on a better apprehension of the elements that went towards forming Lady McReith as a personality: a personality now so changed in my eyes. However, all that happened was that we danced together until the record came to an end, when she whirled finally round and threw herself down again on the sofa, where Babs still lay: and a second later put her arm round Babs's neck. Stripling came across the room and poured out for himself another whisky. He said: 'We must find some way of ragging old Sunny. He is getting too pleased with himself by half.'

Lady McReith went off into such peals of laughter at this, wriggling and squeezing, that Babs, freeing herself, turned and shook her until she lay quiet, still laughing, at last managing to gasp out: 'Do think of something really funny this time, Jimmy.' I asked what had happened on earlier occasions when Sunny Farebrother had been ragged. Peter outlined some rather mild practical jokes, none of which, in retrospect, sounded strikingly amusing. Various suggestions were made, but nothing came of them at the moment; though the discussion might be said to have laid the foundation for a scene of an odd kind enacted on the last night of my stay.

Looking back at the Horabins' dance that took place on that last night, the ball itself seemed merely a prelude to the events that followed. At the time, the Horabins' party itself was important enough, not only on account of the various sequels enacted on our return to the Templers' house—fields in which at that time I felt myself less personally concerned, and, therefore, less interested—but because of the behaviour of Jean Templer at the dance, conduct which to some extent crystallised in my own mind my feelings towards her; at the same time precipitating acquaintance with a whole series of emotions and apprehensions, the earliest of numberless similar ones in due course to be undergone. The Horabins for long after were, indeed, momentous to me simply for that reason. As it happens, I cannot even remember the specific incident that clarified, in some quite uncompromising manner, the positive recognition that Jean might prefer someone else's company to my own; nor, rather unjustly, did the face of this superlatively lucky man —as he then seemed—remain in my mind a year or two later. I have, however, little doubt that the whole matter was something to do with cutting a dance; and that the partner she chose, in preference to myself, persisted dimly in my mind as a figure certainly older, and perhaps with a fair moustache and reddish face. Even if these circumstances are described accurately, it would undoubtedly be true to say that nothing could be less interesting than the manner in which Jean's choice was brought home to me. There was not the smallest reason to infer from anything that had taken place in the course of my visit that I possessed any sort of prescriptive rights over her: and it may well be that the man with the moustache had an excellent claim. Such an argument did not strike me at the time; nor were the disappointment and annoyance, of which I suddenly became aware in an acute degree, tempered by the realisation, which came much later, that such feelings—like those experienced during the incident with Lady McReith—marked development in transmutation from one stage of life to another.

One of the effects of this powerful, and in some ways unexpected, concentration on the subject of Jean at the dance was to distract my attention from everything not immediately connected with her; so that, by the time we were travelling home, several matters that must have been blowing up in the course of the evening had entirely escaped my notice. I was in the back of a chauffeur-driven car, Peter by the far window, and Lady McReith between us. I was conscious that for the first part of the drive these two were carrying on some sort of mutual conflict under the heavy motoring rug that covered the three of us; but I had not noticed how or why she had become separated from the Striplings. Probably the arrangement had something to do with transport to their homes of some other guests who had dined at the Templers' house for the ball. Whatever the reason, one of the consequences of the allotment of seats had been that Jean and Sunny Farebrother had been carried in the Striplings' Mercedes. We rolled along under the brilliant stars, even Peter and Lady McReith at last silent, perhaps dozing: though like electric shocks I could feel the almost ceaseless vibration of her arm next to mine, quivering as if her body, in spite of sleep, knew no calm.

I did not feel at all anxious to retire to bed when we arrived at the house. On the following day I was to travel to London. Farebrother was going on the same train. We were making a late start in order to rest on a little into the morning after the exertions of the ball. Peter, for once, seemed ready for bed, saying good-night and going straight upstairs. The Striplings had arrived before us, and were shifting about restlessly, talking of 'raiding the kitchen', bacon and eggs, more drink, and, in general, showing unwillingness to bring the party to an end. Lady McReith asserted that she was worn out. Sunny Farebrother, too, was evidently anxious to get some sleep as soon as possible. They went off together up the stairs. Finally Babs found her way to the kitchen, and returned with some odds and ends of food: that would for the time postpone the need to bring the night's entertainment to a close. Her husband walked up and down, working himself up into one of his rages against Sunny Farebrother, who had, it appeared, particularly annoyed him on the drive home. Jean had at first gone up to her room; but on hearing voices below came downstairs again, and joined the picnic that was taking place.

'Did you hear what he said about the car on the way back?' Stripling asked. 'Like his ruddy cheek to offer advice about the acceleration. He himself is too mean to have anything but an old broken-down Ford that you couldn't sell for scrap-iron; and he doesn't even take that round with him, but prefers to cadge lifts.'

'Have you seen Mr. Farebrother's luggage?' said Jean. 'It is all piled up outside his room ready to go down to the station first thing in the morning. It looks as if he were going big-game hunting.'

I wondered afterwards whether she said this with any intention of malice. There was not any sign on her part of a desire to instigate trouble; but it is not impossible that she was the true cause of the events that followed. Certainly this remark was responsible for her sister saying: 'Let's go and have a look at it. Jimmy might get an idea for one of his jokes. Anyway, I'm beginning to feel it's time for bed.'

There was, undeniably, a remarkable load of baggage outside Farebrother's bedroom door: several suitcases; a fishing rod and landing net; a cricket bat and pads; a tennis racket in a press; a gun case; and a black tin box of the kind in which deeds are stored, marked in white paint: 'Exors: Amos Farebrother, Esquire'. On the top of this edifice of objects, on the whole ancient, stood the leather hat-box, said by its owner to contain the hat required by tradition for City ritual. Babs pointed to this. Her husband said: 'Yes—and have you seen it? A Jewish old clothes man would think twice about wearing it.'

Stripling tiptoed to the hat-box, and, releasing the catch, opened the lid, taking from within a silk hat that would have looked noticeably dilapidated on an undertaker. Stripling inspected the hat for several seconds, returned it to the box, and closed the lid; though without snapping the fastening. Lowering his voice, he said: 'Get out of sight where you can all watch. I am going to arrange for old Sunny to have a surprise when he arrives at the office.'

My room was next to Peter's at one end of the passage: Farebrother's half-way down: the Striplings slept round the corner beyond. Jean was somewhere farther on still. Stripling said: 'It is a pity Gwen and Peter won't be able to see this. They will enjoy hearing about it. Find a place to squint from.'

He nodded to me, and I moved to my room, from where I regarded the passage through a chink in the door. Stripling, Babs and Jean passed on out of sight; and I suppose the two women remained in the intersecting passage, in a place from which they could command a view of Farebrother's luggage. I waited for at least five minutes, peering through the crack of the barely open door. It was daylight outside, and the passages were splashed with patches of vivid colour, where the morning sun streamed through translucent blinds. I continued to watch for what seemed an age. I had begun to feel very sleepy, and the time at last appeared so long that I was almost inclined to shut the door and make for bed. And then, all at once, Jimmy Stripling came into sight again. He was stepping softly, and carried in his hand a small green chamber-pot.

As he advanced once more along the passage, I realised with a start that Stripling proposed to substitute this object for the top-hat in Farebrother's leather hat-box. My immediate thought was that relative size might prevent this plan from being put successfully into execution; though I had not examined the inside of the hat-box, obviously itself larger than normal (no doubt built to house more commodious hats of an earlier generation), the cardboard interior of which might have been removed to make room for odds and ends. Such economy of space would not have been out of keeping with the character of its owner. In any case it was a point upon which Stripling had evidently satisfied himself, because the slight smile on his face indicated that he was absolutely certain of his ground. No doubt to make an even more entertaining spectacle of what he was about to do, he shifted the china receptacle from the handle by which he was carrying it, placing it between his two hands, holding it high in front of him, as if it were a sacrificial urn. Seeing it in this position, I changed my mind about its volume, deciding that it could indeed be contained in the hat-box. However, before this question of size and shape could be settled one way or the other, something happened that materially altered the course that events seemed to be taking; because Farebrother's door suddenly swung open, and Farebrother himself appeared, still wearing his stiff shirt and evening trousers, but without a collar. It occurred to me that perhaps he knew of some mysterious process by which butterfly collars, too, could be revived, as well as those of an up-and-down sort, and that he was already engaged in metamorphosing the evening collar he had worn at the Horabins'.

Stripling was taken completely by surprise. He stopped dead: though without changing the position of his hands, or the burden that they carried. Then, no doubt grasping that scarcely any other action was open to him, he walked sharply on down the passage, passing my door and disappearing into the far wing of the house, where Mr. Templer's room was situated. Sunny Farebrother watched him go, but did not speak a word. If he were surprised, he did not show it beyond raising his eyebrows a little, in any case a fairly frequent facial movement of his. Stripling, on the other hand, had contorted his features in such a manner that he looked not so much angry, or thwarted, as in actual physical pain. When he strode past me, I could see the sweat shining on his forehead, and at the roots of his rather curly hair. For a moment Farebrother continued to gaze after him down the passage, as if he expected Stripling's return. Then, with an air of being hurt, or worried, he shut his door very quietly. I closed mine too, for I had begun to feel uncommonly tired.

Peter was in the garden, knocking about a golf ball with his mashie, when I found him the following day. Although late on in the morning, no one else had yet appeared from their rooms. I was looking forward to describing the scene Peter had missed between Farebrother and Stripling. As I approached he flicked his club at the ball, which he sent in among the fir trees of the park. While we walked towards the place where it fell, I gave some account of what had happened after he had retired upstairs on returning from the dance. We found the ball in some bracken, and Peter scooped it back into the centre of the lawn, where it lay by the sundial. To my surprise he seemed scarcely at all interested in what had seemed to me one of the most remarkable incidents I had ever witnessed. I thought this attitude might perhaps be due to the fact that he felt a march had been stolen on him for once; though it would have been unlike him to display disappointment in quite that manner.

'I suppose I really ought to have slipped into your room and warned you that something was on.'

'You might not have found me,' he said.

'Why not?'

'I might not have been there.'

His eyes began their monotonous, tinny glistening. I saw that he was very satisfied with himself about something: what was this secret cause for complacency, I did not immediately grasp. I made no effort to solve the enigma posed by him. We talked about when we should meet again, and the possibility of having a party in London with Stringham at Christmas.

'Don't spoil the French girls,' said Peter.

It was only by the merest chance that a further aspect of the previous evening's transactions was brought to my notice: one which explained Peter's evident air of self-satisfaction. The time had come for us to catch our train. Neither the Striplings nor Lady McReith had yet appeared, but Peter's father was pottering about and said: 'I trust you've enjoyed yourself, Jenkins, and that it hasn't been too quiet for you. Peter complains there is never anything to do here.'

Jean said good-bye.

'I hope we meet again.'

'Oh, yes,' she said, 'we *must*.'

Just as I was getting into the car, I remembered that I had left a book in the morning-room.

'I'll get it,' said Peter. 'I know where it is.'

He went off into the house, and I followed him, because I had an idea that its whereabouts was probably behind one of the cushions of the armchair in which I had been sitting. As I came through the door, he was standing on the far side of the morning-room, looking about among some books and papers on a table. He was not far from another door on the opposite side of the room, and, as I reached the threshold, this farther door was opened by Lady McReith. She did not see me, and stood for a second smiling at Peter, but without speaking. Then suddenly she said: 'Catch,' and impelled through the air towards him some small object. Peter brought his right hand down sharply and caught, within the palm, whatever had been thrown towards him. He said: 'Thanks, Gwen. I'll remember next time.'

I saw now that he was putting on his wrist-watch. By this time I was in the room, and making for the book—*If Winter Comes*—which lay on one of the window-seats. I said good-bye to Lady McReith, who responded with much laughter, and Peter returned with me to the car, saying: 'Gwen is quite mad.' Sunny Farebrother was still engaged in some final business arrangement with Mr. Templer, which he brought to a close with profuse thanks. We set out together on the journey to the station.

The manner of Lady McReith's return of Peter's watch was the outward and visible sign to me of his whereabouts after we had returned from the Horabins'. The fact that an incisive step of one sort or another had been taken by him in relation to Lady McReith was almost equally well revealed by something in the air when they spoke to each other: some definite affirmation which made matters, in any case, explicit enough. The propulsion of the watch was merely a physical manifestation of the same thing. In the light of Peter's earlier remark on the subject of absence from his room during the attempted ragging of Sunny Farebrother, this discovery did not perhaps represent anything very remarkable in the way of intuitive knowledge: especially in view of Lady McReith's general demeanour and conversational approach to the behaviour of her friends. At the same time—as in another and earlier of Peter's adventures of this kind—his enterprise was displayed, confirming my conception of him as a kind of pioneer in this increasingly familiar, though as yet still largely unexplored country. It was about this time that I began to think of him as really a more forceful character than Stringham, a possibility that would never have presented itself in earlier days of my acquaintance with both of them.

These thoughts were cut short by Sunny Farebrother, who whispered to me (though two sheets of glass divided us from the chauffeur): 'Were you going to give this chap anything?' Rather surprised at his curiosity on this point, I admitted that two shillings was the sum I had had in mind. I hoped he would not think that I ought to have suggested half a crown. However, he nodded gravely, as if in complete approval, and said: 'So was I; but I've only got a bob in change. Here it is. You add it to your florin and say it's from both of us.'

When the moment came, I forgot to do more than hand the coins to the chauffeur, who, perhaps retaining memories of earlier visits, did not appear to be unduly disappointed.

In spite of the accumulation of luggage, extraordinary exertions on Farebrother's part made it possible to dispense with the assistance of a porter.

'Got to look after the pennies, you know,' he said, as we waited for the train. 'I hope you don't travel First Class, or we shall have to part company.'

As no such difficulty arose, we found a Third Class compartment to ourselves, and stacked the various items of Farebrother's belongings on the racks. They almost filled the carriage.

'Got to be prepared for everything,' he said, as he lifted the bat and pads. 'Do you play this game?'

'Not any longer.'

'I'm not all that keen on it nowadays myself,' he said. 'But a cricketer always makes a good impression.'

For about three-quarters of an hour he read *The Times*. Then we began to talk about the Templers, a subject Farebrother introduced by a strong commendation of Peter's good qualities. This favourable opinion came as something of a surprise to me; because I was accustomed to hear older persons speak of Peter in terms that almost always suggested improvement was absolutely necessary, if he were to come to any good in life at all. This was not at all the view held by Farebrother, who appeared to regard Peter as one of the most promising young men he had ever run across. Much as I liked Peter by that time, I was quite unable to see why anything in his character should appeal so strongly to Farebrother, whose own personality was becoming increasingly mysterious to me.

'Peter should do well,' Farebrother said. 'He is a bit wild. No harm in that. He knows his way about. He's alive. Don't you agree?'

This manner of asking one's opinion I had already noticed, and found it flattering to be treated without question as being no longer a schoolboy.

'Of course his father is a fine old man,' Farebrother went on. 'A very fine old man. A hard man, but a fine one.'

I wondered what had been the result of their business negotiations together, in which so much hardness and fineness must have been in operation. Farebrother had perhaps begun to think of this subject too, for he fell into silence for a time, and sighed once or twice; at last remarking: 'Still, I believe I got the best of him this time.'

As that was obviously a matter between him and his host, I did not attempt to comment. A moment later, he said: 'What did you think of Stripling?'

Again I was flattered at having my opinion asked upon such a subject; though I had to admit to myself that on the previous night I had been equally pleased when Stripling had, as it were, associated me with his projected baiting of Farebrother. Indeed, I could not help feeling, although the joke had missed fire, that I was not entirely absolved from the imputation of being in some degree guilty of having acted in collusion with Stripling on that occasion. I was conscious, therefore, unless I was to appear in my own eyes hopelessly double-dealing, that some evasive answer was required. Accordingly, although I had not much liked Stripling, I replied in vague terms, adding some questions about the relative success of his motor-racing.

'I don't really understand the fellow,' Farebrother said. 'I quite see he has his points. He has plenty of money. He quite often wins those races of his. But he always seems to me a bit too pleased with himself.'

'What was Babs's first husband like?'

'Quite a different type,' said Farebrother, though without particularising.

He lowered his voice, just as he had done in the car,

though we were still alone in the compartment.

'A rather curious thing happened when we got in from that dance last night,' he said. 'As you know, I went straight up to my room. I started to undress, and then I thought I would just cast my eye over an article in *The Economist* that I had brought with me. I find my brain seems a bit clearer for that kind of thing late at night.'

He paused for a moment, and shook his head, suggesting much burning of midnight oil. Then he went on: 'I thought I heard a good deal of passing backwards and forwards and what sounded like whispering in the passage. Well, one year when I stayed with the Templers they made me an apple-pie bed, and I thought something like that might be in the wind. I opened the door. Do you know what I saw?'

At this stage of the story I could not possibly admit that I knew what he had seen, so there was no alternative to denial, which I made by shaking my head, rather in Farebrother's own manner. I had begun to feel a little uncomfortable.

'There was Stripling, marching down the passage holding *a jerry* in front of him as if he were taking part in some ceremony.'

I shook my head again; this time as if in plain disbelief. Farebrother was not prepared to let the subject drop. He said: 'What could he have been doing?'

'I can't imagine.'

'He was obviously very put out at my seeing him. I mean, what the hell could he have been doing?'

Farebrother leant forward, his elbows on his knees, confronting me with this question, as if he were an eminent counsel, and I in the witness box.

'Was it a joke?'

'That was what I thought at first; but he looked quite

serious. Of course we are always hearing that his health is not good.'

I tried to make some non-committal suggestions that might throw light on what had happened.

'Coupled with the rest of his way of going on,' said Farebrother, 'it made a bad impression.'

We journied on towards London. When we parted company Sunny Farebrother gave me one of his very open smiles, and said: 'You must come and lunch with me one of these days. No good my offering you a lift as I'm heading Citywards.' He piled his luggage, bit by bit, on to a taxi; and passed out of my life for some twenty years.

3

Being in love is a complicated matter; although anyone who is prepared to pretend that love is a simple, straightforward business is always in a strong position for making conquests. In general, things are apt to turn out unsatisfactorily for at least one of the parties concerned; and in due course only its most determined devotees remain unwilling to admit that an intimate and affectionate relationship is not necessarily a simple one: while such persistent enthusiasts have usually brought their own meaning of the word to something far different from what it conveys to most people in early life. At that period love's manifestations are less easily explicable than they become later: often they do not bear that complexion of being a kind of game, or contest, which, at a later stage, they may assume. Accordingly, when I used to consider the case of Jean Templer, with whom I had decided I was in love, analysis of the situation brought no relief from uneasy, almost obsessive thoughts that filled my mind after leaving the Templers' house. Most of all I thought of her while the train travelled across France towards Touraine.

The journey was being undertaken in fiery sunshine. Although not my first visit to France, this was the first time I had travelled alone there. As the day wore on, the nap on the covering of the seats of the French State Railways took on the texture of the coarse skin of an over-heated animal: writhing and undulating as if in an effort to find relief from the torturing glow. I lunched in the restaurant car, and drank some red *vin ordinaire* that tasted unexpectedly sour. The carriage felt hotter than ever on my return: and the train more crowded. An elderly man with a straw hat, black gloves, and Assyrian beard had taken my seat. I decided that it would be less trouble, and perhaps cooler, to stand for a time in the corridor. I wedged myself in by the window between a girl of about fifteen with a look of intense concentration on her pale, angular features, who pressed her face against the glass, and a young soldier with a spectacled, thin countenance, who was angrily explaining some political matter to an enormously fat priest in charge of several small boys. After a while the corridor became fuller than might have been thought possible. I was gradually forced away from the door of the compartment, and found myself unstrategically placed with a leg on either side of a wicker trunk, secured by a strap, the buckle of which ran into my ankle, as the train jolted its way along the line. All around were an immense number of old women in black, one of whom was carrying a feather mattress as part of her luggage.

At first the wine had a stimulating effect; but this sense of exhilaration began to change after a time to one of heaviness and despair. My head buzzed. The soldier and the priest were definitely having words. The girl forced her nose against the window, making a small circle of steam in front of her face. At last the throbbings in my head became so intense that I made up my mind to eject the man with the beard. After a short preliminary argument in which I pointed out that the seat was a reserved one, and, in general, put my case as well as circumstances and my command of the language would allow, he said briefly: *'Monsieur, vous avez gagné,'* and accepted dislodgment with resignation and some dignity. In the corridor, he moved skilfully past the priest and his boys; and, with uncommon agility for his age and size, climbed on to the wicker trunk, which he reduced almost immediately to a state of complete dissolution: squatting on its ruins reading *Le Figaro.* He seemed to know the girl, perhaps his daughter, because once he leaned across and pinched the back of her leg and made some remark to her; but she continued to gaze irritably out at the passing landscape, amongst the trees of which an occasional white château stood glittering like a huge birthday cake left out in the woods after a picnic. By the time I reached my destination there could be no doubt whatever that I was feeling more than a little sick.

The French family with whom I was to stay was that of a retired infantry officer, Commandant Leroy, who had known my father in Paris at the end of the war. I had never met him, though his description, as a quiet little man dominated by a masterful wife, was already familiar to me; so that I hoped there would be no difficulty in recognising Madame Leroy on the platform. There was, indeed, small doubt as to her identity as soon as I set eyes on her. Tall and stately, she was dressed in the deepest black. A female companion of mature age accompanied her, wearing a cone-shaped hat trimmed with luxuriant artificial flowers. No doubt I was myself equally unmistakable, because, even before descending passengers had cleared away, she made towards me with eyebrows raised, and a smile that made me welcome not only to her own house, but to the whole of France. I shook hands with both of them, and Madame Leroy made a gesture, if not of prevention and admonition, at least of a somewhat deprecatory nature, as I took the hand of the satellite, evidently a retainer of some sort, who removed her fingers swiftly, and shrank away from my grasp, as if at once offended and fearful. After this practical repudiation of responsibility for my arrival, Rosalie, as she turned out to be called, occupied herself immediately in some unfriendly verbal exchange with the porter, a sickly-looking young man Madame Leroy had brought with her, who seemed entirely under the thumb of these two females, emasculated by them of all aggressive traits possessed by his kind.

After various altercations with station officials, all more or less trifling, and carried off victoriously by Madame Leroy, we climbed into a time-worn taxi, driven by an ancient whose moustache and peaked cap gave him the air of a Napoleonic grenadier, an elderly *grognard,* fallen on evil days during the Restoration, depicted in some academic canvas of patriotic intention. Even when stationary, his taxi was afflicted with a kind of vehicular counterpart of St. Vitus's dance, and its quaverings and seismic disturbances must have threatened nausea to its occupants at the best of times. On that afternoon something far less convulsive would have affected me adversely; for the weather outside the railway station seemed warmer even than on the train. The drive began, therefore, in unfavourable circumstances so far as my health was concerned: nor could I remember for my own use any single word of French: though happily retaining some measure of comprehension when remarks were addressed to me.

Madame Leroy had evidently been a handsome proposition in her youth. At sixty, or thereabouts, she retained a classical simplicity of style: her dimensions comprehensive, though well proportioned: her eye ironical, but not merciless. She seemed infinitely prepared for any depths of poverty in the French language, keeping up a brisk line of talk, scarcely seeming to expect an answer to questions concerning the health of my parents, the extent of my familiarity with Paris, the heat of the summer in England, and whether crossing the Channel had spoiled a season's hunting. Rosalie was the same age, perhaps a little older, with a pile of grey hair done up on the top of her head in the shape of a farmhouse loaf, her cheeks cross-hatched with lines and wrinkles like those on the side of Uncle Giles's nose: though traced out here on a larger scale. From time to time she muttered distractedly to herself: especially when clouds of white dust from the road blew in at the window, covering us with blinding, smarting powder, at the same time obscuring even more thoroughly the cracked and scarred windscreen, which seemed to have had several bullets put through it in the past: perhaps during the retreat from Moscow. With much stress, and grunting of oaths on the part of the veteran, the car began to climb a steep hill: on one of the corners of which it seemed impossible that the engine would have the power to proceed farther. By some means, however, the summit was achieved, and the taxi stopped, with a final paroxysm of vibration, in front of a door in a whitewashed wall. This wall, along the top of which dark green creeper hung, ran for about fifty yards along the road, joining the house, also white, at a right-angle.

'*Voilà,*' said Madame Leroy. 'La Grenadière.'

Below the hill, in the middle distance, flowed the river, upon which the sun beat down in stripes of blue and gold. Along its banks minute figures of a few fishermen could just be seen. White dust covered all surrounding vegetation; and from a more solid and durable form of this same white material the house itself seemed to have been constructed. The taxi still throbbed and groaned and smelt very vile. To vacate it for the road brought some relief. Madame Leroy led the way through the door in the wall in the manner of a sorceress introducing a neophyte into the land of faërie: a parallel which the oddness of the scene revealed by her went some way to substantiate.

We entered a garden of grass lawns and untidy shrubs,

amongst the stony paths of which a few rusty iron seats were dotted about. In one corner of this pleasure ground stood a summer-house, covered with the same creeper that hung over the outer wall, and hemmed in by untended flower beds. At first sight there seemed to be a whole army of people, including children, wandering about, or sitting on the seats, reading, writing, and talking. Madame Leroy, like Circe, moved forward through this enchanted garden, ignoring the inhabitants of her kingdom as if they were invisible, and we passed into the house, through a glass-panelled door. The hall was as black as night, and I fell over a dog asleep there, which took the accident in bad part, and was the object of much vituperation from Rosalie. Mounting several flights of stairs, Madame Leroy still leading the way, we at last entered a room on the top floor, a garret containing a bed, a chair, and a basin, with its accessories, in blue tin, set on a tripod. A view of the distant river appeared once more, through a port-hole in this austere apartment, one wall of which was decorated with a picture, in cheerful colours, of St. Laurence and his grid-iron; intended perhaps in jocular allusion to the springs of the bed. Rosalie, who had followed us up the stairs bearing a small jug, now poured a few drops of lukewarm water, lightly tinted by some deposit, into the basin on the tripod: intoning a brief incantation as she did this. Madame Leroy stood by, waiting apparently for this final ministration: and, satisfied no doubt that I had become irrevocably subject to her occult powers, she now glided towards the door, having indicated that we might meet again in the garden in due course. As she retired, she said something about '*l'autre monsieur anglais*' having the bedroom next door. At that moment I could scarcely have felt less interest in a compatriot.

When the door shut, I lay for a time on the bed. Something had gone wrong, badly wrong, as a result of luncheon on the train. At first I attributed this recurrent feeling of malaise to the wine: then I remembered that some sort of fish in the hors d'œuvres had possessed an equivocal flavour. Perhaps heat and excitement were the true cause of my feeling unwell. There was a slight improvement after a lapse of about twenty minutes, at the end of which time I rose and peered through the port-hole on to a landscape through which the river ran as straight as a canal, among trees, and white houses similar in size and shape to La Grenadière. I washed my hands in the tin basin, and set off, rather gingerly, down the stairs.

As I reached the hall, the door on the left opened suddenly, and Madame Leroy reappeared. She smiled meaningly, as if to give assurance of her satisfaction in accepting a new catachumen; and pointed to the garden, evidently with a view to undertaking further preliminaries of initiation. We stepped out into the evening sunshine, and, side by side, moved towards the groups gathered together in knots at different points on the grass: from one of which her husband, Commandant Leroy, at once detached himself and came towards us. He was a small man, several inches shorter than his wife, with dark blue glasses and a really colossal moustache. Speaking good English (I remembered he had been an interpreter) he enquired about the journey, explaining that he had been unable to come to the station because his health was not good: he had been gassed, though not seriously, he added, at one of the German attacks on Ypres early in the war, and he was suffering at present from pains in various parts of his body. Madame Leroy heard him with impatience: at length telling him sharply to go and lie down. He shook hands again, and pottered off towards the house. Madame Leroy inclined her head, apparently to express regret that control over her husband even after these many years, was still incomplete. She told me that she had one son, Emile, whom they saw occasionally because he was an instructor at the Cavalry School at Saumur: another, Marcel, serving in Morocco with the Chasseurs d'Afrique: and a daughter, Victorine, married to an army doctor in Saigon.

'Une vraie famille de soldats.'

'Une vraie famille d'officiers,' corrected Madame Leroy, though not unkindly.

We cruised about the garden. The persons assembled there, a trifle less numerous than had at first appeared, were of different classification: some guests, some members of the family. The next introduction was to Berthe, one of the Leroy nieces, a plump brunette, sitting on one of the seats, watching life through sly, greenish eyes set far apart in a face of fawn-coloured rubber. She was engaged, Madame Leroy explained, to the son of the Chef de Cabinet of the Sous-Secrétaire de Marine. Her aunt took this opportunity of speaking a few improving words on the subject of marriage in general, received by Berthe with a tightly compressed smirk; and we passed on to Suzette, another niece, who was writing letters in mauve ink at one of the iron tables. Suzette was small and fair, not a beauty, but dispensing instantaneously, and generously, emotional forces that at once aroused in me recollections of Jean Templer; causing an abrupt renewal—so powerful that it seemed almost that Jean had insinuated herself into the garden—of that restless sense of something desired that had become an increasing burden upon both day and night. Suzette shook hands and smiled in such a manner as to put beyond doubt, were the metaphor to be used, any question of butter melting in the mouth. Then she sat down again and continued her letter, evidently a composition that demanded her closest attention.

Two boys, perhaps great-nephews, followed, somewhere between nine and twelve years of age, with strongly marked features, broadly ironical like Madame Leroy's, to whose side of the family they belonged. Heavy black eyebrows were grafted on to white faces, as if to offset the pattern of dark blue socks against sallow, skinny legs. Both were hard at work with lexicons and notebooks; and, after shaking hands very formally, they returned to work, without looking up again as we passed on from their table. Their names were Paul-Marie and Jean-Népomucène.

Leaving these ramifications of the Leroy household, we approached the outskirts of a Scandinavian pocket in the local community, first represented in the person of a tall young man—in size about six foot three or four—wearing a black suit, light grey cap, and white canvas shoes, who was reading *Les Misérables* with the help of a dictionary. This figure, explained Madame Leroy, as I escaped from his iron grip, was Monsieur Örn—so, at least, after many changes of mind, I decided his name, variously pronounced by his fellow boarders, must be spelt, for during the whole of my stay at La Grenadière I never saw it written down—who was a Norwegian, now learning French, though in principle studying in his own country to be an engineer. From Monsieur Örn's vacant blue eyes a perplexed tangle of marked reactions seemed to signal uncertainly for a second or two, and then die down. I had seen a provincial company perform *The Doll's House* not many months before, and felt, with what I now see to have been quite inadmissible complacency, that I knew all about Ibsen's countrymen.

As Monsieur Örn seemed to be at a loss for words, we proceeded to Monsieur Lundquist, a Swede in dark grey knickerbockers, mending a bicycle. Monsieur Lundquist, although formality itself—he was almost as formal as Paul-

Marie and Jean-Népomucène had been—was much more forthcoming than Monsieur Örn. He repeated several times: *'Enchanté, Monsieur Yenkins,'* putting his heels together, and holding his bicycle-pump as if it were a sword and he were about to march past in review, while he smiled and took Madame Leroy's hand in his after he had let go of my own. His dark curly hair and round chubby face gleamed in the sun, seeming to express outwardly Monsieur Lundquist's complete confidence in his own powers of pleasing.

As we strolled on towards the summer-house, built with its entrance facing obliquely from the centre of the lawn—if the central part of the garden could really be so called—Madame Leroy explained that within this precinct would be found Monsieur and Madame Dubuisson, who had been married only a short time. Having called this fact to mind, she tapped loudly on one of the supports of the arbour before venturing to escort me through its arch. After taking this precaution, she advanced in front of me, and peeped through one of the embrasures in the wall, pausing for a moment, then beckoning me on, until at last we entered the heart of the retreat in which the Dubuissons were sitting side by side.

Afterwards I discovered that Monsieur Dubuisson was only about forty. At first sight he struck me as much older, since the skin of his face fell in diamond-shaped pouches which appeared quite bloodless. Like Monsieur Örn, he wore a cap, a very flat, very large, check cap, with a long peak, like that in which *apaches* used to be portrayed in French comic papers or on the stage. Under this headgear, rank and greying, almost lavender-coloured hair bunched out. He held a book on his knee, but was not reading. Instead he sat gazing with a look of immense and ineradicable scepticism on his face, towards what could be seen of the garden. His long upper lip and general carriage made me think of a French version of the Mad Hatter. His bride, a stocky little woman, younger than her husband, was dressed in white from head to foot: looking as if she had prepared herself for an afternoon's shopping in Paris, but had decided instead to spend her time knitting in the summerhouse. This very domestic occupation seemed scarcely to harmonise with the suggestion—conveyed in some manner by her face, even more than her clothes—that she was not, temperamentally, a domestic person: not, at any rate, in the usual meaning of that term. As Stringham had said of Peter Templer, she did not appear to be intended by nature for 'home life'. Whatever domesticity she might possess seemed superimposed on other, and perhaps more predatory, characteristics.

Though still feeling decidedly bilious, I had done my best to make myself agreeable to each of the persons in turn produced by Madame Leroy; and, such is the extraordinary power of sentiment at that age, the impact of Suzette's personality, with its reminder of Jean, had made me forget for a while the consequences of the hors d'œuvres. However, when Monsieur Dubuisson held out to me the book lying on his knee, and said dryly, in excellent English: 'I should be interested to hear your opinion on this rendering,' my head began to go round again. The title on the cover, *Simples Contes des Collines,* for the moment conveyed nothing to me. Fortunately Monsieur Dubuisson did not consider it necessary to receive an answer to his question, because, almost immediately, he went on to remark: 'I read the stories in French merely as—as a matter of interest. For you see I find no—no difficulty at all in expressing myself in the language of the writer.'

The pauses were evidently to emphasise the ease with which he spoke English, and his desire to use the absolutely appropriate word, rather than on account of ignorance of phrasing. He went on: 'I like Kipling. That is, I like him up to a point. Naturally one finds annoying this—this stress on nationalism. Almost blatant nationalism, I should say.'

All this conversation was now becoming a little overwhelming. Madame Leroy, engaged with Madame Dubuisson on some debate regarding *en pension* terms, would in any case, I think, have cut short the development of a serious literary discussion, because she was already showing indications of restlessness at Monsieur Dubuisson's continued demonstration of his command of English. However, a new—and for me almost startling—element at that moment altered the temper of the party. There was the sound of a step behind us, and an additional personage came under the rustic arch of the entrance, refocusing everyone's attention. I turned, prepared for yet another introduction, and found myself face to face with Widmerpool.

Monsieur Dubuisson, quite shrewd in his way, as I learnt later, must have realised at once that he would have to wait for another occasion to make his speech about Kipling, because he stopped short and joined his wife in her investigation of the *en pension* terms. Possibly he may even have felt that his support was required in order that the case for a reduction might be adequately presented. It was evidently a matter that had been discussed between the three of them on a number of earlier occasions, and, so soon as Madame Leroy had spoken of the surprise and pleasure that she felt on finding that Widmerpool and I were already acquainted, she returned vigorously to her contest with the Dubuissons.

Widmerpool said in his thick, flat voice: 'I thought it might be you, Jenkins. Only yours is such a common name that I could not be sure.'

We shook hands, rather awkwardly. Widmerpool had tidied himself up a little since leaving school, though there was still a kind of exotic drabness about his appearance that seemed to mark him out from the rest of mankind. At a later stage of our sojourn at La Grenadière, he confided to me that he had purchased several ties during an afternoon spent in Blois. He was wearing one of these cravats of the country when he came into the summer-house, and its embroidered stripes insinuated that he might not be English, without adding to his appearance the least suggestion of French origins. His familiar air of uneasiness remained with him, and he still spoke as if holding a piece of india-rubber against the roof of his mouth. He also retained his accusing manner, which seemed to suggest that he suspected people of trying to worm out of him important information which he was not, on the whole, prepared to divulge at so cheap a price as that offered. All this uncomfortable side of him came into my mind, and I could think of nothing to say. Madame Leroy was now deeply involved with the Dubuissons regarding the subject of some proposed financial readjustment, and it looked as if the matter was going to come to a head, one way or the other. At last the three of them went off together, talking hard. I was left alone with Widmerpool. He did not speak.

'How long have you been here?' I asked.

He stared hard at me from the solid glass windows through which he observed the world; frowning as if some important canon of decency had already been violated by my ineptitude: and that this solecism, whatever it was, grieved rather than surprised him. Then he said: 'You know we are supposed to talk *French* here, Jenkins.'

It was hard to guess how best to reply to this admonition. To say: '*Oui,* Widmerpool,' would sound silly, even a trifle flippant; on the other hand, to answer in English would be to aggravate my incorrect employment of the language; and might at the same time give the appearance of trying to increase the temptation for Widmerpool to relapse into his native tongue, with which my arrival now threatened to compromise him. In spite of his insignificance at school, I still felt that he might possess claims to that kind of outward deference one would pay to the opinion of a boy higher up in the house, even when there was no other reason specially to respect his views. In any case the sensation of nausea from which I had once more begun to suffer seemed to be increasing in volume, adding to the difficulty of taking quick decisions in so complicated a question of the use of language. After a long pause, during which he appeared to be thinking things over, Widmerpool spoke again.

'It would probably be simpler,' he said, 'if I showed you round first of all *in English*. Then we can talk French for the rest of the time you are here.'

'All right.'

'But tell me in the first place how you knew of La Grenadière?'

I explained about Commandant Leroy and my father. Widmerpool seemed disappointed at this answer. I added that my parents had thought the terms very reasonable. Widmerpool said: 'My mother has always loved Touraine since she visited this country as a girl. And, of course, as you know, the best French is spoken in this part of France.'

I said I had heard a Frenchman question that opinion; but Widmerpool swept this doubt aside, and continued: 'My mother was always determined that I should perfect my French among the châteaux of the Loire. She made enquiries and decided that Madame Leroy's house was far the best of the several establishments for paying-guests that exist in the neighbourhood. Far the best.'

Widmerpool sounded quite challenging; and I agreed that I had always heard well of the Leroys and their house. However, he would not allow that there was much to be said for the Commandant: Madame, on the other hand, he much admired. He said: 'I will take you round the garden first, and introduce you.'

'No, for Heaven's sake—Madame Leroy has already done that.'

Widmerpool looked offended at this speech, and seemed uncertain what should be the next move. He temporised by asking: 'What sort of a journey did you have?'

'Hot.'

'You look a bit green.'

'Let's go into the house.'

'Did you have a change,' he said. 'I came straight through by a clever piece of railway management on my part.'

'Where can I be sick?'

'What do you mean?'

'Where can I be sick?'

At length he understood; and soon after this, with many expressions of sympathy from Madame Leroy, and some practical help from Rosalie, who unbent considerably now that I was established as a member of the household—and an indisposed one—I retired to bed: lying for a long time in a state of coma, thinking about Widmerpool and the other people in the garden. The images of Jean Templer and Suzette hovered in the shadows of the room, until they merged into one person as sleep descended.

How all the inhabitants of La Grenadière were accommodated in a house of that size was a social and mathematical problem, so far as I was concerned, never satisfactorily elucidated during my stay there. I could only assume that there were more bedrooms than passage doors on the upper storeys, and that these rooms led one from another. The dining-room was on the left of the main entrance: the kitchen on the right. In the sunless and fetid segment between these two rooms, Rosalie presided during meals, eating her own portion from a console table that stood on one side of the hall, facing a massive buhl cabinet on the other: the glass doors of this cabinet revealed the ragged spines of a collection of paper-backed novels. This segregation in the hall symbolised Rosalie's footing in the house, by imposing physical separation from her employers on the one hand, and, on the other, from Marthe, a girl of eighteen, showing signs of suffering from goitre, who did the cooking: and did it uncommonly well.

Two dogs—Charley and Bum—shared with Rosalie her pitchy vestibule: a state of perpetual war existing between the three of them. Charley was so named on account of the really astonishing presumption that he looked like an English dog: whereas his unnaturally long brown body, short black legs, and white curly tail, made it almost questionable whether he was indeed a dog at all, and not a survival of a low, and now forgotten, form of prehistoric life. Bum, a more conventional animal, was a white wire-haired terrier. He carried his name engraved on a wide leather collar studded with brass hob-nails. Every Monday he was placed on a table in the garden, and Madame Leroy would bathe him, until his crisp coat looked as if it were woven from a glistening thread of white pipe-cleaners. Charley was never washed, and resenting this attention to his fellow, would on this account pick a quarrel with Bum every seven days. Rosalie was for ever tripping over the dogs in the passage, and cursing them: the dogs squabbling with each other and with Rosalie: at times even stealing food from her plate when she was handing on the next course into the dining-room: where we all sat at a large round table that nearly filled the room.

Most of the talking at meals was done by Madame Dubuisson, Berthe and Paul-Marie, the last of whom was said, by almost everyone who referred to him, to be unusually full of *esprit* for his age: though I was also warned that his remarks were sometimes judged to be *'un peu shocking'*. When he spoke, his black eyebrows used to arch, and then shoot together, and a stream of words would pour out, sending Madame Dubuisson and Berthe, especially, into fits of laughter at his sallies. These sometimes caused Madame Leroy to shake her head in mild reproval: though Madame Leroy herself would often smile admiringly at the ease with which Paul-Marie succeeded in hitting off life's paradoxical situations: especially those connected with the relations of the sexes. For my own part I understood only a small proportion of Paul-Marie's jokes on account of the speed with which he spat out his sentences, and also because of his colloquial manner of expressing himself; but I gathered their general import, which was to the effect that women, owing to their cunning ways, were to be approached with caution. Whether or not they were good jokes I am now in no position to say. I imagine that they belonged, on the whole, to that immense aggregation of synthetic humour on this subject that serves the French pretty well, being adapted to most cases that arise. Indeed, Paul-Marie's synthetic jokes might perhaps be compared with Uncle Giles's synthetic scepticism, both employable for many common situations. Jean-Népomucène was much quieter. With heavy-lidded eyes, he used to watch his brother, and give a short, very grown-up laugh at appropriate moments. Most of the time at table Jean-Népomucène's manner was absent, suggesting that his mind was engaged on preoccupations of his own, perhaps of a similar order to his brother's reflections, but more gravely considered. Berthe and Madame Dubuisson would sometimes try and tease him about his silences, saying: *'Ah, Jean-Népomucène, il est bavard, lui,'* in this way provoking a verbal attack from Paul-Marie, which usually required their combined forces to beat off.

Commandant Leroy rarely spoke. His wife kept him on a diet, and he sat, almost hidden, behind a colossal bottle of Contrexeville water, that always stood in front of him, from which, after every meal, he took a few drops, mixed with grey powder, in a spoon. Monsieur Dubuisson also conversed little at meals, no doubt because he felt his conversation wasted in the intellectual surroundings available at La Grenadière. He would, however, occasionally read aloud some item of news from the papers (his only extravagance seemed to be buying newspapers), after which he would laugh satirically as he qualified these quotations by supplying details of the individual, country, or political group, that provided funds for the journal in question. He used to listen to Paul-Marie's chatter with a look of infinite sourness on his face.

The position of the Dubuissons at La Grenadière always remained something of a mystery. It was evident that they had come there merely to enjoy a cheap holiday, and that Monsieur Dubuisson considered that life owed him something superior to the accommodation to be found with the Leroys. Berthe and Suzette used to have some joke together about Madame Dubuisson, who was apparently held to own a past not to be too closely scrutinised. They were talking the matter over, in whispers, one day, when sitting behind me on the way back from an expedition to Loches. They seemed to have no very definite information, but their conclusions—as I rather dimly understood them—

seemed to be that Madame Dubuisson had been her husband's mistress for a number of years: having at last induced him to marry her. At that time such a subject, illustrated by the practical circumstances of a couple who seemed to me to be so lacking in romance as the Dubuissons, appeared to be of only the most academic interest: to have little or nothing to do with the practical problems of life. At a later date I should have been more curious regarding their story. Madame Dubuisson used to giggle, and behave generally in a fairly free manner, especially when her husband was not present; and I felt that —if an analogy could be drawn between two such different households—she represented at La Grenadière something comparable to Lady McReith's position when staying at the Templers'. Madame Dubuisson was, for example, the guest whom Commandant Leroy undoubtedly liked best, and the boys, too, seemed to get on with her well. I never discovered her husband's occupation. It appeared that—like Sunny Farebrother—he had distinguished himself during the war: or, at least, he mentioned this fact to me on one or two occasions; and at one period he seemed to have taught, or lectured, at some provincial university. He said that at present he was in business, but without specifying its nature.

'I am a very busy man, building up for my corporation, and trying to materialise along the same lines a few ideas regarding the financing of certain needs which actually are most difficult to meet,' he remarked to me soon after my arrival.

He must have suspected that I required further enlightenment before I could answer, because he added: 'I might even come to London, when, and if, certain—certain negotiations pending with British houses mature.'

I asked if he knew London well.

'Probably better than yourself,' he replied; 'being nearly at the head of a finance corporation, I am trying to assure a certain percentage of the insolvency risk which might arise when I guarantee credits by endorsing bills.'

'I see.'

'You must not think,' Monsieur Dubuisson continued, smiling and showing a barrier of somewhat discoloured teeth, 'that I am merely—merely a commercial gent. I am also developing my activity as a newspaperman, and publish weekly one, or a couple, of articles. I hope to be circulated in England soon.'

'Do you write in English?'

'Of course.'

I inquired about the subjects on which he wrote. Monsieur Dubuisson said: 'I sent lately to the *National Review* a longish article entitled "Cash Payments; or Productive Guarantees?" speaking my views on the actual and future relations of France, Great Britain, and Germany. I have had no answer yet, but I have a manuscript copy I can lend you to read.'

He paused; and I thanked him for this offer.

'As a matter of fact I write along three very different lines,' Monsieur Dubuisson went on. 'First as a financial expert: second, summaries of big problems looked upon from an independent threefold point of view—political, military, economic: finally in consideration of the growth of the social idea in English literature.'

All this left me little, if at all, wiser on the subject of the Dubuisson background, but there could be no doubt that Monsieur Dubuisson had plenty of confidence in his own qualifications. Outwardly, he never showed much interest in his wife, though they spent a good deal of their time together: since neither of them took any part in the collective recreations of La Grenadière, such as the excursions to places of interest in the neighbourhood. This lack of public attention from her husband did not appear to worry Madame Dubuisson at all. She chattered away all the time to anyone who happened to find themselves next to her; and without any regard for the question of whether or not her listener understood what she was talking about: a habit perhaps acquired from her husband.

The two Scandinavians did not 'get on' with each other. Both Berthe and Suzette warned me of this, in diplomatic terms, soon after I came to La Grenadière. According to the girls, Monsieur Örn complained that Monsieur Lundquist was 'too proud'; while Monsieur Lundquist had actually stated openly that he considered Monsieur Örn to be lacking in *chic.* Monsieur Örn, like Monsieur Dubuisson, rarely spoke, spending most of his time writing lists of French words in a notebook. Berthe said that Monsieur Örn had confided to her that all Swedes were proud, often for no reason at all; Monsieur Lundquist especially so, for no better cause than that his father happened to be an official at the Law Courts. Monsieur Lundquist himself was going to become a journalist, and Monsieur Örn had told Berthe that Monsieur Lundquist was much inclined to exaggerate the social position that this calling would bring him. Although Monsieur Örn did not talk a great deal, he would sometimes look sternly across the table at Monsieur Lundquist, the whole of his craggy face slowly setting into a gloomy, hostile state: *'comme un Viking'*, Berthe used to call this specially organised physiogonomy. As a matter of fact Berthe had a weak spot for Monsieur Örn, because he was so good at tennis. If she happened to be cutting the melon at luncheon, she would always give him the largest slice, or help him generously to *pot-au-feu.*

Apart from his regret that Monsieur Örn was so hopelessly ill-equipped so far as *chic* was concerned—an opinion of which, I found, he made no secret, expounding the view freely to everyone in the house—Monsieur Lundquist seemed quite unaware of the vigour of Monsieur Örn's disapproval of his own attitude towards the world, which both of them agreed to be characteristically Swedish; nor was he prepared to accept Monsieur Örn's repeated assertions that he did not understand the Swedish language. Monsieur Lundquist, transgressing the rule of La Grenadière, whenever he found his French inadequate to make his meaning clear, would often make use of Swedish. Monsieur Örn would then listen, adjusting his firm features in such a way as to indicate utter failure to comprehend that such outlandish—or, perhaps it was, such affected—sounds could possibly have any meaning at all: even for Swedes. Monsieur Örn would finally make some remark in his notably individual French, evidently wholly irrelevant to the matter raised by Monsieur Lundquist. On such occasions Monsieur Lundquist would only smile, and shake this head, unable to credit Monsieur Örn's unvarying and oppressive lack of *chic*.

In this circle, Widmerpool had made himself an accepted, if not specially popular, figure. There was no question here of his being looked upon by the rest of the community as the oddity he had been regarded at school. In the weeks that followed I came to know him pretty well. We talked French to each other at meals, and kept up some show of using French during expeditions: alone together—usually late in the evening, when the others had gone to their rooms, to devote themselves to study, or to rest—we used to speak English; although Widmerpool rarely did so without making some reference to the reluctance with which he diverged from the rule of the house. He used to work hard at the language all the rest of the time. In spite of inherent difficulty in making words sound like French, he had acquired a large vocabulary, and could carry on a conversation adequately, provided he could think of something to say; for I found that he had no interest in anything that could not be labelled as in some way important or improving, an approach to conversation that naturally limited its scope. His determination to learn French set an example from which I fell lamentably short. In his rigid application to the purpose for which he came to France, he was undoubtedly the most satisfactory of Madame Leroy's boarders, even including the industrious Monsieur Örn, who never could get his genders right.

Like Monsieur Dubuisson, Widmerpool showed no enthusiasm for Paul-Marie's jokes.

'That boy has a corrupt mind,' he said, not many days after I had been in the house. 'Extraordinary for a child of that age. I cannot imagine what would happen to him at an English school.'

'He's like Stringham as a small French boy.'

I said this without thinking at all deeply about the accuracy of the comparison. I did not, in fact, find in Paul-Marie any startling resemblance to Stringham, though some faint affinity must have existed between them, in so much that more than once I had thought of Stringham, when Paul-Marie had been engaged in one of his torrential outbursts of conversation. However, Widmerpool showed sudden interest in the identification of their two characters.

'You were rather a friend of Stringham's, weren't you?' he asked. 'Of course I was a bit senior to know him. I liked the look of him on the whole. I should say he was an amusing fellow.'

For Widmerpool to imply that it was merely a matter of

age that had prevented him from being on easy terms with Stringham struck me, at that time, as showing quite unjustifiable complacency regarding his own place in life. I still looked upon him as an ineffective person, rather a freak, who had no claim to consider himself as the equal of someone like Stringham who, obviously prepared to live dangerously, was not to be inhibited by the narrow bounds to which Widmerpool seemed by nature committed. It was partly for this reason that I said: 'Do you remember the time when you saw Le Bas arrested?'

'An appalling thing to happen,' said Widmerpool. 'I left soon after the incident. Was it ever cleared up how the mistake arose?'

'Stringham rang up the police and told them that Le Bas was the man they wanted to arrest.'

'What do you mean?'

'The criminal they were after looked rather like Le Bas. We had seen a picture of him outside the police-station.'

'But why——'

'As a hoax.'

'Stringham?'

'On the telephone—he said he was Le Bas himself.'

'I never heard anything like it,' said Widmerpool. 'What an extraordinary thing to have done.'

He sounded so furious that I felt that some sort of apology was called for—in retrospect the episode certainly seemed less patently a matter for laughter, now that one was older and had left school—and I said: 'Well, Le Bas was rather an ass.'

'I certainly did not approve of Le Bas, or of his methods of running a house,' said Widmerpool: and I remembered that Le Bas had particularly disliked him. 'But to do a thing like that to his own housemaster . . . And the risk he ran. He might have been expelled. Were you concerned in this too, Jenkins?'

Widmerpool spoke so sternly that for a moment I thought he intended to sit down, there and then, and, in a belated effort to have justice done, report the whole matter in writing to Le Bas or the headmaster. I explained that personally I had had no share in the hoax, beyond having been out walking with Stringham at the time. Widmerpool said, with what I thought to be extraordinary fierceness: 'Of course Stringham was thoroughly undisciplined. It came from having too much money.'

'I never noticed much money lying about.'

'Stringham may not have been given an abnormal amount himself,' said Widmerpool, irritably, 'but his family are immensely wealthy. Glimber is a huge place. My mother and I went over it once on visiting day.'

'But he is not coming in to Glimber.'

I felt glad that I had been supplied by Templer with this piece of information.

'Of course he isn't,' said Widmerpool, as if my reply had been little short of insulting. 'But there are all his mother's South African gold holdings. That divorce of hers was a very unfortunate affair for someone so well known.'

I should have liked to hear more of this last matter, but, Stringham being a friend of mine, I felt that it would be beneath my dignity to discuss his family affairs with someone who, like Widmerpool, knew of them only through hearsay. Later in life, I learnt that many things one may require have to be weighed against one's dignity, which can be an insuperable barrier against advancement in almost any direction. However, in those days, choice between dignity and unsatisfied curiosity was less clear to me as a cruel decision that had to be made.

'And that thin, rather good-looking boy,' Widmerpool

continued, 'who used to be about a lot with you and Stringham?'

'Peter Templer.'

'Was he in the Le Bas affair too?'

'He was out for a walk with us on the same afternoon.'

'He did not have too good a reputation, did he?'

'Not too good.'

'That was my impression,' said Widmerpool. 'That he was not a good influence in the house.'

'You and he were mixed up in the Akworth row, weren't you?' I asked, not from malice, or with a view to keeping him in order on the subject of my friends, so much as for the reason that I was inquisitive to know more of that affair: and, considering the way that Widmerpool had been talking, I felt no particular delicacy about making the enquiry.

Widmerpool went brick-red. He said: 'I would rather not speak of that, if you don't mind.'

'Don't let's, then.'

'I suppose Templer got sacked in the end?' Widmerpool went on: no doubt conscious that he might have sounded over-emphatic, and evidently trying to bring some jocularity into his tone.

'More or less asked to leave.'

'How badly used he really to behave?'

He moistened his lips, though scarcely perceptibly. I thought his mixture of secretiveness and curiosity quite intolerable.

'He had a woman before he left.'

If Widmerpool had been upset by the news that Stringham had played the Braddock alias Thorne trick on Le Bas, and more personally embarrassed by reference to the Akworth scandal, this piece of information, regarding Templer's crowning exploit, threw him almost entirely off his balance. He made a strange sound, half-way between a low laugh and a clearing of the throat, simultaneously swallowing hard. He also went, if possible, redder than ever. Took off his spectacles and began to polish them, as he usually did when his nerves were on edge. I did not feel entirely at ease with the subject myself. To help out the situation, I added: 'I have just been staying with the Templers as a matter of fact.'

Widmerpool clearly welcomed this shift of interest in our conversation, enquiring almost eagerly about the Templers' house, and the manner in which they lived. We talked about the Templers for a time, and I found to my surprise that Widmerpool knew Sunny Farebrother by name, though they had never met. He said: 'A very sharp fellow, they tell me.'

'I liked him.'

'Naturally you did,' said Widmerpool. 'He can make himself very agreeable.'

I found Widmerpool's remarks in this vein so tiresome that I was almost inclined to try and shock him further by describing in detail the various incidents that had taken place while I was staying at the Templers'. In the end I decided that those happenings needed too much explanation before they could be appreciated, anyway by Widmerpool, that there was nothing to be gained by trying to impress him, or attempting to modify his point of view. I told him that Peter was going straight into business, without spending any time at the university. Rather unexpectedly, Widmerpool approved this decision, almost in Sunny Farebrother's own phrase.

'Much better get down to work right away,' he said. 'There was not much money when my father died, so I talked things over with my mother—she has a wonderful grasp of business matters—and we decided we would do the same thing, and cut out Oxford or Cambridge.'

By using the first person plural, he made the words sound as if there had been some question of his mother going up to the university with him. He said: 'This effort to polish up my French is merely in the nature of a holiday.'

'A holiday from what?'

'I am articled to a firm of solicitors.'

'Oh, yes.'

'I do not necessarily propose to remain a solicitor all my life,' said Widmerpool. 'I look to wider horizons.'

'What sort?'

'Business. Politics.'

This all seemed to me such rubbish that I changed the subject, asking where he lived. He replied, rather stiffly, that his mother had a flat in Victoria. It was convenient, he said; but without explaining the advantages. I enquired what life was like in London.

'That depends what you do,' said Widmerpool, guardedly.

'So I suppose.'

'What profession are you going to follow?'

'I don't know.'

It seemed almost impossible to make any remark without in one manner or another disturbing Widmerpool's equanimity. He was almost as shocked at hearing that I had no ready-made plans for a career as he had been scandalised a few minutes earlier at the information regarding the precocious dissipation of Templer's life.

'But surely you have some bent?' he said. 'An ambition to do well at something?'

This ideal conception—that one should have an aim in life—had, indeed, only too often occurred to me as an unsolved problem; but I was still far from deciding what form my endeavours should ultimately take. Being at that moment unprepared for an *a priori* discussion as to what the future should hold, I made several rather lame remarks to the effect that I wanted one day 'to write': an assertion that had not even the merit of being true, as it was an idea that had scarcely crossed my mind until that moment.

'To write?' said Widmerpool. 'But that is hardly a profession. Unless you mean you want to be a journalist—like Lundquist.'

'I suppose I might do that.'

'It is precarious,' said Widmerpool. 'And—although we laugh, of course, at Örn for saying so, right out—there is certainly not much social position attached: unless, for example, you become editor of *The Times,* or something of that sort. I should think it over very carefully before you commit yourself.'

'I am not absolutely determined to become a journalist.'

'You are wise. What are your other interests?'

Feeling that the conversation had taken a turn that delivered me over to a kind of cross-examination, I admitted that I liked reading.

'You can't earn your living by reading,' said Widmerpool, severely.

'I never said you could.'

'It doesn't do to read too much,' Widmerpool said. 'You get to look at life with a false perspective. By all means have some familiarity with the standard authors. I should never raise any objection to that. But it is no good clogging your mind with a lot of trash from modern novels.'

'That was what Le Bas used to say.'

'And he was quite right. I disagreed in many ways with Le Bas. In that one, I see eye to eye with him.'

There was not much for me to say in reply. I had a novel—*If Winter Comes,* which I had now nearly finished

—under my arm, and it was impossible to deny that I had been reading this book. Widmerpool must have noticed this, because he continued in a more kindly tone: 'You must meet my mother. She is one of those rare middle-aged women who have retained their youthful interest in matters of the mind. If you like books—and you tell me you do—you would thoroughly enjoy a chat with her about them.'

'That would be nice.'

'I shall arrange it,' said Widmerpool. *'Et maintenant, il faut se coucher, parce-que je compte de me reveiller de bonne heure le matin.'*

In the course of subsequent conversations between us he talked a good deal about his mother. On the subject of his father he was more reticent. Sometimes I had even the impression that Widmerpool *père* had earned a living in some manner of which his son—an only child—preferred not to speak: though, one evening, in a burst of confidence, he mentioned that his paternal grandfather had been a Scotch business man called Geddes, who had taken the name of Widmerpool after marrying a wife of that name, who was—so Widmerpool indicated in his characteristic manner—of rather higher standing than himself. There seemed to have been some kind of financial crisis when Widmerpool's father had died, either on account of debts, or because the family's income had been thereby much reduced. Life with his mother appeared to be very quiet and to consist of working all day and studying law after dinner most nights; though Widmerpool took care to explain to me that he deliberately took part in a certain amount of what he called 'social life'. He said, with one of his rare smiles: 'Brains and hard work are of very little avail, Jenkins, unless you know the right people.'

I told him that I had an uncle who was fond of saying

the same thing; and I asked what form his relaxations generally took.

'I go to dances,' said Widmerpool; adding, rather grandly: 'in the Season, that is.'

'Do you get a lot of invitations?' I asked, divided between feeling rather impressed by this attitude towards the subject in hand and, at the same time, finding difficulty in believing that he could be overwhelmed by persons wishing to share his company.

Widmerpool was evasive on this point, and muttered something about invitations being 'just a question of getting on a list'. As he seemed unwilling to amplify this statement, I did not press him further, having myself a somewhat indistinct comprehension of what he meant: and appreciating that the relative extent of his invitations, as for anyone, might be, perhaps, a delicate matter.

'I don't get much time for games now,' he said. 'Though once in a way I make a point of going down to Barnes, and driving a ball into a net.'

I was, for some reason, conscious of an odd sense of relief that he should no longer consider himself compelled to undergo those protracted and gruelling trials of endurance against himself for which he still remained chiefly notable in my mind. Driving a golf ball into a net presented an innocuous, immensely less tortured, picture to the mind than that offered by those penitential exertions with which I had formed the habit of associating his hours of recreation. This mitigated strain became even more apparent to me later on, when we used to play tennis, though his old enthusiasm was still quite strong enough.

Tennis at La Grenadière—or rather in the grounds of a ruined nineteenth-century mansion in Renaissance style situated about a mile and a half away on the outskirts of the town—was certainly of a kind to give small opportunity for a parade of that feverish keenness which had made the sight of Widmerpool playing games at school so uncomfortable to watch: although, so far as possible, he always insisted upon a high standard of athletic formality being observed whenever we played. The tennis-court was, however, the stage for him to reveal to me quite another side of his character: an unsuspected strength of personality and power of negotiation. This was in connexion with the rupture of relations between Monsieur Örn and Monsieur Lundquist, both of whom, as it turned out, took their game with seriousness at least equal to Widmerpool's; in spite of the comparatively unprofessional circumstances in which these contests were held.

The several hard tennis courts in this garden, which had been taken over as a park by the municipality, had never been properly kept up since becoming public property; so that in the course of time the soil had receded from the metal bars that formed the lines of demarcation, leaving solid boundaries that protruded so far above the ground that it was easy to catch one's foot in them when running about the court. If the ball hit one of these projecting strips of metal, it might become wedged beneath, or fly off at an unexpected angle; accordingly counting as a 'let'. Both of these types of 'let' took place with fair frequency, somewhat slowing up the cadence of the game, and making it hard to play with the concentration with which Widmerpool liked to approach all forms of sport. In addition to this local impediment to rapid play, neither Berthe nor Suzette were very proficient at the game; and they—with Paul-Marie and Jean-Népomucène, also beginners—always had to be worked into the fours.

Being no great performer myself, I rather enjoyed tennis played in these leisurely, at times undoubtedly eccentric, conditions; but Widmerpool was perpetually grumbling about 'the game not being taken seriously', a complaint that was, from his point of view, fully justified: although he was himself in no sense a good player. If he could possibly manage to do so, he would try to arrange a 'men's four', which usually resulted in one of us partnering a Scandinavian; and it soon became clear that, however much Monsieur Örn and Monsieur Lundquist might be able to cloak their mutual antipathy in the common intercourse of everyday life, their hatred for each other on the tennis court was a passion far less easily curbed. As it happened, a 'men's four' was not so simple for Widmerpool to contrive as might be supposed, because Berthe and Suzette were inclined to resent having to play in a four with Paul-Marie and Jean-Népomucène—another instance of excessive insistence on dignity defeating its own ends, for in that manner the girls would have gained practice which they greatly needed—and also, a more potent reason, because there were at best only four tennis balls; one of which had a gash in its outer covering which adversely affected the bounce. These balls not uncommonly became mislaid in the thickets of the garden; and, although Paul-Marie and Jean-Népomucène were themselves not above playing a single with only one ball (provided this were not the damaged one), the rest of the party looked upon a couple of sound balls as a minimum; and preferred, if possible, to have the use of all available. Sometimes either Berthe or Suzette was '*souffrante*', and wanted to sit out for a set or two. This rarely occurred to both of them on the same day, so that, as it happened, competition between Monsieur Örn and Monsieur Lundquist, although each occasionally played against the other partnering one of the girls, took on its most violent aspect when both were engaged in a 'men's four': a 'single' between them being, naturally, unthinkable.

If a 'single' had ever taken place, it would undoubtedly have been won by Monsieur Örn, a better player than Monsieur Lundquist, taller and quicker in movement. There was, however, another element that entered into these games, especially when four were playing. This was knowledge of the peculiarities of the court, and their uses in winning a set, of which Monsieur Lundquist had a far keener grasp than Monsieur Örn. Monsieur Lundquist was also accustomed to practice a trick which had for some reason the effect of making Monsieur Örn abandon his normal state of vague, silent acceptance of the hardships of life and become decidedly irritable. This stratagem was for Monsieur Lundquist suddenly to change the style of his service, from a fairly brisk delivery that sent the grit flying about the court, to a gentle lob that only just cleared the net: a stroke which, quite unaccountably, always took Monsieur Örn by surprise, invariably causing him to lose the point.

Monsieur Lundquist never employed this device more than once in the course of an afternoon: often not at all. However, on one unusually hot day, after I had been at La Grenadière for several weeks, he did it twice in the same set, catching out Monsieur Örn on both occasions. It so happened that earlier in the same afternoon a ball lodged itself four or five times under the back line, a particularly annoying circumstance for the player—in every case Monsieur Örn—who certainly would otherwise have won the point. After the last of these 'lets', Monsieur Lundquist served his second lob—an unheard-of thing—catching Monsieur Örn unawares for the second time, with—so far as I was concerned—entirely unexpected effect on the Norwegian's temper.

The actual word, or words, employed by Monsieur Örn never came publicly to light, even after the whole matter had been closed: nor was it ever established whether the epithet, or designation, had been expressed in Swedish, Norwegian, or in some opprobrious term, or phrase, common to both languages. Whatever was said, Monsieur Örn spoke quietly, with closed lips, almost muttering to himself; although in a manner apparently audible to Monsieur Lundquist, who lost all at once his look of enormous self-satisfaction, went red in the face, and walked quickly round to the other side of the net. Widmerpool, his partner, shouted: '*Mais qu'est-ce que vous faites, Monsieur Lundquist? J'en ai ici deux balles. C'est assez?*'

Monsieur Lundquist took no notice of him. It was at least clear to me that, whatever else he might want, he had not crossed the court in search of tennis balls. He went straight up to Monsieur Örn and—I suppose—demanded an apology. 'I thought those northern races did not get hysterical,' Widmerpool said to me afterwards, when we were discussing the distressing scene that followed; which ended with Monsieur Lundquist marching away from the rest of us, jumping on his bicycle, and riding at breakneck speed over the dusty pot-holes that punctuated the drive's steep descent. At one moment, as he rounded the corner, I felt sure that he was going to come off; but he recovered his balance, and passing rapidly through the open gates of wrought iron that led to the road, he disappeared from sight. I agreed with Widmerpool that if he had supposed that hysteria formed no part of the Scandinavian temperament, he had—to use a favourite phrase of his own—based his opinion on insufficient data.

This scene, though in itself a violent one, did not take long to play out. Before its close, Berthe and Suzette had both risen from the seat upon which they had been resting, and done their best to join in. They were only partially successful in this, though they contrived to add appreciably to the hubbub. Finally, we were all left standing in the centre of the court beside Monsieur Örn, who had limited himself throughout the commotion almost entirely to monosyllables. He now began to speak in a deep, strident voice, which after a minute or two showed signs of shaking with emotion. At first Widmerpool and I were unable to grasp the root of the trouble, partly because Monsieur Lundquist's lobbing technique was sufficiently common for none of the rest of us specially to have noticed it that afternoon: partly because at that age I was not yet old enough to be aware of the immense rage that can be secreted in the human heart by cumulative minor irritation. However, the subject of the dispute began to reveal itself in due course after Monsieur Lundquist had left the gardens. In fact Monsieur Örn at length demonstrated the origin of his annoyance by himself tapping a ball—the gashed one—lightly over the net in Monsieur Lundquist's manner, where it fell flat, like a stone, on the reddish dust. '*Jamais,*' said Monsieur Örn, now very quietly, after performing this action several times. '*Jamais—jamais.*' Whether his words were intended to convey that no one should ever practice tricks of that sort, or whether he was expressing an intention never again to play tennis with Monsieur Lundquist was not certain.

The result of all this was a breach between Monsieur Örn and Monsieur Lundquist which there seemed no possibility of closing. By the time we reached the house, I had satisfactorily reconstructed the situation in my own mind; and I imagined—as it turned out, quite incorrectly—that I had grasped its intricacies more thoroughly than Widmerpool. It is doubtful whether the two girls ever understood the true source of the disturbance, though neither of them was backward in explaining what had gone wrong, and how it should be put right. There is no knowing what sort of an account Madame Leroy was given of the trouble, because she heard the first version from Berthe and Suzette as soon as we arrived back at La Grenadière.

Whatever was said was, in any case, sufficient to prepare her for a trying time at dinner that evening, during which meal Monsieur Örn and Monsieur Lundquist spoke no word to each other and very little to anyone else: projecting between them across the table a cloud of hatred that seemed to embarrass even Madame Leroy, not easily disconcerted in her own house. Her husband, it is true, did not show any concern whatever, or, indeed, awareness that something might be amiss; and Paul-Marie and Jean-Népomucène, at first greatly delighted by the grown-up quarrel, soon forgot the Scandinavians in some elaborate and secret diversion of their own. Berthe, Suzette, and Madame Dubuisson were in a state of acute excitement, shooting each other glances intended to be full of meaning; while they conversed in a kind of hissing undertone. Widmerpool, also, was plainly agitated. The only person whole-heartedly amused, and pleased, by what had happened was Monsieur Dubuisson, who talked more than was his custom throughout the meal, amplifying a little the *exposé* he had given on the previous day of one of his favourite subjects, the development of water-power in Morocco. So far as I was concerned myself, these circumstances made me feel very uneasy, and I could see no way for matters to right themselves; nor for normal life to be carried on, except by the hand-to-mouth method symbolised by passing to Monsieur Örn or Monsieur Lundquist whatever food or drink each was likely to need, for which neither would ask the other. This state of affairs lasted throughout the following day, and the next; until there seemed no solution to the problem of how to restore the relationship between Monsieur Örn and Monsieur Lundquist to its old footing, imperfect as this may have been.

To my great surprise, Monsieur Dubuisson began to discuss this situation with me one evening, when we found ourselves alone together in the garden. It had been another bakingly hot day, and the white dust lay thick on the leaves of the shrubs, and over the battered seat upon which I was sitting. I was reading *Bel-Ami,* discovered among the books —on the whole not a very exciting collection—kept in the glass cabinet in the hall. Monsieur Dubuisson had been walking up and down one of the paths, studying a newspaper. Now he came across the withered grass, and sat down beside me, at the same time taking from the pocket of his black alpaca coat his pipe, of which—like Peter Templer—he was, for some reason, immensely proud. As usual he cleared his throat several times before speaking, and then, leaning backwards, spat sideways over the seat. In his slow, disapproving voice he said: 'I think it would be a—a little absurd if I talked French to you in view of our —our relative mastery of each other's tongue. Do you agree, Jenkins, yes?'

'Absolutely.'

One had to admit that he spoke English remarkably well, in spite of the hesitations made necessary by the subtlety of his processes of thought. There could be no doubt that every sentence was intended to knock you down by its penetrative brilliance. Smiling quietly to himself, as if at some essentially witty conception that he was inwardly playing with, and withheld only because its discernment was not for everybody, he began slowly to fill his pipe with tobacco —again like Peter's—that smelt peculiarly abominable.

'There seems to be a regular falling-out between our good friends from the north,' he said.

I agreed.

'You and I,' said Monsieur Dubuisson, 'belong to nations

who have solved their different problems in different ways.'

I admitted that this assertion was undeniable.

'Our countries have even, as you would say, agreed to differ. You lean on tradition: we on logic.'

I was not then aware how many times I was to be informed of this contrast in national character on future occasions by Frenchmen whose paths I might happen to cross; and again I concurred.

'As I understand the affair,' went on Monsieur Dubuisson, 'as I understand the circumstances of the matter, it would be difficult to achieve something in the nature of a reconciliation.'

'Very difficult, I——'

'It would be difficult, because it would be hard to determine whether an appeal should be made, on the one hand, to your congenital leaning towards tradition: or, on the other, to our characteristic preference for logic. Do you agree? The way may even lie near some Scandinavian fusion of these two ideas. You read Strindberg?'

'I have heard of him.'

'I think our Swedish friend, Lundquist, is quite pleased with himself,' said Monsieur Dubuisson, allowing me no opportunity to interrupt his train of thought: at the same time nodding and smiling, as a speaker personally familiar with the exquisite sensations that being pleased with oneself could impart to the whole being. 'Örn, on the other hand, always seems to have the blues. During the war I knew some of your countrymen of that type. Always down at the mouth.'

'Did you see a lot of the British Army?'

'Towards the end, quite a lot. It was obvious, speaking English as I do. For three months I was second-in-command to a battalion. I was wounded twice and have four citations.'

I asked if he had ever come across my father in Paris; but, although Monsieur Dubuisson was unwilling to admit that they had never met—and assured me that he had heard Commandant Leroy speak of my father in the highest terms—it seemed probable that the two of them had never run across one another. On the other hand, Monsieur Dubuisson remarked: 'Much of my work was done with Captain Farebrother, whom you have perhaps met in England. He was called Sunny Farebrother by his comrades in the army.'

'But how astonishing—I have met him.'

As a matter of fact, I had thought of Farebrother almost as soon as Monsieur Dubuisson had mentioned his own war record, because it had immediately occurred to me how much Jimmy Stripling would have loathed Monsieur Dubuisson, with his wounds and citations. Besides, Monsieur Dubuisson's treatment of the circumstances of his war career made Farebrother's references to his own military past seem infinitely fastidious.

'But why should you think it astonishing?' asked Monsieur Dubuisson, with one of his withering smiles, which spread over the whole of his face, crinkling the features into the shape of a formal mask of comedy, crowned with greyish-mauve locks. 'Captain Farebrother is a man I know to go about a great deal in society. What could be more natural than that you should have met him?'

I did not know in those days that it was impossible to convince egoists of Monsieur Dubuisson's calibre that everyone does not look on the world as if it were arranged with them—in this case Monsieur Dubuisson—at its centre; and, not realising that, in his eyes, the only possible justification for my turning up at La Grenadière would be the fact that I had once met someone already known to him, I tried to explain that this acquaintanceship with Farebrother seemed to me an extraordinary coincidence. In addition to this, if I had been old enough to have experienced something of the world of conferences and semi-political affairs, in effect a comparatively small one, it would have seemed less unexpected that their meeting had taken place.

'He was a good fellow,' said Monsieur Dubuisson. 'There was, as a matter of fact, a small question in which Captain Farebrother had shown himself interested, and of which I later heard nothing. Perhaps you know his address?'

'I am afraid not.'

'It is of no consequence,' said Monsieur Dubuisson. 'I can easily trace him.'

All the same he cleared his throat again, rather crossly. I felt that all this talk about the war, by reviving old memories, had put him out of his stride. He pulled at his pipe for a time, and then returned to the subject of Monsieur Örn and Monsieur Lundquist.

'Now you were present when this falling-out took place,' he said. 'Can you recite to me the pertinent facts?'

I told him how matters had looked to me as a witness of them. He listened carefully to the story, which sounded—I had to admit to myself—fairly silly when told in cold blood. When I came to the end he knocked out his pipe against the leg of the seat, and, turning towards me, said quite tolerantly: 'Now look here, Jenkins, you know you and I cannot believe eyewash of that sort. Grown-up men do not quarrel about such things.'

'What were they quarrelling about, then?'

Monsieur Dubuisson gave his slow, sceptical smile. He shook his head several times.

'You are no longer a child, Jenkins,' he said. 'I know that in England such matters are not—not stressed. But you have no doubt noticed at La Grenadière the presence of two charming young ladies. You have?'

I conceded this.

'Very good,' said Monsieur Dubuisson. 'Very good.'

He rose from the seat, and stood looking down at me, holding his hands behind his back. I felt rather embarrassed, thinking that he had perhaps guessed my own feelings for Suzette.

'Then what is there to be done about it?' I asked, to break the silence.

'Ah, *mon vieux*,' said Monsieur Dubuisson. 'Well may you ask what is to be done about it. To me—troubled as I am with a mind that leaps to political parallels—the affairs seems to me as the problems of Europe in miniature. Two young girls—two gentlemen. Which gentleman is to have which young girl? Your Government wishes mine to devalue the franc. We say the solution lies in your own policy of export.'

He shrugged his shoulders.

'I shrug my shoulders,' he said, 'like a Frenchman on the London stage.'

I was entirely at a loss to know how to reply to his presentation of this political and international allegory in relation to the matter in hand: and I found myself unable to grasp the implications of the parallel he drew with sufficient assurance to enable me to express either agreement or disagreement. However, Monsieur Dubuisson, as usual, appeared to expect no reply. He said: 'I appreciate, Jenkins, that you have come here to study. At the same time you may need something—what shall I say?—something more stimulating than the conversation which your somewhat limited fluency in the French language at present allows you to enjoy. Do not hesitate to talk with me when we are alone together on any subject that may happen to interest you.'

He smiled once again; and, while I thanked him, added: 'I am conversant with most subjects.'

As he strolled back across the lawn towards the house, he stowed away his pipe, which he seemed to use as a kind of emblem of common sense, in the pocket of his black alpaca jacket, which he wore over fawn tussore trousers.

I remained on the seat, thinking over his remarks, which required some classification before judgment could be passed on them. I could not accept his theory that jealousy about the girls, at least jealousy in any straightforward form, was at the bottom of the quarrel; because, in so much as the Scandinavians were to be thought of in connexion with Berthe and Suzette, each had paired off—if such an expression could be used of so amorphous a relationship—with a different girl: and everyone seemed perfectly happy with this arrangement. Berthe, as I have said, undoubtedly possessed a slight weakness for Monsieur Örn, which he recognised by markedly chivalrous behaviour towards her, when any such questions arose as the pumping-up of tyres of her bicycle, or carrying parcels back from the village when she did the shopping. Like Berthe, Monsieur Örn, too, was engaged; and he had, indeed, once handed round a small, somewhat faded, snapshot of himself sitting in ski-ing costume in the snow with his fiancée, who came from Trondhjem. Monsieur Lundquist, on the other hand, although interest in himself allowed him to show no more than moderate preference towards girls, or anyone else, seemed distinctly inclined towards Suzette. In so much as this allocation could be regarded as in any way part of a system, it also appeared to be absolutely satisfactory to everyone concerned. Indeed, the only person I knew of who might be said to have suffered from emotions that fell within the range of those suggested by Monsieur Dubuisson was myself; because, although the episode of the tennis court represented the more dramatic side of life at La Grenadière, the image of Suzette played in fact a far more preponderant part in my thoughts than the affairs of the Scandinavians, however unrestrained their behaviour.

I sometimes tried to sort out these feelings that had developed towards Suzette, which had certainly aroused from time to time a sensation of annoyance that Monsieur Lundquist should be talking animatedly to her, or helping her down the spiral staircase of some medieval building that we might be visiting. These were, I was aware, responses to be compared with those aroused by Jean Templer, with whom, as I have said, I now thought of myself as being 'in love'; and I was somewhat put out to find that recurrent projections in the mind of the images of either of them, Jean or Suzette, did not in the least exclude that of the other. That was when I began to suspect that being in love might be a complicated affair.

Naturally these reflections linked themselves with the general question of 'girls', discussed so often in my presence by Stringham and Templer. The curious thing was that, although quite aware that a sentiment of attraction towards Suzette was merely part of an instinct that had occasioned Peter's 'unfortunate incident'—towards which I was conscious of no sense of disapproval—my absorption in the emotional disturbance produced by Jean and Suzette seemed hardly at all connected with the taking of what had been, even in Templer's case, a fairly violent decision. I did not view his conduct on that London afternoon either as a contrast to my own inability to tackle the problem posed by these girls; nor even, for that matter, as an extension—or cruder and more aggravated version—of the same motive. My own position in the matter seemed, even to myself, to be misty: half-pleasant, half-melancholy. I was, however, struck by the reflection that undoubted inconvenience was threatened if this apparently recurrent malady of the heart was to repeat itself throughout life, with the almost dizzy reiteration that had now begun to seem unavoidable.

Suzette herself remained, so far as I was concerned, almost as enigmatic as Jean. Sometimes I thought she liked me to sit beside her at meals, or play as her partner at the strange games of auction bridge that sometimes took place in the evening, bearing the same relation to ordinary card playing that our tennis bore to ordinary tennis; and once there seemed a chance that her preference was shown even a little more definitely. This happened one Monday afternoon, when Bum was having his bath on the table in the garden, and, Madame Leroy suffering from migraine, Suzette was conducting this ceremony.

She had asked me to hold the dog, while he was being soaped all over. Bum usually enjoyed his bath, standing quietly with legs apart, until it was time for him to be dried with a rough towel; then he would run off, wagging his tail. That day, however, he stood on the table peacefully until the soap-suds reached half-way down his back, when, at that point, he suddenly escaped from my hands, and jumped on to the ground. Shaking himself excitedly, he set off across the garden, having decided, evidently, that he had had enough of this bath. At that moment Charley appeared from the front door. I have mentioned that Charley was never bathed, and resented this attention paid to Bum's handsome coat. Charley began to growl, and the two dogs ran round the paths, snarling, though fairly amicably, at each other, chased by Suzette and myself. At last Charley disappeared into the bushes, and we headed Bum into the summer-house. As we came in there after him, he jumped on to the seat, and out of the window. Suzette sat down, rather breathless, shaking her head to show that she proposed to pursue him no farther. I sat down beside her, and found my hand resting on hers. She continued to laugh, and did not remove her fingers from under mine. Whether or not this fortuitous preliminary might have developed along more positive lines is hard to say. I had no plan of campaign in mind, though I knew this to be a moment that would commit us one way or the other. Suzette probably—indeed, certainly—knew far better what it was all about. However, there was no time for the situation to develop because, at that moment, Widmerpool appeared in the summer-house; just as he had done on the day of my arrival.

'*Mais qu'est-ce que c'est que ce bruit effroyable?*' he said. '*On doit penser que tout le monde a devenu fou.*'

'*Tout le monde est fou,*' Sudette said. '*Naturellement, tout le monde est fou.*'

Our hands had separated as Widmerpool came through the door. He sat down between us and began to talk of *Les Misérables,* which he had borrowed from Monsieur Örn. Suzette resumed her well-behaved, well-informed exterior, with which I was by now so familiar, and for a time she discoursed, almost as boringly as Widmerpool himself, on the subject of Victor Hugo. The occasion was past; but in the days that followed I thought often about that moment in the summer-house when our hands had been together, regretting that I had not managed to turn that chance to some account.

The words just spoken by Monsieur Dubuisson while sitting by me on the seat had, therefore, a peculiarly powerful effect in confirming, not only the overwhelming impact of this new, perhaps rather alarming, ascendancy of the emotions; but also my consciousness of the respect which Monsieur Dubuisson obviously paid to these forces, as coming first when any human relationship was to be analysed. I did not feel that I could discuss such things with Widmerpool; and it never occurred to me that he himself might feel equally attracted towards Berthe or Suzette. I still saw him only in the crude, and inadequate, terms with which I had accepted him at school.

If I had decided to discuss Suzette with Widmerpool, I should have had an opportunity that evening, because he mentioned in his more formal manner, after dinner, that he would like to have a word with me alone, before I went off to bed. He showed every sign of being particularly pleased about something, when he spoke to me, and he was rubbing together his 'gritty little knuckles', as Peter Templer had called them. Except at meals, I had seen nothing of him all day. I imagined that he had been working in his bedroom, where he would sometimes disappear for hours on end, while he translated the French classics, or otherwise studied the language.

Everyone, except Commandant Leroy, went off to their rooms early that night; probably because the atmosphere of disquiet spread by Monsieur Örn and Monsieur Lundquist, although perhaps a shade less crushing than on the previous day, was still discouraging to general conversation. After the rest of the household had gone upstairs, Widmerpool, pursing his lips and blowing out his cheeks, kept on looking in the commandant's direction, evidently longing to get rid of him; but the old man sat on, turning over the tattered pages of a long out-of-date copy of *L'Illustration*, and speaking, disjointedly, of the circumstances in which he had been gassed. I liked Commandant Leroy. The fact that he was bullied by his wife had not prevented him from enjoying a life of his own; and, within the scope of his world of patent medicines and pottering about the garden, he had evolved a philosophy of detachment that made his presence restful rather than the reverse. Widmerpool despised him, however, chiefly, so far as I could gather, on the grounds that the commandant had failed to reach a higher rank in the army. Madame Leroy, on the other hand, was respected by Widmerpool. 'She has many of the good qualities of my own mother,' he used to say; and I think he was even a trifle afraid of her.

Commandant Leroy sat describing in scrupulous detail how his unit had been ordered to move into the support line along a network of roads that were being shelled, according to his account, owing to some error committed by the directing staff. He had gone forward to inspect the ground himself, and so on, and so forth. The story came to an end at last, when he found himself in the hands of the army doctors, of whom he spoke with great detestation. Widmerpool stood up. There was another long delay while Bum was let out of the room into the garden: and, after Bum's return, Commandant Leroy shook hands with both of us, and shuffled off to bed. Widmerpool shut the door after him, and sat down in the commandant's chair.

'I have settled the matter between Örn and Lundquist,' he said.

'What on earth do you mean?'

Widmerpool made that gobbling sound, not unlike an engine getting up steam, which meant that he was excited, or put out, about something: in this case unusually satisfied. He said: 'I have had conversations with each of them —separately—and I think I can confidently predict that I am not far from persuading them to make things up.'

'What?'

'In fact I have reason to suppose that within, say, twenty-four hours I shall have achieved that object.'

'Did you tell them not to be such bloody fools?'

This was quite the wrong comment to have made.

Widmerpool, who had previously shown signs of being in a far more complacent mood than was usual in his conversations with me, immediately altered his expression, and, indeed, his whole manner. He said: 'Jenkins, do you mind home truths?'

'I don't think so.'

'First,' said Widmerpool, 'you are a great deal too fond of criticising other people: secondly, when a man's self-esteem has been injured he is to be commiserated with—not blamed. You will find it a help in life to remember those two points.'

'But they have both of them been behaving in the most pompous way imaginable, making life impossible for everyone else. I quite see that Lundquist should not have sent sneaks over the net like that, but Örn ought to be used to them by now. Anyway, if Örn did rap out something a bit stiff, he could easily have said he was sorry. What do you think the word meant?'

'I have no idea what the word meant,' said Widmerpool, 'nor am I in the least interested to learn. I agree with you that Lundquist's play from a certain aspect—I repeat from a *certain* aspect—might be said to leave something to be desired; that is to say from the purest, and, to my mind, somewhat high-flown, sportsmanship. On the other hand there was no question of *cheating*.'

'It is a pretty feeble way of winning a service.'

'Games,' said Widmerpool, 'are played to be won, whatever people may say and write to the contrary. Lundquist has never found that service to fail. Can he, therefore, be blamed for using it?'

He folded his arms and stared fixedly past me, as if he were looking out into the night in search of further dialectical ammunition, if I were to remain unconvinced by his argument.

'But you wouldn't use that service yourself?'

'Everyone has his own standards of conduct,' said Widmerpool. 'I trust mine are no lower than other people's.'

'Anyhow,' I said, as I was getting tired of the subject, 'what did you do to bring them together?'

'First of all I went to Lundquist,' said Widmerpool, relaxing a little the stringency of his manner; 'I explained to him that we all understood that Örn should not have spoken as he did.'

'But we don't know what Örn said.'

Widmerpool made a nervous movement with his hands to show his irritation. He seemed half-inclined to break off his narrative, but changed his mind, and went on: 'I told him that we all knew Örn was a bit of a rough diamond, as Lundquist himself understood, as much—or even more—than the rest of us. It was therefore no good expecting anything very courtly from Örn in the way of behaviour.'

'How did Lundquist take that?'

'He fully agreed. But he emphasised that such defects, attributed by him to inherent weaknesses in the Norwegian system of education, did not alter the fact that his, Lundquist's, honour had been insulted.'

Widmerpool stopped speaking at this point, and looked at me rather threateningly, as if he was prepared for such a statement on Lundquist's part to arouse comment. As I remained silent, he continued: 'That argument was hard to answer. I asked him, accordingly, if I had his permission to speak to Örn on the same subject.'

'What did he say to that?'

'He bowed.'

'It all sounds very formal.'

'It *was* very formal,' said Widmerpool. 'Why should it have been otherwise?'

Not knowing the answer, I did not take up this challenge; thinking that perhaps he was right.

'I went straight to Örn,' said Widmerpool, 'and told him that we all understood his most justifiable annoyance at Lundquist's service; but that he, Örn, must realise, as the rest of us did, that Lundquist is a proud man. No one could be in a better position to appreciate that fact than Örn himself, I said. I pointed out that it could not fail to be painful to Lundquist's *amour-propre* to lose so frequently—even though he were losing to a better tennis-player.'

'Did all this go on in French?'

Widmerpool took no notice of this question; which, both Scandinavians knowing some English, seemed to me of interest.

'Örn was more obstinate than Lundquist,' said Widmerpool. 'Örn kept on repeating that, if Lundquist wished to play pat-ball with the girls—or little boys, he added—there was plenty of opportunity for him to do so. He, Örn, liked to play with men—*hommes*—he shouted the word rather loud. He said that, in his own eyes, *hommes* might be stretched to include Paul-Marie and Jean-Népomucène, but did not include Lundquist.'

Widmerpool paused.

'And he stuck to that?' I asked.

Widmerpool shook his head slowly from side to side, allowing his lips to form a faint smile. He said: 'Örn took a lot of persuading.'

'Then he agreed?'

'He agreed that I should come again tomorrow to renew the discussion.'

'You are certainly taking a lot of trouble about them.'

'These things are worth trouble,' said Widmerpool. 'You may learn that in time, Jenkins.'

I followed him up the stairs, more than a little impressed.

There was something about the obstinacy with which he pursued his aims that could not be disregarded, or merely ridiculed. Even then I did not recognise the quest for power.

The consequence of Widmerpool's efforts was to be seen a couple of nights later, when Monsieur Örn and Monsieur Lundquist sat together, after dinner, at one of the tables in the garden, finishing off between them a bottle of Cognac: after giving a glass to Madame Leroy, Madame Dubuisson, and myself, and two glasses to Monsieur Dubuisson: everyone else, for one reason or another, refusing the offer. Long after I was in bed and asleep that night, I was woken by the sound of the Scandinavians stumbling up to their room, now apparently on the best of terms. It had been a triumph of diplomacy on Widmerpool's part. The enterprise he had shown in the matter displayed a side of his character the existence of which I had never suspected. I had to admit to myself that, in bringing Monsieur Örn and Monsieur Lundquist together again, he had achieved a feat that I should never have ventured even to attempt.

The sense of tension that had prevailed during the period of the row was now replaced by one of perhaps rather strained amiability, in which all but Monsieur Dubuisson joined. Monsieur Dubuisson accepted the brandy as the outward and visible sign of reconciliation, but he showed no vestige of surprise at the changed situation certainly none of satisfaction. Madame Leroy was, of course, delighted; though I do not think that she ever had any idea of how concord had once more been brought about: attributing it entirely to a change of heart on the part of the couple concerned. For the rest of us, there could be no doubt of the improvement. The latter part of my stay at La Grenadière was passed, on the whole, in an atmosphere of good will on all sides: with the exception of a comparatively minor incident which involved Widmerpool only. There was undoubtedly a suggestion of nervous relaxation when Monsieur Lundquist moved, a few days later, to Bonn, where he was to continue his studies. Monsieur Örn shook him very heartily by the hand, and they agreed to meet when Monsieur Örn visited Stockholm, as he assured Monsieur Lundquist he had always intended to do sooner or later; but I do not think there was any doubt that Monsieur Örn was as heartily glad to see the Swede's back as Monsieur Lundquist to escape from Monsieur Örn.

Curiously enough, Widmerpool, although the sole author of the reconciliation, received little or no credit for his achievement. During the few days left to them after they had made things up, Monsieur Örn and Monsieur Lundquist used sometimes to walk up and down in the garden together, when Widmerpool would occasionally try to join them; but I noticed that they would always stroll away from him, or refuse to speak English, or French, which debarred him from conversation. It was hard to say whether or not he noticed this; his last week at La Grenadière being, in any case, blighted by another matter, in its way, sufficiently provoking for him. This was the appearance on the wall of the *cabinet de toilette* of a crude, though not unaccomplished, representation of himself—somewhat in the style of the prehistoric drawings of the caves in the Dordogue—in this case scratched on the plaster with a sharp instrument.

Two things about this composition seemed to me certain: first, that it was intended as a portrait of Widmerpool: secondly, that the artist was French. Beyond these external facts, that seemed to admit of no critical doubt, I was completely at sea as to where responsibility might lie; nor could I be sure of the moment when the design was completed. At the time when I first became aware of its existence, Widmerpool had been out of temper all the previous day; so that his eye had probably fallen on the picture some twenty-four hours or more before it came to my own notice. I could not help wondering whether he would mention the subject.

That evening he remarked: 'I really think something should be done about those two French boys.'

'What have they been up to now?'

'Haven't you noticed a drawing on one of the walls?'

'A sort of scrawl?' I asked, rather dishonestly.

'I don't know what it is meant to be,' said Widmerpool. 'And although it is not exactly indecent, it is suggestive, which is worse. I hardly like to mention it to Madame Leroy, though I certainly think it should be removed.'

'How would you remove it?'

'Well, paint over it, or something like that. It is Paul-Marie, I suppose.'

He said no more about the picture; but I knew that its existence embittered his remaining days at La Grenadière. I felt some curiosity myself as to the identity of the draughtsman, and was not at all sure that Widmerpool was right in recognising the work of Paul-Marie. If one of the boys was to be suspected, I should have put my money on Jean-Népomucène, who might easily have felt a sudden need to express himself in some graphic medium, in order to compete with the conversational gifts in which his elder brother excelled. However, there was no reason to suppose that he was good at drawing, and, especially on account of the facility displayed, the possibility that neither of the boys was responsible could not be disregarded.

I thought in turn of the other persons in the house. On the whole it was hardly likely to be attributable to Madame Leroy, or her husband. Berthe, it was true, had sometimes boasted of her sketches in water-colour: though this would have been an oblique and perverse manner of advertising her talent. I could not even bear to consider that the hand might have been Suzette's, dismissing all consideration of such a thing from my mind. Rosalie worked too hard all day to have had time to make the deep incisions in the wall: she was also short-sighted. Marthe was invariably in the kitchen, and she could hardly ever have had the opportunity to observe Widmerpool's appearance with sufficient thoroughness to have achieved so striking a likeness. It was doubtful whether Madame Dubuisson possessed the creative imagination: though there could be no question that the drawing must have appealed, especially, to her own brand of humour. Monsieur Dubuisson sometimes cleaned out his pipe with a sharp, stiletto-like instrument that could have been used as an etching-point.

There remained the contingency that Widmerpool might have derived some obscure gratification in the production of a self-portrait in such inappropriate circumstances: though here, as an objection, one came up against the essential Frenchness of the design. If Widmerpool himself had indeed been the artist, his display of annoyance had been a superb piece of acting: and it was not credible to me that anything so improbable was at the root of the mystery. Perplexity was increased a day or two later by the addition to the picture of certain extraneous details, in pencil, which, personally, I should have been prepared to swear belonged in spirit to a school of drawing other than that of the originator. However, these appendages may not have been attributable to any single individual. They were mannered, and less sure of touch. This business was never referred to in my presence by anyone except Widmerpool, and then only on that single occasion; though I had reason to suppose that Paul-Marie and Jean-Népomucène used to joke with each other privately on the subject.

When Widmerpool left for England, soon after this, the riddle remained unsolved. He was by then full of a project he had in mind for rearranging his legal books and papers; and, although he muttered that he hoped we might meet again, if I ever came to London, he was preoccupied, evidently thinking of more important matters. It was as if he had already dismissed from his mind the frivolities of Touraine, and peculiarities of the inhabitants of La Grenadière, even before he climbed into the *grognard's* taxi: which had not yet begun its habitual panting and heaving, as its owner was accustomed to coast downhill for the first part of the journey, with a view to saving petrol.

The space left at La Grenadière by the withdrawal of Monsieur Lundquist was filled by Dr. Szczepanowski, a quiet Pole, with gold pince-nez, who wore the rosette of the Légion d'Honneur in his button-hole. Monsieur Dubuisson used to take him for walks, during which, no doubt, he explained some of his theories, including the Moroccan hydraulic scheme. The morning after Widmerpool's departure, another visitor arrived, though for a few days only. This was the father of Paul-Marie and Jean-Népomucène, who was the double of the Frenchman with the Assyrian beard who had occupied my seat in the train on the journey from Paris. Perhaps it was even the man himself: if so, he made no reference to the incident. His presence had a sedative effect on his two sons. Monsieur Dubuisson did not approve of his handling of the French language; warning me not to imitate their father's construction of his sentences, especially in connexion with his use of the preterite. Madame Leroy, on the other hand, greatly admired her relative.

'Quel brave Papa,' she used to say, gazing at him, as he

used to set off down the hill in his straw hat and black gloves.

I never discovered precisely what relation each was to the other, but Madame Leroy's glance seemed to imply that life might have had more compensations if she had married some bearded, titanic figure of this kind, rather than Commandant Leroy. Familiarity with her had not dispelled my impression that she was a kind of sorceress. Life at La Grenadière was not altogether like life in the outer world. Its usage suggested a stage in some clandestine order's ritual of initiation. For a time the presence of Widmerpool had prolonged the illusion that he and I were still connected by belonging to the community of school: and that all that had happened since I had seen him last was that each of us was a year or two older. As the weeks passed at La Grenadière, the changes that had clearly taken place in Widmerpool since he had ceased to be a schoolboy emphasised the metamorphosis that had happened within myself. Now that he had moved on, his absence from La Grenadière made amputation from that earlier stage of life complete; and one day, when Suzette asked me something or other about the way lessons were taught in England, I was surprised to find forgotten the details of what had been for so long a daily routine.

It was, I suppose, an awareness of this change in circumstance that made me increasingly conscious, as the close of my stay in France approached, of the necessity to adopt an attitude towards life, in a general way, more enterprising. This aim owed something to remarks Widmerpool had addressed to me at one time or another; but it was directed particularly towards the project of taking some active step—exactly what step remained undecided—in solving the problem of Suzette: who had established herself as a dominating preoccupation, to which any recollection of

Jean Templer was now, on the whole, subordinate. In spite of prolonged thought devoted to this subject, I managed to devise no more resolute plan than a decision to make some sort of declaration to her when the day came to leave the house: a course of action which, although not remarkable for its daring, would at any rate mark some advance from a state of chronic inaction in such matters from which escape seemed so difficult. The question was: how best to arrange this approach?

Having seen other guests depart from La Grenadière, I knew that the entire household was accustomed to gather round, saying good-bye, and waiting to watch the taxi slide precipitously down the hill. If the question were to arise, for example, of kissing anyone good-bye, it was clear that there might be imminent risk of having to kiss—if such a hypothetical case as kissing were to be considered at all—the whole of the rest of the party gathered together at the door in the wall. Certainly, it might be safely assumed that nothing of the sort would be expected by anyone so anglicised as Monsieur Dubuisson: but I was not at all sure what French etiquette might prescribe in the case of guest and host: though suspecting that anything of the sort was, in general, limited to investitures. It was equally possible that any such comparatively intimate gesture might be regarded as far more compromising in France than in England; and, quite apart from any embarrassing, or unacceptable, situations that might be precipitated if kissing were to become general at my departure from La Grenadière, any hope of making a special impression on Suzette would undoubtedly be lost by collective recourse to this manner of saying good-bye: however pleasant in Suzette's individual case such a leave-taking might be. Some plan was, therefore, required if a hasty decision was to be avoided.

Accordingly, I finished packing early upon the day I was to return to England, and went downstairs to survey the house and garden. The hot weather had continued throughout my stay, and the sun was already beating down on the lawn, where no one except Dr. Szczepanowski was to be seen. I noticed that Suzette's big straw sun-bonnet was gone from the hall, where she was accustomed to leave it on the console table. Bum had once found it there, carrying the hat into the garden and gnawing away some of the brim. Dr. Szczepanowski was writing letters, and he smiled in a friendly manner. Jean-Népomucène at one of the tables appeared a moment later, and requested help in mending an electric torch, as Dr. Szczepanowski was skilled in such matters. Both of them retired to the house to find suitable implements to employ in making the repairs. There was just a chance that Suzette might be sitting in the summer-house, where she occasionally spent some of the morning reading.

I crossed the grass quickly, and went under the arch, preparing to withdraw if Monsieur Dubuisson should turn out to be settled there with his pipe. The excitement of seeing Suzette's straw bonnet was out of all proportion to the undecided nature of my project. She was sitting half-turned from the entrance, and, judging that, if I lost time in talk, I might be manœuvred into a position of formality which could impose insuperable restraint, I muttered that I had come to say good-bye, and took her hand, which, because her arm was stretched along the back of the seat, lay near me. As she turned, I immediately realised that the hand was, in fact, Madame Dubuisson's, who, as she left the house, must have taken up Suzette's straw hat to shield her eyes while she crossed the garden.

It was now too late to retreat. I had prepared a few sentences to express my feelings, and I was already half-way through one of them. Having made the mistake, there was nothing for it but to behave as if it were indeed Madame Dubuisson who had made my visit to La Grenadière seem so romantic. Taking her other hand, I quickly used up the remaining phrases that I had rehearsed so often for Suzette.

The only redeeming feature of the whole business was that Madame Dubuisson herself gave not the smallest sign of being in the least surprised. I cannot remember in what words she answered my halting assurance that her presence at La Grenadière would remain for me by far its sweetest memory; but I know that her reply was entirely adequate: indeed so well rounded that it seemed to have been made use of on a number of earlier occasions when she must have found herself in somewhat similar circumstances. She was small and round and, I decided, really not at all bad-looking. Her contribution to the situation I had induced was, at least from my own point of view, absolutely suitable. She may even have allowed me to kiss her on the cheek, though I could not swear to this. She asked me to send her a picture of Buckingham Palace when I returned to England.

This scene, although taking up only a few minutes, exhausted a good deal of nervous energy. I recognised that there could now be no question of repeating anything of the same sort with Suzette herself, even if opportunity were to present itself in the short time left to me. That particular card had been played, and the curious thing was that its effect had been to provide some genuine form of emotional release. It was almost as if Madame Dubuisson had, indeed, been the focus of my interest while I had been at La Grenadière. I began to feel quite warmly towards her, largely on the strength of the sentiments I had, as it were, automatically expressed. When the time came to say good-bye, hands were shaken all round. Suzette gave mine a little extra squeeze, after relaxing the first grip. I felt that this small attention was perhaps more than I deserved. The passage with Madame Dubuisson seemed at any rate a slight advance in the right direction when I thought things over in the train. It was nearly Christmas before I found the postcard of Buckingham Palace, which perhaps never reached her, as the Dubuissons must, by then, have moved on from La Grenadière.

4

PROLONGED, lugubrious stretches of Sunday afternoon in a university town could be mitigated by attending Sillery's tea-parties, to which anyone might drop in after half-past three. Action of some law of averages always regulated numbers at these gatherings to something between four and eight persons, mostly undergraduates, though an occasional don was not unknown. Towards the middle of my first term I was introduced to them by Short, who was at Sillery's college, a mild second-year man, with political interests. Short explained that Sillery's parties had for years played an established rôle in the life of the university; and that the staleness of the rock-buns, which formed a cardinal element of these at-homes, had become so hackneyed a subject for academical humour that even Sillery himself would sometimes refer to the perennially unpalatable essence of these fossils salvaged from some forgotten cake-world. At such moments Sillery would remind his guests of waggish or whimsical remarks passed on the topic of the rock-buns by an earlier generation of young men who had taken tea with him in bygone days: quoting in especial the galaxy of former undergraduate acquaintances who had risen to some eminence in later life, a class he held in unconcealed esteem.

Loitering about the college in aged sack-like clothes and Turkish slippers, his snow white hair worn longer than that of most of his colleagues, Sillery could lay claim to a venerable appearance: though his ragged, Old Bill moustache (which, he used laughingly to mention, had once been compared with Nietszche's) was still dark. He was, indeed, no more than entering into his middle fifties: merely happening to find convenient a façade of comparative senility. At the beginning of the century he had published a book called *City State and State of City* which had achieved some slight success at a time when works popularising political science and economic theory were beginning to sell; but he was not ambitious to make his mark as an author. In fact one or two of his pupils used to complain that they did not receive even adequate tuition to get them through the schools at anything but the lowest level. This was probably an unjust charge, because Sillery was not a man to put himself easily in the wrong. In any case, circumstances had equipped him with such dazzling opportunity for pursuing his preponderant activity of interfering in other people's business that only those who failed to grasp the extent of his potentiality in his own chosen sphere would expect—or desire—him to concentrate on a pedestrian round of tutorial duties.

Before my first visit, Short described some of this background with care; and he seemed to feel certain qualms of conscience regarding what he termed 'Sillers's *snobisme*'. He explained that it was natural enough that Sillery should enjoy emphasising the fact that he numbered among his friends and former pupils a great many successful people; and I fully accepted this plea. Short, however, was unwilling to encounter too ready agreement on this point, and he insisted that 'all the same' Sillery would have been 'a sounder man'—sounder, at any rate, politically—if he had made a greater effort to resist, or at least conceal, this temptation to admire worldly success overmuch. Short himself was devoted to politics, a subject in which I took little or no interest, and his keenest ambition was to become a Member of Parliament. Like a number of young men of that period, he was a Liberal, though to which of the various brands of Liberalism, then rent by schism, he belonged, I can no longer remember. It was this Liberal enthusiasm which had first linked him with Sillery, who had been on terms with Asquith, and who liked to keep an eye on a political party in which he had perhaps once himself placed hopes of advancement. Short also informed me that Sillery was a keen propagandist for the League of Nations, Czechoslovakia, and Mr. Gandhi, and that he had been somewhat diverted from earlier Gladstonian enthusiasms by the success of the Russian Revolution of 1917.

Short had taken me to Sillery's two or three times before I found myself—almost against my own inclination—dropping in there on Sunday afternoon. At first I was disposed to look on Sillery merely as a kind of glorified schoolmaster—a more easy going and amenable Le Bas—who took out the boys in turn to explore their individual characteristics to know better how to instruct them. This was a manner of regarding Sillery's entertaining so crude as to be positively misleading. He certainly wanted to find out what the boys were like: but not because he was a glorified schoolmaster. His understanding of human nature, coarse, though immensely serviceable, and his unusual ingenuity of mind were both employed ceaselessly in discovering undergraduate connexions which might be of use to him; so that from what he liked to call 'my backwater'—the untidy room, furnished, as he would remark, like a boarding-house parlour—he sometimes found himself able to exercise a respectable modicum of influence in a larger world. That, at least, was how things must have appeared to Sillery himself, and in such activities his spirit was concentrated.

Clay, for example, was the son of a consul in the Levant. Sillery arranged a little affair through Clay which caused inconvenience, minor but of a most irritating kind, to Brightman, a fellow don unsympathetic to him, at that time engaged in archæological digging on a site in the Near East. Lakin, outwardly a dull, even unattractive young man, was revealed as being related through his mother to an important Trade Union official. Sillery discovered this relative—a find that showed something like genius—and managed to pull unexpected, though probably not greatly important, strings when the General Strike came in 1926. Rajagopalaswami's uncle, noted for the violence of his anti-British sentiments, was in a position to control the appointment of a tutor to one of the Ruling Princes; Sillery's nominee got the place. Dwight Wideman's aunt was a powerful influence in the women's clubs in America: a successful campaign was inaugurated to ban the American edition of a novel by an author Sillery disliked. Flannigan-Fitzgerald's brother was a papal chamberlain: the Derwentwater annulment went through without a hitch. These, at least, were the things that people said; and the list of accessories could be prolonged with almost endless instances. All were swept into Sillery's net, and the undergraduate had to be obscure indeed to find no place there. Young peers and heirs to fortune were not, of course, unwelcome; though such specimens as these—for whose friendship competition was already keen—were usually brought into the circle through the offices of secondary agents rather than by the direct approach of Sillery himself, who was aware that in a society showing signs of transition it was essential to keep an eye on the changing focus of power. All the same, if he was known to incline, on the whole, to the Right socially, politically he veered increasingly to the Left.

In the course of time I found that much difference of opinion existed as to the practical outcome of Sillery's scheming, and I have merely presented the picture as first displayed to me through the eyes of Short. To Short, Sillery was a mysterious, politically-minded cardinal of the academical world, 'never taking his tea without an intrigue' (that was the phrase Short quoted); for ever plotting behind the arras. Others, of course, thought differently, some saying that the Sillery legend was based on a kind of kaleidoscope of muddled information, collected in Sillery's almost crazed brain, that his boasted powers had no basis whatever in reality: others again said that Sillery certainly knew a great number of people and passed round a lot of gossip, which in itself gave him some claim to consideration as a comparatively influential person, though only a subordinate one. Sillery had his enemies, naturally, always anxious to denigrate his life's work, and assert that he was nothing more than a figure of fun; and there was probably something to be said at least for the contention that Sillery himself somewhat exaggerated the effectiveness of his own activities. In short, Sillery's standing remained largely a matter of opinion; though there could be no doubt about his turning out to be an important factor in shaping Stringham's career at the university.

Stringham had been due to come into residence the same term as myself, but he was thrown from a horse a day or two before his intended return to England, and consequently laid up for several months. As a result of this accident, he did not appear at his college until the summer, when he took against the place at once. He could scarcely be persuaded to visit other undergraduates, except one or two that he had known at school, and he used to spend hours together sitting in his room, reading detective stories, and complaining that he was bored. He had been given a small car by his mother and we would sometimes drive round the country together, looking at churches or visiting pubs.

On the whole he had enjoyed Kenya. When I told him about Peter Templer and Gwen McReith—an anecdote that seemed to me of outstanding significance—he said: 'Oh, well, that sort of thing is not as difficult as all that,' and he proceeded to describe a somewhat similar incident, in which, after a party, he had spent the night with the divorced wife of a coffee planter in Nairobi. In spite of Madame Dubuisson, this story made me feel very inexperienced. I described Suzette to him, but did not mention Jean Templer.

'There is absolutely nothing in it,' Stringham said. 'It is just a question of keeping one's head.'

He was more interested in what I had to report about Widmerpool, laughing a lot over Widmerpool's horror on hearing the whole truth of Le Bas's arrest. The narrative of the Scandinavians' quarrel struck him only on account of the oddness of the tennis-court on which we had been playing the set. This surprised me, because the incident had seemed of the kind to appeal to him. He had, however, changed a little in the year or more that had passed since I had seen him; and, although the artificial categories of school life were now removed, I felt for the first time that the few months between us made him appreciably older than myself. There was also the question of money—perhaps suggested by Widmerpool's talk on that subject—that mysterious entity, of which one had heard so much and so often without grasping more than that its ownership was desirable and its lack inconvenient: heard of, certainly, without appreciating that its possession can become as much part of someone as the nose on the face. Even Uncle Giles's untiring contortions before the altar of the Trust, when considered in this light, now began to appear less grotesque than formerly; and I realised at last, with great clearness, that a sum like one hundred and eighty pounds a year might indeed be worth the pains of prolonged and acrimonious negotiation. Stringham was, in fact, not substantially richer than most undergraduates of his sort, and, being decidedly free with his money, was usually hard-up, but from the foothills of his background was, now and then, wafted the disturbing, aromatic perfume of gold, the scent which, even at this early stage in our lives, could sometimes be observed to act intoxicatingly on chance acquaintances; whose unexpected perseverance, and determination not to take offence, were a reminder that Stringham's mother was what Widmerpool had described as 'immensely wealthy'.

Peter Templer, as I have said, rarely wrote letters, so that we had, to some extent, lost touch with him. Left to himself there could be little doubt that he would, in Stringham's phrase, 'relapse into primeval barbarism'. Stringham often spoke of him, and used to talk, almost with regret, of the adventures they had shared at school: already, as it were, beginning to live in the past. Some inward metamorphosis was no doubt the cause of Stringham's melancholia, because his attacks of gloom, although qualified by fairly frequent outbursts of high spirits, could almost be given that name. There was never a moment when he became reconciled to the life going on round him. 'The buildings are nice,' he used to say. 'But not the undergraduates.'

'What do you expect undergraduates to be like?'

'Keep bull-pups and drink brandies-and-soda. They won't do as they are.'

'Your sort sound even worse.'

'Anyway, what can one do here? I am seriously thinking of running away and joining the Foreign Legion or the

North-West Mounted Police—whichever work the shorter hours.'

'It is the climate.'

'One feels awful if one drinks, and worse if one's sober. I knew Buster's picture of the jolly old varsity was not to be trusted. After all he never tried it himself.'

'How is he?'

'Doing his best to persuade my mother to let Glimber to an Armenian,' said Stringham, and speaking with perhaps slightly more seriousness: 'You know, Tuffy was very much against my coming up.'

'What on earth did it have to do with her?'

'She takes a friendly interest in me,' said Stringham, laughing. 'She behaved rather well when I was in Kenya as a matter of fact. Used to send me books, and odds and ends of gossip, and all that sort of thing. One appreciates that in the wide open spaces. She is not a bad old girl. Many worse.'

He was always a trifle on the defensive about Miss Weedon. I had begun to understand that his life at home was subject to exterior forces like Buster's disapproval, or Miss Weedon's regard, which brought elements of uncertainty and discord into his family life, not only accepted by him, but almost enjoyed. He went on: 'There has been talk of my staying here only a couple of years and going into the Foot Guards. You know there is some sort of arrangement now for entering the army through the university. That was really my mother's idea.'

'What does Miss Weedon think?'

'She favours coming to London and having a good time. I am rather with her there. The Household Cavalry has been suggested, too. One is said—for some reason—to "have a good time in The Tins".'

'And Buster's view?'

'He would like me to remain here as long as possible—four years, post-graduate course, research fellowship, anything so long as I stay away—since I shattered his dream that I might settle in Kenya.'

It was after one of these conversations in which he had complained of the uneventfulness of his day that I suggested that we should drop in on Sillery.

'What is Sillery?'

I repeated some of Short's description of Sillery, adding a few comments of my own.

'Oh, yes,' said Stringham. 'I remember about him now. Well, I suppose one can try everything once.'

We were, as it happened, first to arrive at that particular party. Sillery, who had just finished writing a pile of letters, the top one of which, I could not avoid seeing, was addressed to a Cabinet Minister, was evidently delighted to have an opportunity to work over Stringham, whom he recognised immediately on hearing the name.

'How is your mother?' he said. 'Do you know, I have not seen her since the private view of the Royal Academy in 1914. No, I believe we met later at a party given by Mrs. Hwfa Williams, if my memory serves me.'

He continued with a stream of questions, and for once Stringham, who had shown little interest in coming to the party, seemed quite taken aback by Sillery's apparent familiarity with his circumstances.

'And your father?' said Sillery, grinning, as if in spite of himself, under his huge moustache.

'Pretty well.'

'You were staying with him in Kenya?'

'For a few months.'

'The climate suits him all right?'

'I think so.'

'That height above sea-level is hard on the blood-pressure,'

Sillery said; 'but your father is unexpectedly strong in spite of his light build. Does that shrapnel wound of his ever give trouble?'

'He feels it in thundery weather.'

'He must take care of it,' said Sillery. 'Or he will find himself on his back for a time, as he did after that spill on the Cresta. Has he run across Dicky Umfraville yet?'

'They see a good deal of each other.'

'Well, well,' said Sillery. 'He must take care about that, too. But I must attend to my other guests, and not talk all the time about old friends.'

I had the impression that Sillery regarded Stringham's father as a falling market, so far as business was concerned; and, although he did not mention Buster, he was evidently far more interested in Mrs. Foxe's household than that of her former husband. However, the room was now filling up, and Sillery began introducing some of the new arrivals to each other and to Stringham and myself. There was a sad Finn called—as nearly as I could catch—Vaalkiipaa: Honthorst, an American Rhodes Scholar, of millionaire stock on both sides of his family: one of Sillery's pupils, a small nervous young man who never spoke, addressed as 'Paul', whose surname I did not discover: and Mark Members, of some standing among the freshmen of my year, on account of a poem published in *Public School Verse* and favourably noticed by Edmund Gosse. Up to that afternoon I had only seen Members hurrying about the streets, shaking from his round, somewhat pasty face a brownish, uneven fringe that grew low on his forehead and made him look rather like a rag doll, or marionette: an air augmented by brown eyes like beads, and a sprinkling of freckles. His tie, a broad, loose knot, left the collar of his shirt a little open. I admired this lack of self-consciousness regarding what I then—rather priggishly—looked on as eccentricity of dress. He appeared to have known Sillery all his life, calling him 'Sillers', a form of address which, in spite of several tea-parties attended, I had not yet summoned courage to employ. The American, Honthorst's, hair was almost as uncontrolled as that of Members. It stood up on the top of his head like the comb, or crest, of a hoopoe, or cassowary; this bird-like appearance being increased by a long, bare neck, ending in a white collar cut drastically low. Honthorst had a good-natured, dazed countenance, and it was hard to know what to say to him. Vaalkiipaa was older than the rest of the undergraduates present. He had a round, sallow face with high cheekbones, and, although anxious to be agreeable, he could not understand why he was not allowed to talk about his work, a subject always vetoed by Sillery.

Conversation was now mostly between Sillery and Members; with the awkward long silences which always characterised the teas. During one of these pauses, Sillery, pottering about the room with the plate of rock-buns, remarked: 'There is a freshman named Quiggin who said he would take a dish of tea with me this afternoon. He comes from a modest home, and is, I think, a little sensitive about it, so I hope you will all be specially understanding with him. He is at one of the smaller colleges—I cannot for the moment remember which—and he has collected unto himself sundry scholarships and exhibitions, which is—I think you will all agree—much to his credit.'

This was a fairly typical thumb-nail sketch of the kind commonly dispensed by Sillery, in anticipation of an introduction: true as far as it went, though giving little or no clue to the real Quiggin: even less to the reason why he had been asked to tea. Indeed, at that period, I did not even grasp that there was always a reason for Sillery's invitations, though the cause might be merely to give opportunity for preliminary investigation: sometimes not worth a follow-up.

No one, of course, made any comment after this speech about Quiggin, because there was really no suitable comment to make. The mention of scholarships once more started off Vaalkiipaa on the subject of his difficulties in obtaining useful instruction from attendance at lectures; while Honthorst, almost equally anxious to discuss educational matters in a serious manner, joined in on the question of gaps in the college library and—as he alleged—out-of-date methods of indexing. Honthorst persisted in addressing Sillery as 'sir', in spite of repeated requests from his host that he should discard this solecism. Sillery was deftly circumventing combined Finnish-American attack, by steering the conversation toward New England gossip by way of hunting in Maine—while at the same time extracting from Vaalkiipaa apparently unpalatable facts about the anti-Swedish movement in Finland—when Quiggin himself arrived: making his presence known by flinging open the door suddenly to its fullest extent, so that it banged against one of the bookcases, knocking over a photograph in a silver frame of three young men in top-hats standing in a row, arm-in-arm.

'Come in,' said Sillery, picking up the picture, and setting it back in its place. 'Come in, Quiggin. Don't be shy. We shan't eat you. This is Liberty Hall. Let me introduce you to some of my young friends. Here is Mr. Cheston Honthorst, who has travelled all the way from America to be a member of my college: and this is Mr. Jenkins, reading history like yourself: and Mr. Stringham, who has been to East Africa, though his home is that beautiful house, Glimber: and Mr. Vaalkiipaa—rather a difficult name, which we shall soon find that we have all got so used to that we shan't be able to understand how we ever found it difficult—and Paul, here, you probably know from Brightman's lectures, which he tells me he loyally attends just as you do; and I nearly forgot Mr. Mark Members, whose name will be familiar to you if you like modern verse—and I am sure you do—so make a place on the sofa, Mark, and Quiggin can sit next to you.'

At first sight, Quiggin seemed to be everything suggested by Sillery's description. He looked older than the rest of us: older, even, than Vaalkiipaa. Squat, and already going bald, his high forehead gave him the profile of a professor in a comic paper. His neck was encircled with a starched and grubby collar, his trousers kept up by a belt which he constantly adjusted. For the first time since coming up I felt that I was at last getting into touch with the submerged element of the university, which, I had sometimes suspected, might have more to offer than was to be found in conventional undergraduate circles. Mark Members was evidently impressed by a similar—though in his case unsympathetic—sense of something unusual so far as Quiggin was concerned; because he drew away his legs, hitherto stretched the length of the sofa, and brought his knees right up to his chin, clasping his hands round them in the position shown in a picture (that used to hang in the nursery of a furnished house we had once inhabited at Colchester) called The Boyhood of Raleigh; while he regarded Quiggin with misgiving.

'Couldn't find the way up here for a long time,' said Quiggin.

He sat down on the sofa, and, speaking in a small, hard voice with a North Country inflexion, addressed himself to Members: seeming to be neither embarrassed by the company, nor by Sillery's sledge-hammer phrases, aimed, supposedly, at putting him at his ease. He went on: 'It's difficult when you're new to a place. I've been suffering a bit here'—indicating his left ear which was stuffed with yellowish cotton-wool—'so that I may not catch all you say too clearly.'

Members offered the ghost of a smile; but there could be no doubt of his uneasiness, as he tried to catch Sillery's eye. However, Sillery, determined that his eye was not to be caught by Members, said: 'The first year is a great period of discovery—and of self-discovery, too. What do you say, Vaalkiipaa? Can you find your way about yet?"

'I make progress,' said Vaalkiipaa, unsmiling: to whom it was perhaps not clear whether Sillery's question referred to discovery in the topographical sense or the more intimate interior examination with which Sillery had linked it. There was a silence, at the end of which Members put in, rather at random: 'Sillers, it is too clever of you to buy a suit the same colour as your loose covers.'

Quiggin sat sourly on the extreme edge of the sofa, glancing round the room like a fierce little animal, trapped by naturalists. He had accepted a rock-bun from Sillery, and for some minutes this occupied most of his attention. Honthorst said: 'They tell me the prospects for the college boat are pretty good, Professor Sillery.'

'Good,' said Sillery, making a deprecatory gesture in our direction to suggest his own unworthiness of this style of address. 'Good. Very good.'

He said this with emphasis, though without in any way committing his opinion on the subject of current aquatics. It was evident that at present Quiggin was the guest who chiefly interested him. Stringham he must have regarded as already in his power because, although he smiled towards him in a friendly manner from time to time, he made no further effort to talk to him individually. Quiggin finished his rock-bun, closely watched by Sillery, picked some crumbs from his trousers, and from the carpet round him:

afterwards throwing these carefully into the grate. Just as Quiggin had dealt with the last crumb, Members rose suddenly from the sofa and cast himself, with a startling bump, almost full length on the floor in front of the fireplace: exchanging in this manner his Boyhood-of-Raleigh posture for that of the Dying Gladiator. Sillery, whose back was turned, started violently, and Members pleaded: 'You don't mind, Sillers? I always lie on the floor.'

'I like my guests to feel at home, Mark,' said Sillery, recovering himself immediately, and playfully pinching the nape of Members's neck between his finger and thumb, so that Members hunched his shoulders and squeaked shrilly. 'And you, Quiggin, are you happy?' Sillery asked.

Quiggin shook his head at the rock-buns, held out towards him once more; and, apparently taking the question to have a more general application than as a mere enquiry as to whether or not he wanted another cup of tea, or was comfortable sitting, as he was, at the springless end of the sofa, said in reply: 'No, I'm not.'

Sillery was enchanted with this answer.

'Not happy?' he said, as if he could not believe his ears.

'Never seem to get enough peace to get any work done,' said Quiggin. 'Always somebody or other butting in.'

Sillery beamed, proffering the plate once more round the room, though without success. Quiggin, as if something had been released within him, now began to enlarge on the matter of his own exasperation. He said: 'All anyone here seems interested in is in messing about with some game or other, or joining some society or club, or sitting up all night drinking too much. I thought people came to the university to study, not to booze and gas all the time.'

'Very good, Quiggin, very good,' said Sillery. 'You find we all fall woefully short of your own exacting standards—formed, no doubt, in a more austere tradition.'

He smiled and rubbed his hands, entranced. It even seemed that he might have been waiting for some such outburst on Quiggin's part: and Quiggin himself somehow gave the air of having made the same speech on other occasions.

'What an extraordinary person,' said Members, under his breath, a remark probably audible only to myself, owing to the fact that the extreme lowness of the armchair in which I was sitting brought my ear almost level with Members's mouth, as he rested with his elbow on the floor. Sillery said: 'What do you think, Mark? Do you find that we are too frivolous?'

Members began to say: 'My dear Sillers——' but, before he could speak the phrase, Sillery cut him short by adding: 'I thought you might be in agreement with Quiggin as your homes are so close, Mark.'

After he had said this, Sillery stood back a bit, as if to watch the effect of his words, still holding the plate of rock-buns in his hand. If he had hoped to strike dismay into the hearts of his listeners, he could hardly have expected a more successful result so far as Quiggin and Members were concerned. Members, thoroughly put out, went pink in the face; Quiggin's expression became distinctly sourer than before, though he did not change colour. 'I had a suspicion that neither of you was aware of this,' said Sillery. 'But you must live *practically* in the same street.'

He nodded his head several times, and changed the subject; or, at least, varied it by asking if I had ever read *Jude the Obscure*. I realised, without achieving any true comprehension of what Sillery was about, that the object of revealing publicly that Members and Quiggin lived close to each other during the vacation was intended in some manner to bring both to heel: in any case I did not know enough of either at the time to appreciate that each might prefer that any details regarding his home life should be doled out by himself alone.

Sillery abandoned the subject after this demonstration of strength on his part, so that the rest of his guests were left in ignorance even of the name of the town Members and Quiggin inhabited. The American and the Finn slipped away soon after this, on the plea that they must work; in spite of protests from Sillery that no one could, or should, work on Sunday evening. As they were leaving, another visitor could be heard coming up the stairs. He must have stood aside for them to pass him, because a moment later, speaking in a resonant, musical voice, like an actor's or practised after-dinner speaker's, he said, as he came through the door: 'Hullo, Sillers, I hoped I might catch you at home.'

This new arrival I recognised as Bill Truscott, who had gone down two or three years before. I had never previously met him, but I had seen him and knew his name well, because he was one of those persons who, from their earliest years, are marked down to do great things; and who so often remain a legend at school, or university, for a period of time after leaving the one or the other: sometimes long after any hope remains, among the world at large, that promise of earlier years will be fulfilled. Sillery was known to be deeply attached to Bill Truscott, though to what extent he inwardly accepted the claims put forward for Truscott's brilliant future, it was not easy to say. Outwardly, of course, he was a strong promoter of these claims; and, in some respects, Truscott could be described as the most characteristic specimen available of what Sillery liked his friends to be; that is to say he was not only successful and ambitious, but was also quite well off for a bachelor (a state he showed no sign of relinquishing), as his father, a Harley Street specialist, recently deceased, had left him a respectable capital. He had gained a good degree, though only by the skin of his teeth, it was rumoured, and, since academical honours represented a good deal of his stock-in-trade, this close shave regarding his 'first' was sometimes spoken of as an ominous sign. However, the chief question seemed still to be how best his brilliance should be employed. To say that he could not make up his mind whether to become in due course Prime Minister, or a great poet, might sound exaggerated (though Short had so described Truscott's dilemma), but in general he was at any rate sufficiently highly regarded in the university, by those who had heard of him, to make him appear a fascinating, and almost alarming, figure.

After sitting down beside Sillery, Truscott at first hardly spoke at all; but at the same time his amused smile acted as a sort of charm on the rest of the company, so that no one could possibly have accused him, on the grounds of this silence, of behaving in an ungracious manner. He was tall and dark, with regular features, caught rather too close together, and the most complete self-assurance that can be imagined. His clothes and hair, even his face, seemed to give out a kind of glossiness, and sense of prosperity, rather like Monsieur Lundquist's. He was already going a little grey, and this added to his air of distinction, preventing him from looking too young and inexperienced. I addressed a remark to him which he acknowledged simply by closing and opening his eyes, making me feel that, the next time I spoke, I ought to make an attempt to find something a trifle less banal to say: though his smile at the same time absolved me from the slightest blame in falling so patently short of his accustomed standards. I was not conscious of being at all offended by this demeanour: on the contrary, Truscott's comportment seemed a kind of spur to encourage all who came to win his esteem; although

—and perhaps because—he was obviously prepared to offer nothing in return.

If Bill Truscott's arrival in the room made a fairly notable impression on myself, chiefly on account of the glowing picture Short had drawn of his charm and brilliance, the rest of Sillery's party treated Truscott, if possible, with even closer attention. Members moved unobtrusively from the floor to a chair, and Quiggin, one of the legs of whose trousers had rucked up, revealing long hirsute pants of grey material, pulled the end of his trouser down towards a black sock, and sat more upright on the sofa. Both he and Members evidently felt that the opportunity had now arrived for Sillery's disclosure regarding the adjacency of their respective homes to be forgotten in discussion of more important matters. Stringham turned out to know Truscott already. He said: 'Hullo, Bill,' and for a minute or two they spoke of some party in London where they had met a month or two before.

'You must tell us about the polite world, Bill," said Sillery, perching on the side of Truscott's chair and slipping an arm round his shoulder. 'Fancy the hostesses allowing you to steal away from their clutches and drop in to visit us here.'

Sillery made this remark gently, through his teeth, so that it was not easy to say whether he intended a compliment, an enquiry, or even an expression of disparagement of the fact that Truscott could spare time for dons and undergraduates at this stage of the Season; when a career had still to be carved out. Truscott certainly accepted the words as tribute to his popularity, and he threw his head back with a hearty laugh to express how great a relief it was for him to escape, even for a short period, from the world of hostesses thus somewhat terrifyingly pictured by Sillery: though he was, at the same time, no doubt aware that a more detailed explanation was required of him to show conclusively that his appearance in the university was due to nothing so ominous as lacking something better to do.

'I have really come on business, Sillers,' he said.

'Indeed?'

'I saw no reason why I should not combine business with pleasure, Eillers. As you know, Pleasure before Business has always been my motto.'

'Pleasure can be so exhausting,' put in Members, fixing Truscott with a winning smile, and thrusting his face forward a little.

However, he seemed a little uncertain, apart from his smile, how best to captivate someone of Truscott's eminence; though clearly determined to make an impression before the opportunity was past. Truscott, for his part, glanced attentively at Members: an appraisal that seemed to result in the decision that, although outwardly Members had not much to offer that was to Truscott's taste, there might be elements not to be despised intellectually. Sillery watched their impact with evident interest. He said: 'I expect you read *Iron Aspidistra,* Bill.'

Truscott nodded; but without producing any keen sense of conviction.

'Mark's poem,' said Sillery. 'It received quite a favourable reception.'

'Surrounded as usual by a brilliant circle of young men, Sillers,' said Truscott, laughing loudly again. 'To tell you the truth, Sillers, I have come up to look for a young man myself.'

Sillery chuckled, pricking up his ears. Truscott stretched out his legs languidly. There was a pause, and muted laughter from the rest of the guests. Truscott looked round, archly.

'For my boss as a matter of fact,' he said.

He laughed quietly to himself this time, as if that were a good joke. Quiggin, who had been silent all the while, though not unattentive, spoke unexpectedly in his grating voice: 'Who is "your boss"?' he asked.

I could not help admiring the cool way in which Truscott turned slowly towards Quiggin, and said, without the slightest suggestion of protest at Quiggin's tone: 'He is called Sir Magnus Donners.'

'The M.P.?'

'I fear that, at the moment, he cannot be so described.'

'But you work for him?' insisted Quiggin.

'Sir Magnus is kind enough to remunerate me as if I worked for him,' said Truscott. 'But you know, really, I scarcely like to describe myself as doing anything that suggests such violent exertions undertaken on his behalf. He is, in any case, the kindest of masters.'

He cocked an eyebrow at Quiggin, apparently not at all displeased by this rather aggressive inquisition. As Truscott had not witnessed Quiggin's arrival and earlier behaviour at the tea-party, I decided that he must find him less odd than he appeared to the rest of us: the thought that perhaps he classed all undergraduate opinion together, as inchoate substance, not to be handled too closely, occurring to me only several years later, after I had come down from the university. Sillery said: 'I don't expect "your master", as you call him, would have much difficulty in returning to the House at any by-election, would he, Bill?"

'His industrial interests take up so much time these days,' said Truscott. 'And really one must admit that ability of his sort is rather wasted in the House of Commons.'

'Isn't he going to get a peerage?' said Stringham, unexpectedly.

Truscott smiled.

'Always a possibility,' he said; and Sillery grinned widely, rubbing his hands together, and nodding quickly several times.

'It's a mortal shame that a big concern like his should be in the hands of a private individual,' said Quiggin, increasing the volume of his North Country accent, and speaking as if he were delivering the opening words of a sermon or address.

'Do you think so?' said Truscott. 'Some people do. Of course, Sir Magnus himself has very progressive ideas, you know.'

'I think you would be surprised, Quiggin, if you ever met Sir Magnus,' said Sillery. 'He has even surprised me at times.'

Quiggin looked as if there was nothing he would like better than to have an opportunity to meet Sir Magnus; but Sillery, who probably feared that conversation might decline from the handling of practical matters, like the disposal of jobs, to one of those nebulous discussions of economic right and wrong, of which he approved in general but obviously considered inopportune at that moment, brought back the subject of Truscott's opening statement by saying: 'And so Sir Magnus wants a man, does he?'

However, Truscott was not disposed to say more of that for the time being. He may even have thought that he had already given away too much. His manner became perceptibly less frivolous, and he said: 'I'll tell you about it later, Sillers.'

Sillery concurred. It was probable that he, too, would prefer the details to be given in private. However, he evidently regarded the acquisition of further information on this matter to be of prime importance; because a minute or two later his impatience got the better of him, and, rising from the arm of Truscott's chair, he announced: 'Bill and I are a pair of very old friends who haven't seen each other for many a long day, so that now I am going to drive you all out into the wind and rain in order that Bill and I can have a chat about matters that would no doubt appear to you all as very tedious.'

He put his head a little on one side. Neither Members nor Quiggin seemed very satisfied by this pronouncement: not at all convinced that they would find any such conversation tedious. Members tried to make some sort of protest by saying: 'Now, Sillers, that is really too bad of you, because you promised that you were going to show me your Gerard Manley Hopkins letter the next time I came to see you.'

'And I wanted to borrow *Fabian Essays,* if it wasn't troubling you,' said Quiggin, very sulky.

'Another time, Mark, another time,' said Sillery. 'And you will find your book in that shelf, Quiggin, with the other Webbs. Take great care of it, because it's a first edition with an inscription.'

Sillery was not at all discomposed, indeed he seemed rather flattered, by these efforts on the part of Members and Quiggin to stay and make themselves better known to Truscott; but he was none the less determined that they should not stand between him and the particulars of why Sir Magnus Donners wanted a young man; and what sort of a young man Sir Magnus Donners wanted. He made a sweeping movement with his hands, as if driving chickens before him in a farmyard, at the same time remarking to Stringham: 'You must come here again soon. There are things I should like to discuss interesting to ourselves.'

He turned quickly, to prevent Quiggin from taking too many of his books, and, at the same time, to say something to the depressed undergraduate called Paul. Stringham and I went down the stairs, followed by Mark Members, who, having failed to prolong his visit, seemed now chiefly interested in escaping from Sillery's without having the company of Quiggin thrust upon him. All three of us left the college through an arched doorway that led to the street. Rain had been falling while we were at tea, but the pavements were now drying under a woolly sky.

'What very Monet weather it has been lately,' said Members, almost to himself. 'I think I must hurry ahead now as I am meeting a friend.'

He disappeared into a side street, his yellow tie caught up over his shoulder, his hands in his pockets and elbows pressed to his sides. In a moment he was lost to sight.

'That must be a lie,' said Stringham. 'He couldn't possibly have a friend.'

'What was Truscott after?'

'He is rather a hanger-on of my mother's,' said Stringham. 'Said to be very bright. He certainly gets about.'

'And Sir Magnus Donners?'

'He was in the Government during the war.'

'What else?'

'He is always trying to get in with my mother, too.'

I had the impression that Stringham was himself quite interested in Bill Truscott, who certainly suggested the existence of an exciting world from which one was at present excluded. We strolled on through the empty streets towards Stringham's college. The air was damp and warm. At the top of the stairs, the sound of voices came from the sitting-room. Stringham paused at the door.

'Somebody has got in,' he said. 'I hope it is not the Boys' Club man again.'

He stood for a moment and listened; then he opened the door. There was a general impression of very light grey flannel suits and striped ties, which resolved itself into three figures, sitting smoking, one of whom was Peter Templer.

'Peter.'

'Bob Duport and Jimmy Brent,' said Peter, nodding towards the other two. 'We thought we would pay a call, to see how your education was getting along.'

He was looking well: perhaps a shade fatter in the face than when I had last seen him; and, having now reached the age for which Nature had, as it were, intended him, he was beginning to lose the look of a schoolboy dressed as a grown man. I should have known Duport and Brent anywhere as acquaintances of Peter's. They had that indefinable air of being up to no good that always characterised Peter himself. Both were a few years older than he; and I vaguely remembered some story of Duport having been involved in a motor accident, notorious for some reason or other. That affair, whatever it was, had taken place soon after he had left school: during my own first year there. He was built on similar lines to Peter, thin and tall, with sandy hair, dressed in the same uncompromising manner, though on the whole less successfully. Brent was big and fat, with spectacles that seemed to have been made with abnormally small circles of glass. Both, it turned out, were business friends, working in the City. They accepted some of Stringham's sherry, and Brent, whose manners seemed on the whole better than Duport's, said: 'What do they rush you for this poison?'

The sum was not revealed, because, almost at the same moment, Duport, who was examining The Pharisee's rider, in one of the pictures that had followed Stringham to this room, remarked: 'I've never seen a jock on land, or sea, sit a horse like that.'

'Put your shirt on him when you do, Bob,' said Peter. 'You may recoup a bit on some of those brilliant speculations of yours that are always going to beat the book.'

'How long are you staying?' asked Stringham, before Duport had time to defend his racing luck.

'Going back to London after dinner.'

I saw that any change that I might have suspected of taking place in the relationship between Templer and Stringham had by now crystallised. It was not that they no longer liked one another, or even that they had ceased to take pleasure in each other's company, so much as the fact that each had grown out of the other's habit of mind: and, in consequence, manner of talking. Stringham had become quieter than he had been at school; though he was, at the same time, more than ever anxious for something new to happen at comparatively short intervals, in order that his attention should be occupied, and depression kept at arm's length. Peter had changed less: merely confirming his earlier attitude towards life. I did not know to what extent, if at all, he was aware of any difference in Stringham. He knew Stringham well, and I could imagine him describing —and laughing over—the warming-up process that seemed to be required that evening: a warming-up that never took place so far as Stringham was concerned. I could, equally, imagine Stringham laughing at the way in which Peter was already shaping along the lines that Stringham had himself so accurately foretold.

'We might all have dinner together,' Stringham said.

'That was the idea.'

In the restaurant, Stringham and I talked to Peter, rather fragmentarily: mainly on the subject of Stringham's stay in Kenya. Duport and Brent grunted to each other from time to time, or, occasionally, to Peter: no sense of fusion quickening the party. Peter told us about his car, recently bought second-hand, and considered a bargain.

'I must take you for a proper run in her,' he said, 'before we go back.'

'Don't forget I want to look in at the Cabaret Club before we hit the hay,' said Brent.

Duport said: 'He's got a girl there who owes him some money.'

'I wish she did,' said Brent: but without elucidating further that cryptic aspiration.

The Vauxhall was, in fact, clearly the foundation of this unpremeditated visit. Peter wanted to try the vehicle out. He continued to assure us how cheap the price had been, inviting admiration of its many good points. This car was adapted for speed, having had the windscreen removed; but it had all the appearance of having passed through a good many hands since the days of its first owner. It certainly put Stringham's two-seater in the shade, and perhaps slightly irritated Stringham on this account. Peter was immensely pleased with the Vauxhall, the purchase of which seemed in some way to have involved Brent. As the evening wore on, Brent's personality became in other respects more determinable. For example, he talked incessantly of women. Peter and Duport treated this preoccupation as something not to be taken at all seriously, making no attempt to hide their concurrent opinion that Brent's attempts to make himself agreeable to girls were entirely unsuccessful: all of which Brent took in fairly good part. His voice managed to be at once deep and squeaky; and he spoke repeatedly of a woman called Flora, who appeared in some manner to have behaved badly to him. On the whole he was undoubtedly preferable to Duport, whose demeanour was aggressive and contradictious. I was not surprised when Duport announced: 'Couldn't stand my place at all. Got sent down my first term. Still it looks worse here.'

I enquired about Jean.

'She's all right,' Peter said. 'In love with a married man twice her age.'

'Is that the sister I'm after?' asked Duport.

'That's the one.'

Towards the end of the meal, things improved a little; though Stringham and I seemed now to know Templer on an entirely different footing from that of the past. Finally, I felt even glad that Duport and Brent had increased the numbers of the party, because their presence alleviated, if it did not conceal, the change that had taken place. Peter was still anxious that we should see how fast the car would travel on a piece of open road, and he promised to deliver us back by midnight; so, after dinner was finished, we agreed to go with him. Stringham and I climbed into the back of the Vauxhall with Duport, not through choice, but because there was more room for everyone if Brent occupied the seat beside the driver. We moved off sharply in the direction of unfrequented roads. I lay back, wishing the seat had been roomy enough to allow sleep. Duport smoked sullenly: Stringham, on the other side of me, was silent: Brent had returned to the subject of Flora, though without receiving much outward sympathy from Peter. We had reached the outskirts of the town, and the car was gathering speed, when—without clearly taking in the meaning of the words —I heard Brent say: 'Let's pick up those two pieces.'

I was scarcely aware that Peter had slowed down, when we stopped with a jerk by the kerb, where, beside a pillar-box at the corner of a side road, two girls were standing. They were wearing flowered dresses, blue and pink respectively, with hats of the same material. Their faces were those of a couple of Dutch dolls. Brent, from the front seat, twisted himself round towards them.

'Would you like to come for half an hour's drive?' he asked, in his unattractive voice, high and oily.

The girls raised no difficulty whatever about falling in with this suggestion. There was not even any giggling to speak of. They jumped in immediately, one of them sitting in front, on Brent's knee; the other joining the three of us at the back, where there was already little enough room to spare. They answered to the names of Pauline and Ena. Ena sat sideways, mainly on Duport, but with her legs stretched across my own knees: her feet, in tight high-heeled shoes, on Stringham's lap. This was a situation similar to many I had heard described, though never previously experienced. In spite of its comparative discomfort, I could not help feeling interest—and some slight excitement—to see how matters would develop. Stringham was obviously not very pleased by the additional company, which left him without the doubtful advantage of any substantial share in either of the girls; but he made the best of things, even attempting some show of pinching Ena's ankles. Neither of the girls had much conversation. However, they began to squeal a little when the car arrived on a more open piece of road, and the engine gathered speed.

'You must admit it was a good buy,' shouted Peter, as we did about seventy-five or eighty.

'All the same we might be returning soon,' said Stringham. 'My physician is insistent that I should not stay up late after my riding accident—especially with anyone, or part of anyone, on my knee.'

'We ought to be getting back, too,' said Duport, freeing himself, apparently dissatisfied, from Ena's long embrace. 'Otherwise it will be tomorrow before we get to London.'

'All right,' said Peter, 'we will turn at the next cross-roads.'

It was on the homeward journey, after making this turn, that the mishap occurred. Peter was not driving specially fast, but the road, which was slippery from rain fallen earlier in the evening, took two hairpin bends; and, as we reached the second of these, some kind of upheaval took place within the car. No one afterwards could explain exactly what happened, though the accepted supposition was that Brent, engaged in kissing Pauline, had disturbed her susceptibilities in some manner, so that she had drawn herself unexpectedly away from him; and, in his effort to maintain their equilibrium, Brent had thrust her against Peter's elbow, in such a way that her head obscured the view. That, at least, was one of the main theories afterwards propounded. Whatever the root of the trouble, the memorable consequence was that Peter—in order to avoid a large elm tree—drove into the ditch: where the car stopped abruptly, making a really horrible sound like a dying monster; remaining stuck at an angle of forty-five degrees to the road.

This was an unpleasant surprise for everyone. The girls could not have made more noise if they had been having their throats cut. Brent, too, swore loudly, in his almost falsetto voice, natural, or assumed to meet the conditions of the moment; though, as it happened, he and Pauline, perhaps owing to their extreme proximity to each other, were the only two members of the party who, when we had at last all succeeded in making our way out of the Vauxhall, turned out to be quite unhurt. Stringham was kicked in the face by Ena, who also managed to give Duport a black-eye by concussion between the back of her head and his forehead. Peter bruised his knuckles against the handle of the door. Ena complained of a broken arm from the violence with which Duport had seized her as the car went over the edge. My own injuries were no worse than a sharp blow on the nose from Ena's knee. However, we were all shaken up more than a little; and, as one of the wheels had buckled, the car clearly could not be driven back that night. There had been some difficulty in getting out of the ditch, and, as I stepped up on to the road, I felt the first drop of rain. Now it began to pour.

This was an exceedingly inconvenient occurrence from

everyone's point of view. Probably Stringham and I were in the most awkward position, as there seemed no prospect of either of us reaching college by the required hour; and it would not be easy to convince the authorities that nothing of which they might disapprove had taken place to make us late: or even to keep us out all night, if things should turn out so badly. The girls were, presumably, accustomed to late hours if they were in the habit of accepting lifts at that time of night; but for them, too, this was an uncomfortable situation. Such recrimination that took place was about equally divided between Peter's two friends and Ena and Pauline: although I knew that, in fact, Stringham was far the angriest person present. Rain now began to fall in sheets. We moved in a body towards the elm tree.

'Of all the bloody silly things to do,' said Brent. 'You might have killed the lot of us.'

'I might easily,' said Peter, who was always well equipped for dealing with friends of Brent's kind. 'I wonder I didn't with a lout like you in the boat. Haven't you ever had a girl sitting on your knee before, that you have to heave her right across the car, just because there is a slight bump in the road?'

'What did you want to get a lot of girls in the car for, anyway?' asked Duport, who was holding a rolled-up handkerchief to his eye. 'If you weren't capable of steering?'

'I didn't ask for them.'

'You ought to have some driving lessons.'

Peter replied with a reference to the time when Duport was alleged to have collided with a lamp-post at Henley; and they both went on like this for some minutes. Pauline and Ena, the former of whom was crying, also made a good deal of noise, while they lamented the difficulty of getting home, certainly an insoluble problem as matters stood.

'How far out are we?' Stringham asked, 'and what is the time?'

The hour was a quarter-past eleven; the general view, that we had come about a dozen miles. There was a chance that a car might pass, but we were a large party to be accommodated. In any case, there was no sign of a car. Stringham said: 'We had better make plans for camping out. Brent, you look good at manual labour—will you set to work and construct a palisade?'

'You didn't ought to have brought us here,' said Pauline.

Ena, still complaining of a torn stocking, and bruises on her arm, cried into her handbag. Peter and Duport moved round the car, pulling and pushing its outer surface, or opening the bonnet to inspect the engine. Brent sat panting to himself on the bank.

Peter said: 'The rain seems to be stopping. We may as well walk in the right direction. There is no point in staying here.'

There was not much enthusiasm for this suggestion; and, when attempted, the heel came off one of Ena's shoes, in any case not adapted to a twelve-mile march.

'Can't we change the wheel?' said Duport.

We struggled with the problem of the wheel from different angles of approach. It was impossible to wind the jack into position under the axle. We only managed to embed the car more firmly than ever in the side of the ditch. While we were engaged in these labours, rain began to fall again, a steady, soaking downpour. Once more we retired to the tree, and waited for the shower to clear.

'What a bloody silly thing to do,' said Duport.

'Almost as brilliant as the time you fell into the orchestra on Boat-Race Night.'

Stringham said: 'For my part, I am now in a perfect condition to be received into one of those oriental religions whose only tenet is complete submission to Fate.'

He joined Brent on the bank, and sat with his head in his hands. A minute or two after this, the miracle happened. There was a grinding noise farther up the road, and the glare of powerful headlights appeared. It was a bus. Brent, with surprising agility for so fat a man, jumped up from where he was sitting, and ran out into the centre of the road, holding his arms wide apart as if in supplication. He was followed by Duport, apparently shaking his fist. I felt little interest in possible danger of their being run over: only a great relief that the bus must in any case come to a standstill, whether they were killed or not.

Stringham said: 'What did I foretell? Kismet. It is the Wheel.'

The bus stopped some yards short of Brent. We all clambered up the steps. Inside, the seats were almost empty, and no one seemed to realise from what untold trouble we had all been rescued. The girls now recovered quickly, and were even anxious to make an assignation for another night. They were, however, both set down (with no more than a promise from Brent that he would look them up if again in that neighbourhood) at a point not far from the pillar-box from which they had embarked on that uniucky drive. We reached the centre of the town: Templer, Brent, and Duport still quarrelling among themselves about which hotel they should patronise, and arguing as to whether or not it was worth ringing up a garage that night to arrange for the repair of the Vauxhall. This discussion was still in progress when we left the bus. Stringham and I said good-night to them.

'I'm sorry to have landed you in all this,' Peter said.

'You must come for a drive with us sometime,' said Stringham. 'Anyway, we'll meet soon.'

But I knew that they would not meet soon; and that this was a final parting. Peter, I think, knew this too. A crescent moon came from behind clouds. The others disappeared from sight. Stringham said: 'What a jolly evening, and what nice friends Peter makes.' The clocks were striking midnight at different places all over the town as I stepped through the door of my college. The rain had cleared. Moonlight gave the grass and towers an air of unreality, as if all would be removed in the morning to make way for another scene. My coat hung on me, shapeless and soggy, the damp working down through the cloth to my shoulders.

This incident with Templer's car had two results, so far as Stringham was concerned: it brought an end to his friendship with Peter, and it immensely strengthened his desire to go down as soon as possible from the university. In fact, he was now unwilling even to consider the possibility of staying in residence long enough to take a degree. It was one of those partings of the ways that happen throughout life: in this case, foretold by Peter himself. No doubt Peter, too, had guessed that something had ended, and that his prophecy had come true, while the rain dripped down on all of us, through the branches of that big elm, while we stood in the shadows of the ditch regarding the stranded Vauxhall.

When I say that their friendship came to an end, I do not mean that Stringham no longer spoke of Templer; nor that, when he talked of him, it was with dislike: nor even, in a sense, with disapproval. On the contrary, he used to refer to Peter as frequently as he had done in the past; and the story of the drive, the crash, Ena and Pauline, Brent and Duport, was embroidered by him until it became a kind of epic of discomfort and embarrassment: at the same time, something immensely funny in the light of Peter's chosen manner of life. Nevertheless, there could be no doubt whatever that metamorphosis had taken place; and, sometimes, it was almost as if Stringham were speaking of a friend who had died, or gone beyond the sea to a place from which he would never return. Once he said: 'How appalling Peter will be in fifteen years' time'; and he never spoke, as formerly he had done, of arranging a meeting between the three of us in London.

I was even aware that, in an infinitely lesser degree, I could not avoid being unfavourably included by Stringham in this reorientation; which, almost necessarily, affected anyone who was at once a friend of Peter's and a fellow undergraduate, fated to remain up for at least three years: both characteristics reminding Stringham of sides of life from which he was determined to cut away. Besides, for my own part I shared none of this sense of having seen the last of Peter; though even I had to admit that I did not care for the idea of spending much of my time with his present acquaintances, if Brent and Duport were typical representatives of his London circle. The extent to which Stringham had resolved to settle his own career was brought home to me one morning, through the unexpected agency of Quiggin, next to whom I found myself sitting, when attending one of Brightman's lectures, at which I had not been appearing so regularly as perhaps I should.

On this occasion Quiggin walked back with me towards my college, though without relaxing the harsh exterior he had displayed when we had first met at Sillery's. He seemed chiefly concerned to find out more about Mark Members.

'Where does his stuff appear?' he asked.

'What stuff?'

'His poems have been published, haven't they?'

'The one I read was in *Public School Verse.*'

'Why *"Public"?'* said Quiggin. 'Why *"Public" School Verse?* Why not just *"School Verse"?'*

I was unable to answer that one; and suggested that such a title must for some reason have appealed to the editors, or publisher, of the volume.

'It is not as if they were "public" schools,' said Quiggin. 'They could not be less "public".'

I had heard this objection voiced before, and could only reply that such schools had to have a name of some sort. Quiggin stopped, stuck his hands into his pockets (he was still wearing his black suit) and poked his head forward. He looked thin and unhealthy: undernourished, perhaps.

'Have you got a copy?' he asked.

'Yes.'

'Can I borrow it?'

'All right.'

'Now?'

'If you like to come with me.'

We undertook the rest of the journey to my rooms in silence. Arrived there, Quiggin glanced round at the furnishings, as if he did not rate very highly the value of the objects provided by the college to sit, or lie, upon. They were, indeed, shabby enough. Standing by the bookcase, he took out the copy of *Public School Verse,* which he had lighted upon immediately, and began to run rapidly through the rest of the books.

'Do you know Members well?' he asked.

'I've met him once, since we were at Sillery's.'

This encounter with Members had been at a luncheon party given by Short, where Members had much annoyed and mortified his host by eating nearly all the strawberries before the meal began. In addition, he had not spoken at all during luncheon, leaving before coffee was served, on the grounds that he had to play the gramophone to himself for half an hour every afternoon; and that, unless he withdrew at once, he would not have time for his music owing to a later engagement. Short, for a mild man, had been quite cross.

'I understand that Members is a coming poet,' said Quiggin.

I agreed that *Iron Aspidistra* showed considerable promise. Quiggin gloomily turned the pages of the collection. He said: 'I'd be glad to meet Members again.'

It was on the tip of my tongue to answer that he was almost certain to do this, sooner or later, if their homes were so close; but, as Quiggin evidently meant there and then, rather than in the vacation, I thought it wiser to leave the remark unmade. I promised to let him know if a suitable occasion should arise, such as Members visiting my rooms, though that seemed improbable after his behaviour at Short's luncheon party.

'Can I take *The Green Hat* too?' asked Quiggin.

'Don't lose it.'

'It is all about fashionable life, isn't it?'

'Well, yes.'

I had myself not yet fully digested the subject matter of *The Green Hat,* a novel that I felt painted, on the whole, a sympathetic picture of what London had to offer: though much of the life it described was still obscure to me. I was surprised at Quiggin asking for it. He went on: 'In that case I do not expect that I shall like it. I hate anything superficial. But I will take the book and look at it, and tell you what I think of the writing.'

'Do.'

'I suppose that it depicts the kind of world that your friend Stringham will enter when he joins Donners-Brebner,' said Quiggin, as he continued to inspect the bookshelf.

'How do you mean?'

'Well you must have heard that he has taken the job that Truscott was talking about at Sillery's. Surely he has told you that?'

'What, with Sir Magnus Donners?'

It was no use pretending that I knew something of this already. I was, indeed, so surprised that only after Quiggin had gone did I begin to feel annoyance.

'I should have thought he would have told you,' said Quiggin.

'Where did you hear this?'

'At Sillery's, of course. Sillery says Stringham is just the man.'

'He probably is.'

'Of course,' said Quiggin, 'I knew at once there would be no chance of Truscott thinking of *me*. Not good enough, by any manner of means, I suppose.'

'Would you have liked the job?'

I did not know what else to say: the idea of Quiggin being the sort of man Truscott was looking for seeming to me so grotesque.

Quiggin did not bother to reply to this question. He merely repeated, with a sniff: 'Not good enough by a long chalk,' adding: 'You might come and see me some time in my college, if you can find the way to it. You won't get any priceless port, or anything like that.'

I said that I was not particularly fond of port; and began to give an account of my likes and dislikes in the matter of wine, which Quiggin, with what I now see as excusable impatience, cut short by saying: 'I live very quietly. I can't afford to do otherwise.'

'Neither can I.'

Quiggin did not answer. He gave me a look of great contempt; as I supposed, for venturing, even by implication, to draw a parallel between a lack of affluence that might, literally, affect my purchase of rare vintages, and a figure of speech intended delicately to convey his own dire want for the bare necessities of life. He remained silent for several seconds, as if trying to make up his mind whether he could ever bring himself to speak to me again; and then said gruffly: 'I've got to go now.'

As he went off, all hunched up on one side with *Public School Verse* and *The Green Hat* under his arm, I felt rather ashamed of myself for having made such a thoughtless remark. However, I soon forgot about this, at the time, in recalling the news I had learnt about Stringham, which I wanted to verify as soon as possible. In general, however, I continued to feel an interest in Quiggin, and the way he lived. He had something of the angry solitude of spirit that held my attention in Widmerpool.

Stringham, when I next saw him, seemed surprised at the importance with which I invested his decision.

'I thought I'd told you,' he said. 'As a matter of fact it isn't finally fixed yet. What awful cheek of your friend Quiggin, if I may say so.'

'What do you think of him?'

'The man is a closed book to me,' Stringham said. 'And one that I confess I have little temptation to open. Bill Truscott, on the other hand, was rather impressed.'

'With Quiggin?'

'Curiously enough.'

'Will you work with Truscott?'

'I shall be the other personal secretary.'

'Did Sillery put up the suggestion?'

'He is very keen on it. He agrees one's family will have to be consulted.'

'Will your family raise difficulties?'

'For once,' said Stringham, 'I don't think they will. My

mother will at last see hopes of getting me settled in life. Buster—most mistakenly—will suppose this to be the first step on the stair to a seat on the Donners-Brebner Board. My father will be filled with frank astonishment that I should be proving myself capable of earning a living in any capacity whatsoever.'

'What about a degree?'

'Bill Truscott reports Sir Magnus as demanding who the hell wants a degree these days; and saying all he needs is men who know the world, and can act and think quickly.'

'Strong stuff.'

'I suppose I can take lessons from Bill.'

'Then you won't come up next term?'

'Not if I can avoid it.'

Sillery's part in this matter was certainly of interest. He might have been expected—as Stringham himself agreed—to encourage as many undergraduates as possible to remain, for as long as possible, within his immediate range. Later on, however, I began to understand something of his reasons for recommending this course. If Stringham remained at the university, it was probable that he would fall under influences other than—and alien to—Sillery's. Even if he remained Sillery's man, he was obviously a person who might easily get involved in some scrape for which Sillery (if too insistent on taking Stringham under his wing) might be held in some degree answerable. Placed in a key position in Donners-Brebner—largely due to Sillery's own recommendation—Stringham could not only supply news of that large concern, but could also keep an eye on Sillery's other man, Truscott. In due course Sillery would no doubt find himself in a position to renew acquaintance in most satisfactory conditions. In short, power without responsibility could hardly be offered to Sillery, within this limited sphere, upon cheaper terms. Such a series of crude images would scarcely have suggested themselves in quite this manner to Sillery's mind—still less did I see them myself in any such clarity—but the apparent paradox of why Sillery threw in his weight on the side of Stringham's going-down became in due course comparatively plain to me.

'Anyway,' said Stringham, 'you'll be in London yourself soon.'

'I suppose so.'

'Then we'll have some fun.'

Somehow, I felt doubts about this. Life no longer seemed to present quite the same uncomplicated façade as at a time when dodging Le Bas and shirking football had been cardinal requirements to make the day tolerable. Although I might not feel, with Stringham, that Peter Templer was gone for good, Peter certainly seemed now to inhabit a world that offered limited attractions. The sphere towards which Stringham seemed to be heading, little as I knew of it, was scarcely more tempting to me. Perhaps Widmerpool had been right in advocating a more serious attitude of mind towards the problem of the future. I thought over some of the remarks he had made on this subject while we had both been staying at La Grenadière.

As it turned out, Mrs. Foxe did not show the complacence Stringham had expected in agreeing, at once, that he should cease to be a member of the university. On the contrary, she wrote to say that she thought him too young to spend all his time in London; even going so far as to add that she had no desire for him to turn into 'something like Bill Truscott': of whom she had always been supposed to approve. However, this was an obstacle not entirely unforeseen; in spite of Stringham's earlier hope that his mother might decide on the spur of the moment that a job was the best possible thing for him.

'Of course that's Buster,' he said, when he spoke of the letter.

I was not sure that he was right. The tone of his mother's remarks did not at all suggest arguments put forward at second-hand. They sounded much more like her own opinions. Stringham reasserted his case. The end of it was that she decided to come and talk things over.

'Really rather good of her,' said Stringham. 'You can imagine how busy she must be at this time of year.'

'Do you think you will persuade her?'

'I'm going to rope in Sillery.'

'Take her to see him?'

'Have him to lunch. Will you come and play for my side?'

'I can't play for your side, if I don't want you to go down.'

'Well, just keep the ring then.'

This was about the stage when I began to become dimly conscious of what Short was trying to convey when he spoke of Sillery's influence, and his intrigues; although, as far as it went, a parent's discussion of her son's future with a don still seemed natural enough. Sillery, I thought, was like Tiresias: for, although predominantly male, for example, in outward appearance, he seemed to have the seer's power of assuming female character if required. With Truscott, for instance, he would behave like an affectionate aunt; while his perennial quarrel with Brightman—to take another instance of his activities—was often conducted with a mixture of bluntness and self-control that certainly could not be thought at all like a woman's row with a man: or even with another woman; though, at the same time, it was a dispute that admittedly transcended somehow a difference of opinion between two men. Certainly Sillery had no dislike for the company of women in the way of ordinary social life, provided they made no personal demands on him. I was anxious to see how he would deal with Mrs. Foxe.

Meanwhile, I continued occasionally to see something of Quiggin, although I came no nearer to deciding which of the various views held about him were true. He was like Widmerpool, as I have said, in his complete absorption in his own activities, and also in his ambition. Unlike Widmerpool, he made no parade of his aspirations, on the contrary, keeping as secret as possible his appetite for getting on in life, so that even when I became aware of the purposeful way in which he set about obtaining what he wanted, I could never be sure where precisely his desires lay. He used to complain of the standard of tutoring, or how few useful lectures were available, and at times he liked to discuss his work in great detail. In fact I thought, at first, that he worked far harder than most of the men I knew. Later I came to doubt this, finding that Quiggin's work was something to be discussed rather than tackled, and that what he really enjoyed was drinking cups of coffee at odd times of day. He had another characteristic with which I became in due course familiar: he was keen on meeting people he considered important, and surprisingly successful in impressing persons—as he seemed to have impressed Truscott—who might have been reasonably expected to take amiss his manner and appearance.

The subject of Quiggin came up at one those luncheons that Short, who had a comfortable allowance, gave periodically. Mark Members, in spite of his behaviour on the earlier occasion, was again of the party (because Short regarded him as intellectually 'sound'); though Brightman was the guest of honour this time. Two undergraduates, called respectively Smethwyck and Humble, were there, and perhaps others. Short was inclined to become sentimental after he had eaten and drunk a fairly large amount in the middle of the day, and he had remarked: 'Quiggin must find it hard to make two ends meet up here. He told me his father used to work on the railway line outside some Midland town.'

'Not a word of truth,' said Brightman, who was the only don present. 'Quiggin is in my college. I went into the whole question of his financial position when he came up. He has certainly no less money than the average—probably more with his scholarships.'

'What *does* his father do then, Harold?' asked Short, who was quite used to being contradicted by Brightman; and, indeed, by almost everyone else in the university.

'Deceased.'

'But what did he do?'

'A builder—keen on municipal politics. So keen, he nearly landed in jail. He got off on appeal.'

Brightman could not help smiling to himself at the ease with which he could dispose of Short.

'But he may have worked on the railway line all the same.'

'The only work Quiggin the Elder ever did on the railway line,' said Brightman, becoming more assertive at encountering argument, 'was probably to travel without a ticket.'

'But that doesn't prove that his son has got any money,' said Humble, who did not care for Brightman.

'He was left a competence,' Brightman said. 'Quiggin lives with his mother, who is a town councillor. Isn't that true, Mark?'

A more vindictive man than Short might have been suspected of having raised the subject of Quiggin primarily to punish Members for his former attack on the strawberries; but Short was far too good-natured ever to have thought of such a revenge. Besides, he would never have considered baiting anyone whom he admired on intellectual grounds.

Brightman, on the other hand, had no such scruples, and he went on to say: 'Come on, Mark. Let's hear your account of Quiggin. You are neighbours, according to Sillers.'

Members must have seen that there was no way of avoiding the subject. Shaking his hair out of his eyes, he said: 'There is a disused railway-siding that was turned into allotments. He probably worked there. It adjoins one of the residential suburbs.'

There was a general laugh at this answer, which was certainly a neat way of settling the questions of both Quiggin and Brightman himself, so far as Members was concerned. Smethwyck began to talk of a play he had seen in London, and conversation took a new course. However, the feelings of self-reproach that contact with Quiggin, or discussions about him, commonly aroused in me were not entirely set at rest by this description of his circumstances. Brightman's information was notoriously unreliable: and Members's words had clearly been actuated by personal dislike. The work on the railway line might certainly have been of a comparatively recreational nature: that had to be admitted in the light of Mark Members's knowledge of the locality; but, even were this delineation of the background true, that would not prevent Quiggin from finding in his life some element chronically painful to him. Even though he might exaggerate to himself, and to others, his lack of means in relation to the financial circumstances of his contemporaries, this in itself pointed to a need for other—and deeply felt—discontents. It was possible that, in the eyes of Quiggin, money represented some element in which he knew himself deficient: rather in the same way that Widmerpool, when he wanted to criticise Stringham, said that he had too much money: no doubt in truth envying the possession of assets that were, in fact, not material ones. It was some similar course of speculation that seemed to give shape to Quiggin's character and outward behaviour.

Short's luncheon took place the day before I was to meet Mrs. Foxe again, and I thought over the question of Quiggin on my way to Stringham's rooms.

'This may be rather a ghastly meal,' Stringham said, while we waited for his mother, and Sillery, to arrive.

Sillery appeared first. He had cleaned himself up a little for the occasion, trimmed his moustache at the corners, and exchanged his usual blue bow for a black silk tie with white spots. Stringham offered him sherry, which was refused. Like many persons more interested in power than sensual enjoyment, Sillery touched no strong drink. Prowling about the room for a minute or two, he glanced at the invitations on the mantelpiece: a London dance or two, and some undergraduate parties. He found nothing there that appeared to interest him, because he turned, and, stepping between Stringham and myself, took each of us by an arm, resting his weight slightly.

'I hear you have been seeing something of Brother Quiggin,' he said to me.

'We met at one of Brightman's lectures, Sillers.'

'You both go to Brightman's lectures, do you?' said Sillery. 'I hope they are being decently attended.'

'Moderate.'

'Mostly women, I fear.'

'A sprinkling of men.'

'I heard they were getting quite painfully empty. It's a pity, because Brightman is such an able fellow. He won golden opinions as a young man,' said Sillery. 'But tell me, how do you find Brother Quiggin?'

I hardly knew what to say. However, Sillery seemed to require no answer. He said: 'Brother Quiggin is an able young man, too. We must not forget that.'

Stringham did not seem much in the mood for Sillery.

He moved away towards the window. A gramophone was playing in the rooms above. Outside, the weather was hot and rather stuffy.

'I hope my mother is not going to be really desperately late,' he said.

We waited. Sillery began to describe a walking tour he had once taken in Sicily with two friends, one of whom had risen to be Postmaster-General: the other, dead in his twenties, having shown promise of even higher things. He was in the middle of an anecdote about an amusing experience they had had with a German professor in a church at Syracuse, when there was a step on the stairs outside. Stringham went to the door, and out on to the landing. I heard him say: 'Why, hullo, Tuffy. Only you?'

Miss Weedon's reply was not audible within the room. She came in a moment later, looking much the same as when I had seen her in London. Stringham followed. 'My mother is awfully sorry, Sillers, but she could not get away at the last moment,' he said. 'Miss Weedon very sweetly motored all the way here, in order that we should not have a vacant place at the table.'

Sillery did not take this news at all well. There could be no doubt that he was deeply disappointed at Mrs. Foxe's defection; and that he did not feel Miss Weedon to be, in any way, an adequate substitute for Stringham's mother. We settled down to a meal that showed no outward prospect of being particularly enjoyable. Stringham himself did not appear in the least surprised at this miscarriage of plans. He was evidently pleased to see Miss Weedon, who, of the two of them, seemed the more worried that a discussion regarding Stringham's future would have to be postponed. Sillery decided that the first step was to establish his own position in Miss Weedon's eyes before, as he no doubt intended, exploring her own possibilities for exploitation.

'Salmon,' he remarked. 'Always makes me think of Mr. Gladstone.'

'Have some, all the same,' said Stringham. 'I hope it's fresh.'

'Did you arrange all this lunch yourself?' asked Miss Weedon, before Sillery could proceed further with his story. 'How wonderful of you. You know your mother was really distressed that she couldn't come.'

'The boys were at choir-practice when I passed this way,' said Sillery, determined that he should enter the conversation on his own terms. 'They were trying over that bit from *The Messiah*'—he hummed distantly, and beat time with his fork—'you know, those children's voices made me mighty sad.'

'Charles used to have a nice voice, didn't you?' said Miss Weedon: plainly more as a tribute to Stringham's completeness of personality, rather than because the matter could be thought to be of any great musical interest.

'I really might have earned my living that way, if it hadn't broken,' said Stringham. 'I should especially have enjoyed singing in the street. Perhaps I shall come to it yet.'

'There's been a terrible to-do about the way you earn your living,' said Miss Weedon. 'Buster doesn't at all like the idea of your living in London.'

Sillery showed interest in this remark, in spite of his evident dissatisfaction at the manner in which Miss Weedon treated him. He seemed unable to decide upon her precise status in the household: which was, indeed, one not easy to assess. It was equally hard to guess what she knew, or thought, of Sillery; whether she appreciated the extent of his experience in such situations as that which had arisen in regard to Stringham. Sitting opposite him, she seemed to have become firmer and more masculine; while Sillery himself, more than ever, took the shape of a wizard or shaman, equipped to resist either man or woman from a bisexual vantage.

This ineffective situation might have continued throughout Miss Weedon's visit, if Moffet—about whom a word should be said—had not handed Stringham a telegram, when he brought the next course. Moffet, a tall, gloomy man, on account of his general demeanour, which was certainly oppressive enough, had in some degree contributed to Stringham's dislike for university life. Stringham used to call Moffet 'the murderer', not on account of anything outwardly disreputable in his appearance, which might have been that of some ecclesiastical dignitary, but because of what Stringham named 'the cold cruelty of Moffet's eye'. If Moffet decided, for one reason or another, that an undergraduate on his staircase was worth cultivating, there was something sacerdotal about the precision with which he never left him free from attentions; as if the victim must be converted, come what may, to Moffet's doctrines. Moffet had at first sight made up his mind that Stringham was one to be brought under his sway.

One of Moffet's tenets was in connexion with the manner in which Stringham arranged several ivory elephants along the top of his mantelpiece. Stringham liked the elephants to follow each other in column: Moffet preferred them to face the room in line. I had been present, on one occasion, when Moffet, having just finished 'doing the room', had disappeared from it. Stringham walked over to the fireplace, where the elephants stood with their trunks in line, and turned them sideways. As he completed this rearrangement, Moffet came in once more through the door. Stringham had the last elephant in his hand. Moffet stared across at him forbiddingly.

'I am afraid I do not arrange ornaments very well, sir,' said Moffet.

'Just a whim of mine regarding elephants.'

'I will try to remember, sir,' said Moffet. 'They take a powerful lot of dusting.'

He retired again, adding: 'Thank you, sir,' as he closed the door. The incident disturbed Stringham. 'Now I shall have to go down,' he said.

However, Moffet was in an excellent mood at having an opportunity to wait on Sillery, of whom, for some reason, he approved more than of most dons. He brought in the telegram with a flourish. The message was from Stringham's mother: she would be arriving, after all: Buster was driving her down. At this, Sillery cheered up at once; and Miss Weedon, too, saw hope that negotiations might now take place. Stringham himself seemed as indifferent as before.

'If Buster is coming,' he said, 'he will certainly queer the pitch.'

'I am looking forward to meeting Buster,' said Sillery, smiling straight across the table to Miss Weedon. 'I think I shall persuade him to our point of view.'

He put the tips of his fingers together. Miss Weedon looked a little surprised at this whole-hearted way in which Sillery offered himself as an ally. She had perhaps assumed that, as a don, he would inevitably attempt to prevent Stringham from going down. She said: 'Commander Foxe's great regret is that he never went to the university.'

I did not know whether this remark was intended to excuse Buster, or to suggest to Sillery a line of attack.

'No doubt he acquired a very useful education in a different sphere,' said Sillery. 'I have made enquiries, and find that we have many friends in common. Bill Truscott, for example.'

Miss Weedon did not feel equally enthusiastic about Bill Truscott. I wondered if they had crossed swords.

'Mr. Truscott has been in the house a lot lately,' she said, guardedly.

'Bill knows the situation perfectly,' said Sillery. 'It would be a great advantage to work in harness with him.'

All Miss Weedon was prepared to admit was the statement that 'Mr. Truscott is always very kind'. However, Sillery's changed mood much improved the atmosphere; luncheon continuing with less sense of strain.

Mrs. Foxe and Buster arrived just as Moffet was clearing the table. They brought with them a hamper; caviare, grapes, a bottle of champagne. The effect of their entrance was immediate. Sillery and Miss Weedon at once abjured a great proportion of the hermaphroditic humours assumed by each of them for the purpose of more convenient association with the other: Miss Weedon relapsing into her normal rôle of attendance on Mrs. Foxe: Sillery steering himself more decidedly towards the part of eccentric professor, and away from the comparatively straightforward manner in which he had been discussing Stringham's affairs. This was the first time I had seen Mrs. Foxe and Buster together. They made an unusual couple. This was not due to the fact that she was a few years the elder of the two, which was scarcely noticeable, because Buster, though he had lost some of his look of anxiety, was distinctly fatter, and less juvenile in appearance, than he had seemed in London a year or more before. He was still dressed with care, and appeared in a more amenable temper than at our earlier meeting.

'We brought some grub down,' he said to Stringham, putting the hamper on a chair; and, turning to me, he remarked: 'I think one can always use caviare, don't you?'

It was clear that he accepted the fact that in the presence of his wife he was a subordinate figure, wherever he might rank away from her. Mrs. Foxe's ownership of

Buster seemed complete when they were in a room together. From time to time she would glance at him as if to make sure that he were behaving himself; but her look was one of absolute assurance that a word from her would be sufficient to quell even the smallest outbreak of conduct of a kind which she might disapprove. I found out, much later, that the circumstances of their marriage had been, so far as they went, respectable enough; and that nothing could have been farther from the truth than Widmerpool's suggestion that her divorce had been a particularly scandalous one. At that time, however, I had not heard any of the story; and I was still curious to know where she and Buster had met, and what romantic climax had been the cause of their going off together.

Sillery now showed great activity. He moved quickly forward to Mrs. Foxe, for a moment or two engaging her in conversation that took up the threads of their acquaintanceship of years before. Then he made for Buster, on whom he evidently intended to concentrate his forces, manœuvring him to the far end of the room; and, after a short while, taking his arm. Moffet had come in to ask if more coffee was required. He was in his element in this somewhat confused scene. Mrs. Foxe and Buster, not yet having lunched, some sort of a picnic was now organised among the remnants of the meal just consumed.

Sillery must have made his point, whatever it was, with Buster almost immediately, because soon he led him back to the food, assuring us that it was extraordinary that, during his war work with the Y.M.C.A., they had never met, though how this meeting could possibly have happened he did not explain. Whatever they had found in common was satisfactory to Buster, too, since he laughed and talked with Sillery as if he had known him for years. I have sometimes wondered whether Sillery made some specific offer on that occasion: a useful business introduction, for example, might have been dangled before Buster, then, as I knew from Stringham, contemplating retirement from the Navy. On the whole it is probable that nothing more concrete took place than that the two of them were aware, as soon as they set eyes on one another, of mutual sympathy: Sillery confining himself to flattery, and perhaps allowing Buster to hear the names of some of the more impressive specimens in his collection. Whatever the reason, Stringham's fate was settled in these first few minutes, because it was then that Buster must have decided to withdraw opposition. How serious this opposition was likely to be, if Sillery had not stepped in, is another question hard to answer. Buster might be in comparative subjection to his wife, but he was not necessarily without influence with her on that account. On the contrary, his subjection was no doubt a source of power to him in such matters. It was not surprising that he was against Stringham going down; his change of heart was much less to be expected. However, by the time Mrs. Foxe decided to leave, after scarcely any discussion over the caviare, champagne and grapes (the last of which Sillery consented to share), it was agreed that Stringham should go down at the end of the term. When he said good-bye, Sillery assured Mrs. Foxe that he was always at her service: when he took Buster's hand he put his own left hand over their combined grip, as if to seal it: to Miss Weedon he was polite and friendly, though less demonstrative. Moffet was waiting on the stairs. Something in the dignity of his bow must have moved Buster, because a coin changed hands.

Although a letter from Uncle Giles was by no means unknown, he did not write often; and only when he wanted something done for him: requiring details of an address he had lost, for example, or transmitting an account of some project in which he was commercially interested at that moment and wished recommended to all persons his relations might come across. He possessed a neat, stiff, old-fashioned handwriting, not at all suggestive of vagaries of character. There was usually a card from him at Christmas, undecorated, and very small in size: sent out in plenty of time. When, towards the end of the Michaelmas term, an envelope arrived addressed in his angular hand, I supposed at first that he had now taken to dispatching these Christmas greetings more than a month in advance. 'I am staying in London for some weeks,' he wrote, 'and I should like to see you one evening. After all, I have only three nephews. I dine every night at the Trouville Restaurant. Just drop in. It is very simple, of course, but you get good value for your money. We must take care of the pennies, these days. Any night will do.' Sunny Farebrother, I remembered, had made the same remark about the pennies. The fact that I might not be in a position to 'drop in' to a restaurant in London 'any night' did not appear to have struck my uncle, never very good at grasping principles that might govern other people's lives and movements. His letter was written from Harrods, so that there was no means of sending an answer; and I made up my mind that, even if I were to visit London—as I was doing, so it happened, the following day, to dine with Stringham—I should not spend the evening at the Trouville Restaurant. Uncle Giles did not state the reason for his wish to meet me, which may have sprung from completely disinterested affection for a member of his family not seen for some time. I suspected, perhaps unjustly, that such was not the motive; and, since at that age behaviour of older people seems, more often than not, entirely meaningless, I dismissed Uncle Giles's letter from my mind, as I now think, rather inexcusably. I had not seen Stringham since the summer, and had heard very little from him on the subject of his job. For one reason or another arrangements to meet had fallen through, and I felt, instinctively, that he was passing into an orbit where we should from now on see less of each other. I was thinking about this subject that afternoon, feeling disinclined for work, watching the towers of the neighbouring college, with the leaden sky beyond, when there was a knock on the door.

'Come in.'

It was Le Bas.

'I've been lunching with your Dean,' he said. 'He mentioned your name. I thought I would look you up.'

For some reason I felt enormously surprised to see him standing there. He had passed so utterly from daily life. This surprise was certainly not due to Le Bas having altered in appearance. On the contrary, he looked the same in all respects: except that he seemed to have shrunk slightly in size, and to have developed a kind of deadness I had not remembered in the texture of his skin. He stood by the door, as if he had just glanced in to make sure that no misbehaviour was in progress, and would proceed immediately on his way to other rooms in the college, to see that there, too, all was well. I asked him to sit down. He came farther into the room, but appeared unwilling to seat himself; standing in one of his characteristic poses, holding up both his hands, one a little above the other, like an Egyptian god, or figure from the Bayeux tapestry.

'How are you getting on, Jenkins?' he asked, at last agreeing, though with apparent reluctance, to occupy an armchair. 'You have a nice view from here, I see.'

He rose again, and stared out of the window for a minute or two, at the place where clouds had begun to darken the sky. The sound of undergraduate voices came up from below. Le Bas turned his gaze down on the passers-by.

'I expect you know the story of Calverley throwing pebbles at the Master of Balliol's window,' he said. 'Just to make him look out for the benefit of some visitors. Parkinson was some sort of a connexion of Calverley's, I believe. I saw Parkinson the other day. In fact I rowed in a Duffers' Eight with him. Parkinson was in your time, wasn't he? Or am I confusing dates?'

'Yes, he was. He only went down from here last year.'

'He missed his "blue", didn't he?'

'I think he was only tried out a couple of times.'

'Who else is there from my house?'

'Stringham went down last term.'

'Went down, did he? Was he sent down?'

'No, he——'

'Of course I remember Stringham,' said Le Bas. 'Wrote a shocking hand. Never saw such a fist. What was he sent down for?'

'He wasn't sent down. He got a job with Donners-Brebner. I am going to see him tomorrow.'

'Who else?' insisted Le Bas, who had evidently never heard of Donners-Brebner.

'I saw Templer not long ago. He is in the City now.'

'Templer?' said Le Bas. 'Oh, yes, Templer. In the City, is he? Did he go up to the university?'

'No.'

'Probably just as well,' said Le Bas. 'Still it might have toned him down a bit. I suppose as it is he will spend the rest of his life wearing those startling socks. It was Templer, wasn't it, who always wore those dreadful socks?'

'Yes—it was.'

'Still, he may grow out of it,' said Le Bas.

'Or them,' I said; and, since Le Bas did not smile, added: 'I stayed in the same French family as Widmerpool, the summer after I left.'

'Ah yes, Widmerpool.'

Le Bas thought for a long time. He climbed up on to the fender, and began to lift himself by the edge of the mantelpiece. I thought for a moment that he might be going to hoist himself right on to the shelf; perhaps lie there.

'I was never quite happy about Widmerpool,' he admitted at last.

This statement did not seem to require an answer.

'As you probably know,' said Le Bas, 'there were jokes about an overcoat in the early days.'

'I remember being told something about it.'

'Plenty of keenness, but somehow——'

'He used to train hard.'

'And a strong—well——' Le Bas seemed rather at a loss, ending somewhat abruptly with the words: 'Certain moral qualities, admirable so far as they went, but——'

I supposed he was thinking of the Akworth affair, which must have caused him a good deal of trouble.

'He seemed to be getting on all right when I saw him in France.'

This statement seemed in the main true.

'I am glad to hear it,' said Le Bas. 'Very glad. I hope he will find his level in life. Which college did you say?'

'He didn't go to the university.'

'What is he going to be?'

'A solicitor.'

'Do none of my pupils consider a degree an advantage in life? I hope you will work hard for yours.'

Facetiously, I held up a copy of Stubbs's *Charters* that happened to be lying at hand on the table.

'Do you know Sillery?' I asked.

'Sillery? Sillery? Oh, yes, of course I know Sillery,' Le Bas said; but he did not rise to this bait.

There was a pause.

'Well, I have enjoyed our talk,' Le Bas said. 'I expect I shall see you on Old Boy Day.'

He got up from the chair, and stood for a few seconds, as if undecided whether or not to bring his visit to an end.

'Friendships have to be kept up,' he said, unexpectedly.

I suppose that his presence had recalled—though unconsciously—the day of Braddock alias Thorne; because for some reason, inexplicable to myself, I said: 'Like Heraclitus.'

Le Bas looked surprised.

'You know the poem, do you?' he said. 'Yes, I remember you were rather keen on English.'

Then he turned and made for the door, still apparently pondering the questions that this reference to Heraclitus had aroused in his mind. Having reached the door, he stopped. There was evidently some affirmation he found difficulty in getting out. After several false starts, he said: 'You know, Jenkins, do always try to remember one thing—it takes all sorts to make a world.'

I said that I would try to remember that.

'Good,' said Le Bas. 'You will find it a help.'

I watched him from the window. He walked quickly in the direction of the main entrance of the college: suddenly he turned on his heel and came back, very slowly, towards my staircase, at the foot of which he stopped for about a minute: then he moved off again at a moderate pace in another quarter: finally disappearing from sight, without leaving any impression of decision as to his next port of call. The episode of Braddock alias Thorne, called up by Le Bas's visit, took on a more grotesque aspect than ever, when thought of now. I wondered whether Le Bas had himself truly accepted his own last proposition. Nothing in his behaviour had ever suggested that his chosen principles were built up on a deep appreciation of the diversity of human character. On the contrary, he had always demanded of his pupils certain easily recognisable conventions of conduct: though, at the same time, it occurred to me that the habit of making just such analyses of motive as this was precisely what Le Bas had a moment before so delicately deprecated in myself.

There are certain people who seem inextricably linked in life; so that meeting one acquaintance in the street means that a letter, without fail, will arrive in a day or two from an associate involuntarily harnessed to him, or her, in time. Le Bas's appearance was one of those odd preludes that take place, and give, as it were, dramatic form to occurrences that have more than ordinary significance. It is as if the tempo altered gradually, so that too violent a change of sensation should not take place; in this case, that some of the atmosphere of school should be reconstructed, although only in a haphazard fashion, as if for an amateur performance, in order that I should not meet Stringham in his new surroundings without a reminder of the circumstances in which we had first known one another.

For some reason, during the following day in London, I found myself thinking all the time of Le Bas's visit; although it was long before I came to look upon such transcendental manipulation of surrounding figures almost as a matter of routine. The weather was bad. When the time came, I was glad to find myself in the Donners-Brebner building, although the innate dejection of spirit of that part of London was augmented by regarding its landscape from this huge and shapeless edifice, recently built in a style as wholly without ostensible order as if it were some vast prehistoric cromlech. Stringham's office was on one of the upper storeys, looking north over the river. It was dark now outside, and lights were reflected in the water, from the oppressive and cheerless, as well as beautiful, riverside. Stringham looked well: better than I had seen him for a long time.

'Let's get out of here,' he said.

'I'm a bit late.'

'We'll have a drink.'

'Where shall we make for?'

For a brief second, for an inexpressibly curtailed efflux of time, so short that its duration could be appreciated only in recollection, being immediately engulfed at the moment of birth, I was conscious of a sensation I had never before encountered: an awareness that Stringham was perhaps a trifle embarrassed. He took a step forward, and made as if to pat my head, as one who makes much of an animal.

'There, there,' he said. 'Good dog. Don't growl. The fact is I am cutting your date. Cutting it in slow motion before your eyes.'

'Well?'

'It is an absolutely inexcusable thing to do. I've been asked to rather a good party at short notice—and have to dine and go to a play first. As the party can hardly fail to be rather fun, I thought you wouldn't mind.'

'Of course not.'

'An intolerable act, I admit.'

'Not if it's a good party.'

'I thought the thing to do would be for you to come back and talk while I changed. Then I could drop you wherever you are going to dine.'

'Let's do that.'

I could pretend to Stringham that I did not mind: within, I was exceedingly annoyed. This was quite unlike him. A rearrangement of plans would now be necessary. His car was parked outside. We drove northward.

'How are things at the old coll.?'

'Le Bas visited me yesterday.'

'Our former housemaster?'

'Braddock alias Thorne.'

'Good heavens, I had forgotten all about that.'

'I wonder if he has.'

'Did you tell him how it happened?'

'No.'

'How extraordinary for him to swim to the surface.'

'He asked about you.'

'No?'

Stringham was not interested. Le Bas was scarcely a memory. I began to realise that considerable changes had indeed been taking place.

'What is it like in London?'

'I'm rather enjoying myself. You must come and live here soon.'

'I suppose I shall in due course.'

'Can't you get sent down? No one could stand three years of university life.'

We arrived at the house, and, passing between the pillars of the doorway, collected drinks in the dining-room. Then we went upstairs. The place seemed less gloomy than on my earlier visit. Stringham's bedroom was a rather comfortless apartment, looking out on to the roofs of another row of large houses.

'Who are you dining with?'

'The Bridgnorths.'

'Haven't I seen pictures of a rather captivating daughter called Lady Peggy Stepney?'

'The last photograph was taken at Newmarket. I've been wondering whether it wasn't time for her to get married and settle down,' said Stringham. 'I seem to have been a bachelor an awfully long time.'

'What does Lady Peggy think about it?'

'There are indications that she does not actively dislike me.'

'Why not, then?'

We talked in a desultory way, Stringham walking to and fro, wearing only a stiff shirt, and some black silk socks, while he washed his hands, and brushed his hair. I did not know how serious he might be with regard to the Bridgnorths' daughter. The idea of one of my friends getting married had scarcely occurred to me, even as a possibility. I saw now that such a thing was not absolutely out of the question. From time to time a footman appeared, offering different collars, because Stringham could find none he liked.

'I suppose this must be one of Buster's,' he said, at last accepting a collar that satisfied him. 'I shall sell the rest of mine off cheap to the clergy to wear back-to-front.'

He slipped on his tail-coat, pulling at the cuffs of his shirt.

'Come on,' he said; 'we'll have another drink on the way out.'

'Where is your dinner-party?'

'Grosvenor Square. Where shall I drop you?'

'Grosvenor Square will do for me.'

'But what will you do?'

'Dine with an uncle of mine.'

'Does he live there?'

'No—but he isn't expecting me just yet.'

'He was expecting you then?'

'A standing invitation.'

'So I really haven't left you too high and dry?'

'Not in the least.'

'You are jolly lucky to have relations you can drop in on at any time,' said Stringham. 'My own are much too occupied with their own affairs to care for that.'

'You met Uncle Giles once. He suddenly arrived one night when we were having tea. It was the day of Peter's "unfortunate incident".'

Stringham laughed. He said: 'I remember about Peter, but not about your uncle.'

We reached the car again, and drove for a time in silence. 'We'll meet soon,' Stringham said. 'I suppose you are going back tonight—otherwise we might have lunched tomorrow.'

'I'll be up in a week or two.'

'We will get together then.'

We had reached Grosvenor Square, and he slowed up.

'Now where?'

'I'll climb down here.'

'I expect it will be a really frightful party, and Peggy will have decided not to turn up.'

He waved, and I waved, as the car went on to the far side of the square.

The evening was decidedly cool, and rain was half-heartedly falling. I knew now that this parting was one of those final things that happen, recurrently, as time passes: until at last they may be recognised fairly easily as the close of a period. This was the last I should see of Stringham for a long time. The path had suddenly forked. With regret, I accepted the inevitability of circumstance. Human relationships flourish and decay, quickly and silently, so that those concerned scarcely know how brittle, or how inflexible, the ties that bind them have become. Lady Bridgnorth, by her invitation that night, had effortlessly snapped one of the links—for practical purposes the main one—between Stringham and myself; just as the accident in Templer's car, in a rather different manner, had removed Templer from Stringham's course. A new epoch was opening: in a sense this night was the final remnant of life at school.

I was glad to have remembered Uncle Giles. It was, I suppose, justification of the family as a social group that, upon such an occasion, my uncle's company seemed to offer a restorative in the accidental nature of our relationship and the purely formal regard paid by him to the fact that I was his nephew. Finding a telephone box, I looked up the address of the Trouville Restaurant, which turned out to be in Soho. It was fairly early in the evening. Passing slowly through a network of narrow streets, and travelling some distance, I came at last to the Trouville. The outside was not inviting. The restaurant's façade was boarded up with dull, reddish shutters. At the door hung a table d'hôte menu, slipped into a brass frame that advertised Schweppes' mineral waters—Blanchailles—Potage Solférino—Sole Bercy—Côtelettes d'Agneau Reform—Glace Néapolitaine—Café. The advertised charge seemed very reasonable. The immense depression of this soiled, claret-coloured exterior certainly seemed to meet the case; for there is always something solemn about change, even when accepted.

Within, the room was narrow, and unnaturally long, with a table each side, one after another, stretching in perspective into shadows that hid the service lift: which was set among palms rising from ornate brass pots. The emptiness, dim light, silence—and, to some extent, the smell—created a faintly ecclesiastical atmosphere; so that the track between the tables might have been an aisle, leading, perhaps, to a hidden choir. Uncle Giles himself, sitting alone at the far end of this place, bent over a book, had the air of a sleepy worshipper, waiting for the next service to begin. He did not look specially pleased to see me, and not at all surprised.

'You're a bit late,' he said. 'So I started.'

It had not occurred to him that I should do otherwise than come straight up to London, so soon as informed that there was an opportunity to see him again. He put his book face-downwards on the tablecloth. I saw that it was called *Some Things That Matter*. We discussed the Trust until it was time to catch my train.